ALSO BY MAGGIE MCPHEE

DEATH IN AUTUMN

AUTUMN IN THE DESERT, BOOK 0 (PREQUEL NOVELLA)

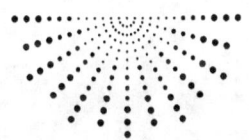

MAGGIE MCPHEE

Cover by: Zoran Petrovic/Fiverr.com name: visual arts

Map of Palm Lakes by: Maria Gandolfo/ Fiverr.com name: Renflowergrapx

ISBN: 978-1-946014-34-4 (Ebook version)

ISBN: 978-1-946014-36-8 (Paperback version)

Sixth Sense Books

150 Buck Run E

Dahlonega, GA 30533

Email address: authormaggiemcphee@gmail.com

For Nigel
Everything is better because you are part of my life

CONTENTS

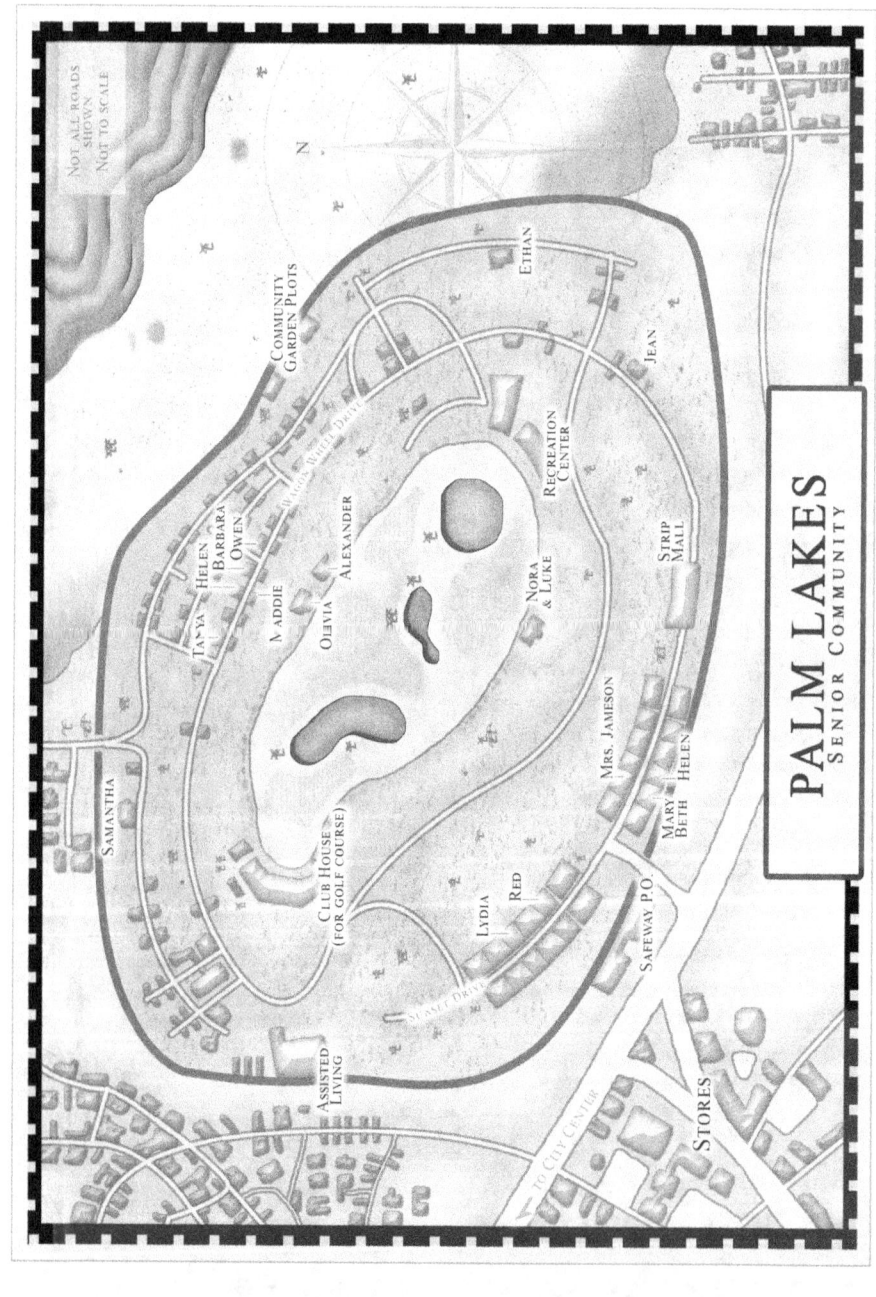

PALM LAKES
SENIOR COMMUNITY

CHARACTERS

Residents Of Palm Lakes
   Maddie and Stanley O'Neill
   Samantha Taylor, the O'Neills' daughter, and her husband Arthur
   Helen Mueller, recent widow
   Alexander Stirling, bachelor
   Serafina Costello, widowed
   Mary Beth Costello, daughter of Serafina, divorced & living
temporarily with Mom, in spite of being too young to legally reside there
   Barbara Blackstone and her husband Ben
   Red Johnson, bachelor and member of The Posse
   Lydia Stern, divorcee
   Tanya Cooper and her husband
   Owen Schmidt, serial killer
   Jean Callahan and her husband Richard

Wagon Wheel Drive residents (single family homes)
   Maddie and Stanley O'Neill
   Barbara and Ben Blackstone, their cat Fluffy and dog Jack
   Tanya Cooper and husband
   Owen Schmidt

Helen Mueller and her cat Sheba

Sunset Drive residents (condos)
Lydia Stern
Serafina and Mary Beth Costello
Later, Helen Mueller
Mrs. Jameson
Red Johnson

Living along the golf course
Alexander Stirling

* * *

PREFACE

It's been a lifelong dream for me to write novels, but I was over 60 before I took the plunge and began writing fiction. Before then, for several years I had written nonfiction books, and I enjoyed being a writer and selling my books, but writing nonfiction didn't quite satisfy my particular writing desire. So I began a science fiction novel. I spent nearly a year on it (part time, as my husband and I were working on our online business then) and finally accumulated about 80,000 words. But something didn't feel quite right, so I set it aside.

I had another story in my head that was begging to be told. It was about the lives of residents of a retirement community in the Arizona desert. I had lived and worked in such a community in the 90s, and I had loads of stories to tell. Funny stories, sad stories, and most of all, inspiring stories. As I approached my autumn years (note the use of the word 'approached'), I felt that movies and books were doing little to acknowledge the existence, let alone active contribution, of senior citizens, and what they did tell painted a grim story or followed overworked stereotypes. The tale they told was you start falling apart as you age, you get aches and pains and physical and mental disabilities. You have to take tons of pills and can't do anything you used to do, becoming a burden to your family and society. And then you die after spending all your money on health care. That perspective would be ludicrous if it weren't being embraced by so many older folks.

I remember a time when aging people were active. They kept house, baked, sewed, participated in clubs and church groups, cared for grandchildren and worked in jobs until they wanted to quit. They gardened, raised and showed dogs and painted or wrote. They were vital, opinionated and active. It was only when they got to be about 90 that they sometimes became weakened or slowed down significantly. Sure, not everyone made that milestone, but it seemed that people *lived* life in those days. When did it all change?

My *Autumn In The Desert* series is meant to reflect how I believe life can be as we age. We still face the challenges of our younger counterparts, but the years often, if we have learned anything, give us a bit of wisdom to soften the blows and point out alternate paths. The grim picture of a decline into death is relatively new in this country, and I choose to reject that portrayal of the aging process. I believe there is another path through the Golden Years, and if we have the courage to act on what our hearts tell us, we can find happiness, success and love unexpectedly late in life.

My series is based on my years living in a retirement community in Arizona. I worked there as well. At the time, I was in my 40s and was one of the youngest legal residents. It gave me an up close but at the same time objective perspective on the lives of other residents. Now that I am of retirement age myself, I see how important it is not to give up on life and start declining just because that's what the media and even the medical establishment preaches at this time.

I don't believe life is meant to be harsher or emptier as we age. I believe each day is a gift, and that we can create whatever we choose if we have the courage to follow our hearts. I hope that my stories inspire hope in my readers and maybe even spur them to take action and reach for their dreams, no matter what their age, because I believe that it's never too late to write a happy ending to your life story.

Maggie McPhee
June 5, 2019

ACKNOWLEDGMENTS

I could never have completed these stories without encouragement and help from my husband, Nigel. He functioned as my editor in spite of admitting that my series wasn't 'his kind of story,' giving me valuable advice and cheering me on when I wondered if it was worth the effort to keep writing. He believed in me when I wrestled with self-doubt during the time when the books did not sell. And when they did, he didn't act surprised. :)

I am indebted to everyone I knew when I lived in Sun City West, Arizona and worked at a local landscaping company. After I learned as much as I could about desert landscaping, I teamed up with another female landscaper to start our own company, Your Gardening Angels, and we continued to serve the seniors in Sun City West and surrounding retirement communities. My work gave me the opportunity to get to know a diverse group of retired folks from all over the US and Canada, many of whom became friends. The several years I spent in Sun City West are the basis for my series, but it is important to point out that these stories are fiction and not intended to portray any real person or incident.

The path of the indie author has been long and crooked for me, but the ups have inspired me never to surrender to the self-doubt during the down times, and the kind words of my readers inspire me to continue to share the story of life in Palm Lakes Senior Community. I am grateful for my readers, who often take the time to tell me they enjoyed my series or were inspired by it. It's the loyal readers who make the effort so worthwhile.

CHAPTER ONE

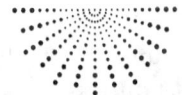

FRIDAY, APRIL 28, 1995

At a truck stop in Arizona, 1:15am

*H*e tramped down the narrow hallway of the RV, naked and still damp from his shower, the makeshift plastic runner shifting slightly under his bare feet. He paused in the doorway to the bedroom, clutching the plastic garbage bag that held his soiled clothes, including an expensive pair of leather sandals. He grimaced at the waste. He'd never forgotten to shed his shoes in the past. Now they were ruined.

Never mind. He had a lot of cleaning up to do; there was no time to dwell on regrets. He began to untape the layers of plastic that shielded his bedroom from splatter, meticulously removing each successive layer to avoid spills, using copious amounts of paper towels to soak up fluids.

His system, perfected over years of experience, was flawless. In less than 45 minutes, he had a sizable hunk of garbage ready for disposal, his bag of clothes separate and destined for another location.

On his way back for a second shower, he rolled up his makeshift runner and bagged it with his clothes. The second shower left him wide awake, clean and smelling fresh. He felt newly born. Humming to himself, he dressed and drove to his pre-chosen site in the desert under a starry sky, as alone as if he were the last human on a post-apocalyptic planet.

The shoulderless two-lane road on the way to nowhere was empty of traffic, as anticipated. The whisper of a warm breeze caressed Owen's face as he trudged to the dump site, the muscles of his strong upper body barely straining with his burden.

Virgin desert stretched to the horizon in all directions, punctuated by the occasional dark slash of an arroyo or a wall of cliffs. Desert trees, teddy bear chollas, saguaros and the occasional fading yellow flowers of brittle bush, ghostly silhouettes drained of color by the night, softened the moonlike landscape.

The new moon gave scant illumination while he dug a shallow hole, dumped the garbage in and backfilled it. He added a few rocks, as large as he could handle, in hopes of discouraging coyotes from excavating. The smaller bag with his clothes, he would toss in a dumpster on the way home.

He examined his work in the starry darkness. The mound resembled a grave, but he'd walked a good distance from the road, and the terrain had plenty of rocks and cacti as well as mesquite and palo verde trees to camouflage it.

Of the few who traveled this way, no one wandered this far from the road, especially in summer. He wasn't concerned that someone would find what was left of her. Some part of him almost wanted discovery, but caution won out, at least this time. He had done his best to leave no evidence, so even if the body got dug up, it wouldn't lead back to him.

He tapped the shovel on the ground one last time to dislodge remaining dirt and took off his work gloves and slapped them against his thigh. A layer of sweat and sandy dirt filmed his face and bare arms, making him itch with annoyance. He hated being dirty. Women. They were fundamentally dirty, the cause of everything irritating in his life.

Back in his RV, he showered a final time and dressed in casual pants, t-shirt and deck shoes without socks. He sat in the captain's chair that was the driver's seat. Once again, he regretted the loss of his nearly-new sandals. But why dwell on what was wrong? His body was pleasantly sore from the night's activity, almost like after a good workout, and he smiled to himself as he held her gold anklet in his hand, tilting it this way and that in the glow of the interior light.

Ruby. Her brassy appearance, puffy bleached blonde hair, low-cut top and tight miniskirt were magnetic. And those heels. How did women walk in them? But to his conscious mind, what had most attracted him was the golden bracelet that glistened on her ankle. Unlike the rest of her, the anklet had turned out to be the real deal. 14K gold and of elegant design, it didn't seem to belong on the Ruby he'd met. Perhaps it was a gift from an admirer.

He had quickly found things to judge. She'd smoked like a forest fire while they had coffee in a secluded booth of the truck stop's large diner. Late at night, there were still patrons, but not so many, and he made sure no one noticed them. She yakked on and on, boring him with her plan of getting to LA and breaking into movies, as if winning the Miss Bumfuck, USA contest in Texas five years ago would give her traction. She was young, not even 25, but still, most of her looks depended on her big tits, trashy clothes and lots of makeup. What did women use for brains? He was doing the world a favor, ridding it of such whores. That's all she was, when you stripped off the silly dreams.

Because she was nothing but a whore, it was child's play to lure her back to his RV for a drink and implied intimacy. She had cracked her gum the whole way across the tarmac to his strategically parked vehicle—away from the building and lights, door facing the desert. God, he hated gum-chewing. She was a real piece of work. By the time they climbed aboard, he was so sick of her mindless stupidity, he didn't wait like he usually did to act. Under the guise of pouring her a drink, he soaked a rag—a clean one—in chloroform and quickly silenced her. Bound and gagged, she waited in the bedroom for his pleasure while he drove, always obeying traffic laws, to a secluded location. There he had his fun, showing her his power and control of the situation. He demonstrated she was nothing. Until she was.

He dropped the anklet into his shirt pocket. He had a special place for souvenirs. This one would be labeled "Ruby." He wasn't sure it was her real name. He hadn't given her his. But it would be the last remembrance of a frivolous, shallow, even venal, life. Women were such trivial bitches. Like Mother.

"Junior! How dare you speak that way!" The cigarette- and booze-hardened voice raked him like claws, coming as if through a tunnel. Had he said anything out loud?

"Just shut up and leave me alone. It's time to go home," he barked.

"I should think so," she said primly, "You sit around much longer, and you might attract attention. Then you'll get caught. You're just like your father was; he couldn't keep his eye on the ball."

"Shut up," he muttered, but he turned off the interior lights and put the vehicle in gear and headed in the direction of home. With luck, he'd be back before dawn. If only Mother would keep quiet until then.

CHAPTER TWO

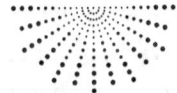

TUESDAY, MAY 9, 1995

Red, 8:00am

*R*ed sipped the bitter brew that passed for coffee at Posse HQ. It wasn't the worst coffee he'd ever had, not by a long shot, but the coffeemaker could probably use descaling. Living in the low desert at Palm Lakes Senior Community had taught him a few things about the side effects of hard water, something he hadn't known about when he moved to Arizona. Someday, he'd install a water softener in his condo like other residents did. He was tired of sticky showers.

Nick Dwyer stepped into the doorway of the tiny break room, and Red raised his mug in salute. An older retiree and veteran of Palm Lake's volunteer police force, Nick was his sometime-partner. "Hey, Nick, how's it hanging?"

Nick grunted and shuffled over to the coffee pot. After his first gulp of coffee, he settled his bearlike frame into the rickety plastic chair at the break table beside Red and ran a hand through his thick, short-cropped white hair. Setting his mug on the formica, Nick let out a sigh. "I guess I'm hanging in there." A frown creased his wrinkled face, and his blue eyes lacked their usual spark.

Red had a talent for reading people, and Nick wasn't himself this morning. "Everything OK?" he ventured, not really sure he would like the answer.

"Not really." Nick drank more coffee, as if weighing his reply. "My wife has cancer."

Red felt as if he'd been hit with a bat. "Oh, shit. That's awful." He wasn't sure what else to say; he didn't really know Nick that well and hadn't socialized with him outside of the Posse. He paused to allow Nick room to speak. His partner was a formidable figure, a couple inches over six feet and solid in a way that was rare for an octogenarian, but simply speaking of the burden he was carrying had shrunk him.

"They say she has six months at most. They want her to do chemo, but they say it won't cure her, so she said no. I don't know what to do. I want to support her, but I want to fight for every day we have left. She says she's chosen quality over quantity." His chin dropped, and his eyes defocused, as if he were deep in thought.

"I'm so sorry, Nick. I'm here if you think of anything I can do to help." Red paused as he processed Nick's news. "What the hell are you doing here, anyway?"

Nick's bright blue eyes filled with tears. "Liz wants me to stay on the Posse. She insists that we go on as normal. That's going to be hard for me, but I guess she's right. Maybe you can help me not to sink into self-pity. I need to be strong for Liz."

"Done," said Red and put a hand on his friend's arm. "Any time you want to unload, I'm here. But until you choose to talk about it, I'll keep you distracted and busy. Speaking of which, did you see the bulletin the staties put out?"

Nick perked up. "No. What's it about?"

"Looks like they have a murderer running loose on the interstate. They found a woman's body buried in the desert not far from a big rest area. Purely a coincidence that a hiker found it; it was way out in the back of beyond. It's fresh, and they're looking at it as a potential serial killer, want all of us to report on missing women. I checked, and Palm Lakes doesn't have any."

Nick grunted and sipped his coffee. Then he said, "Fat chance the murderer lives here! And thank God for that."

Red felt like a dog on a scent, straining at the leash to be released to hunt, but Nick was right; he should be grateful life was so quiet. *So why wasn't he?* "I know you're right, but I'm bored. Nothing ever happens here."

Nick glared at him in disapproval. "I know I was only a small town police chief, but didn't you see enough action working big city homicide?"

Red blew out a sigh. "Sure. I thought I'd love the quiet here. But I miss the chase. I sometimes wonder if my life is over. Doesn't seem to be much worth doing anymore."

Nick's look was appraising, and Red wondered if he sounded like a whiner.

"How about the report about drug dealing on Casino Drive?" his partner asked.

Red barked a laugh. "Right. Alert grandma sees neighbor walking dog with paper bag in hand and immediately assumes he's dealing dope...'this is good shit'." He mimicked holding out a poop bag, grinning at his pun.

Nick smiled and shook his head. "You ask me, a senior community is a great cover. No one expects grandpa to be dealing dope." Nick was finally 100% engaged.

"I'm not sure what we can do, other than cruise that road more often."

"That's what they pay us the big bucks to do," affirmed Nick heartily.

Red snickered. "Yeah, pay. That's what's missing from my life."

"Maybe you need to get a horse. Since my old gelding went to horse heaven, I've been thinking of getting a new one, but at my age, who knows how long I've got. And now with Liz sick, maybe I won't have time to train a new mount."

Red gulped the rest of his coffee. "I don't know. I've only ridden a few times. It might be smarter to get a horse than look for wife #4, though." Instantly, he realized his mistake.

Nick gave him a sharp look. "I suppose I should count myself lucky. Liz and I had a good run."

Red silently cursed himself for his gaffe, then punched Nick's shoulder as he stood up. "Let's cruise Casino Drive and find us some drug dealers."

A weak smile on his face, Nick nodded and followed him to the sink, where they rinsed out their mugs. Out in the parking lot, they stood by their vehicles planning their shift in the warm sunshine. Red deferred to Nick, "How shall we divvy up the territory?"

"Oh, the usual is good. I'll take the north part of town. We can meet for lunch at the hamburger place. Let's make sure we each go down Casino Drive several times. Maybe we can scare them straight."

Red guffawed. "Yeah, we're real scary. But I agree. Nothing much going on otherwise."

Later, when their eventless shift was over, Red headed back to his condo by way of the grocery store. Nick seemed to be holding up well. He was a tough old codger. Other than trying to distract Nick from his trouble, Red had no clue what to do for his friend. His relationships over the years had all revolved around work. Outside of work, he wasn't stellar at social interactions, which was why he was a three-time loser at marriage.

Nick's revelation had him thinking about his life. He pulled into the Safeway parking lot, deep in thought. As he browsed the TV dinners and other frozen meals, he wondered if this was all he had to look forward to. Takeout. TV dinners. Lonely nights drinking. The occasional golf game was OK, and he worked out regularly, but what for? He suddenly realized his life lacked direction and purpose. Most of all, it didn't *feel* like a life.

Annoyed that he was in a funk, he walked out of the grocery store empty-handed. The sun was low on the horizon, and the temperature was perfect, though it had briefly hit 95 degrees earlier. Spring didn't last long here, but it sure was glorious. He hated to see it go.

What he needed was to do things differently. He'd gotten into a rut. He hated eating alone in public, but he needed a real meal for a change, so he drove to the nearby Jade Dragon restaurant and gorged on General Tso's chicken and spring rolls, surrounded by the cacophony of diners having a night out. As was his habit, he watched his surroundings, wondering about the other patrons. Were they enjoying retirement? They seemed to be. It had been ages since he'd been out with friends, but he was comfortable being alone, at least, most of the time. By the time he finished his meal with a glass of plum wine, he felt pleasantly sated and glowing with good will, as if he'd picked up the happy vibes of the other diners.

It was dusk as he cruised down his street and pulled into his driveway. The neighbor two doors down was putting something in her mailbox, but she didn't see him in the fading light as he waited for his garage door to open. He'd noticed her before. She was no more than 5'2" with luscious curves. Usually she wore long skirts and a peasant blouse that showed off her cleavage. Thick, dark hair swept her shoulders, and it appeared damp from recent washing. She looked attractive in scruffy pink sweatpants and a dark T-shirt that stretched tight across her beautiful tits. She was just his type. He shook his head at his thoughts, pulled into the garage and went inside and poured himself a scotch.

That did it. He had a rule. He never dated residents of Palm Lakes. Too much chance of complication, especially if the woman lived close by. If the gypsy girl was becoming so enticing, that meant he needed to make a trip to Vegas for some R&R. Gamble a little, watch a show, find a willing woman with no strings attached.

Sighing, he realized he needed to wait a bit; he'd feel guilty if he abandoned Nick when he needed support. He swirled the ice in his glass and inhaled the peaty fragrance of the scotch, relaxing into his decision. He'd get to Vegas when the time was right.

* * *

Barbara, 9:15am

It was already warmer than Barbara liked, but she'd been putting off planting her pots for days, and it was just going to get hotter. She'd lugged the bags of potting soil and the flats of petunias to the back lanai along with her trowel and an empty bucket, so she was ready to go.

Her calico cat Fluffy had slipped out with her and was exploring the intriguing scents along the edge of the back yard. Being a senior feline with a few extra pounds, Fluffy wasn't much of a hunter, so the quails and rabbits had nothing to worry about.

As Barbara dug out the faded winter flowers and tossed them into the bucket, sweat began to bead on her forehead. Her sunglasses slipped down her nose as it became slick with sweat from her exertions. Who said women 'glow'? She always sweated like a pig. Laughing to herself, she finished preparing the rectangular cement planters and sat back on her heels to catch her breath.

The silence was pierced by a male voice shouting a curse in the next yard, and Fluffy came streaking across the gravel to the patio door, tail as thick as a bottlebrush. Standing on the property line, hands fisted and eyes glaring, stood Fluffy's nemesis, next door neighbor Owen Schmidt. Short, with thinning brown hair and a nondescript face, Owen still managed to make an impression with his rock hard body that quivered with rage. Again.

What was the matter with that man? He'd declined her every invitation to dinner and parties. All her attempts to befriend him were summarily rejected, practically sneered at. She didn't mind him sticking to himself—her neighbors Maddie and Stanley didn't accept her invitations, either, though Maddie made it clear they simply didn't socialize at all—but he did it with such an air of judgment. As if she'd done something unforgivable to him.

She tried to tell herself he was just having a bad day, but she had never seen him happy. "What can I do for you, Owen?" she asked in her most accommodating voice.

"What you can do is what I have asked over and over. Keep your stupid pets off my property. I'm damn well fed up with them messing my yard." There was a tick in a muscle on the right side of his face, and his bare upper arms were ropy with tension. That man needed to learn yoga or meditation.

She put the trowel down, stood slowly and brushed dirt off her gardening gloves, trying to gather herself to deal patiently with his anger. "I don't let them out much. We don't have the money for a fence, but we'll be getting one as soon as we can."

His brown eyes narrowed to slits, matching the downturned slash of his mouth. "It's against the law and the covenants to let them roam."

Barbara sighed at his rigidity. "I feel sorry for Fluffy and Jack, because we had acres in California, and they're used to having freedom." Where was his compassion?

He obviously wasn't moved. "If you don't keep them on your property, I will complain to the HOA or the police. I'm fucking fed up with this nonsense. How hard is it to just keep them inside until you get a fence?" He turned and stomped back across the gravel and into his house, ending the encounter.

That hadn't gone well. He'd never sworn at her before. His anger did seem to be escalating. She wondered if he would go to the trouble of complaining. She turned and walked to the sliding glass door and let Fluffy into the house. She was lucky Jack, her hyperactive Jack Russell, had elected to stay inside this morning. That's all she needed, Owen yelling about both pets.

Owen had shattered her contemplative mood with his anger. She wanted to make excuses for him, but something about him was so... extreme. He scared her a little, but she didn't like to dwell on negative thoughts, so she pushed that aside. She finished planting her petunias and watered all the pots, pleased that the job was done until the fall, when she'd swap them out for something hardier to the cold.

While showering away the soil and ill feelings, she wondered what to do. Surely Owen could be persuaded to be reasonable. They were going to put up a fence eventually, but it wasn't only the cost that held them back. She regretted the thought of breaking up the open feel of the neighborhood. No one else had fences, and it gave them a sense of space. That was something she missed of California, the wide open space. That, and the pleasant summers.

Fluffy had never been purely a house cat, and Jack needed more exercise than he got inside. She wanted peace with her neighbor, but at what price? Would he really turn her in? He certainly sounded serious.

As she toweled her hair dry, her thoughts drifted to the dinner she had planned for tonight. It was Ben's birthday, and she and her husband had a tradition that had lasted throughout their marriage. She loved cooking, and on his birthday, she made him whatever he wanted, no matter how fancy. It made celebrating more fun, because they both could drink, and it was nicely private. She had plenty of time to prepare the meal before he returned from his golf game.

She would start the apple pie now, because a pie from scratch took a good bit of time, and she needed to reserve at least a couple hours for making Ben's favorite homemade pasta and sauce. Humming, she lost herself in the preparations and mercifully forgot Owen's temper tantrum.

* * *

Jean, 9:55am

JEAN PAUSED in the classroom's doorway and scanned the small room. A gentleman with his back to her was laying things on a rectangular table at the front of the room. He was short in stature with a shock of white hair and moved with grace and strength that belied his apparent age. She grinned as she thought of him as a leprechaun come to impart magical information to her.

Despite the rows of chairs, there was only one other student present. She sat in the front row, leaning forward to watch over the instructor's shoulder as he worked. All Jean could see of her was dark shoulder-length hair and a colorful blouse.

Jean wasn't comfortable with strangers and would have preferred to disappear in a crowd, but she was getting acclimated to the tiny classes. Most people in the area simply had no interest in metaphysical subjects; it's not like they were living in California. There had never been more than four students in any of the Reiki classes she'd attended, and she'd enjoyed those, so she was learning to come out of her shell.

She forced herself to march down the aisle to the first row and sat next to the other woman, unnoticed by the instructor, who might have been hard of hearing. As Jean sat down, the woman turned intelligent brown eyes on her. Laugh lines around her eyes and mouth said she had a sense of humor, and her smile revealed beautiful, white teeth. No man would fail to notice the ample cleavage framed by the neckline of the brightly colored peasant blouse, but what caught Jean's attention was the exquisite necklace of turquoise chunks in silver, embellished with red coral and mother of pearl. It had to be worth a fortune. "Wow, that's a beautiful necklace. I'm Jean Callahan."

"Thanks. I love turquoise. My name's Lydia, Lydia Stern. I was beginning to worry I was going to be the only student today." Lydia stared at her with eyes that seemed to see her, really see her in a way that unnerved her a bit.

Shaking her head at her fanciful reaction, Jean smiled back. "This is my first class on dowsing. I was introduced to it in my Karuna Reiki class, and it attracted me in a way that's hard to explain. I just had to learn more about it."

"This is my first dowsing class, too. I read about it in a book I got on crystal healing, and I thought it could be a useful tool in my work."

Their voices either grabbed the leprechaun's attention, or he had finished his preparations. He turned pale blue eyes on them, and a warm smile split his wrinkled face. "What lovely ladies! Welcome to the Basic Dowsing class. I'll be your teacher and guide. My name is Joe Waters."

Joe turned out to be a terrific instructor. He combined just the right mix of inspiring and humorous anecdotes, fundamentals and hands-on practice, and the two hours sped by. By the end, Jean and Lydia were both psyched about taking the intermediate class in June.

Jean had enjoyed the experience so much that she quickly agreed to have lunch with her new friend at the local Italian restaurant. Lucia's Trattoria was located in a strip mall in Palm Lakes Senior Community, where both ladies resided. The eatery's decor was typical of a casual family diner, with plastic red and white checked tablecloths, wine bottles in woven holders with candles stuck in them and red plastic water glasses. Prints of Italian locales hung on the walls, and there was a takeout counter in the back of the room, down a walkway that was separated from the dining room proper by a short wrought iron fence.

"I love this place," said Jean. "It isn't much to look at," she whispered as she glanced around, "but the food is great and the portions generous."

"It's one of my favorites for the same reasons. I think the big portions is the main reason it's such a success. People in Palm Lakes love getting two meals for the price of one. But today I'm so hungry, I won't have anything to take home."

"Me, too," said Jean. "I told Richard I'd run errands after class, so he's not expecting me for lunch. I didn't think I'd be hungry. Maybe something about the class got my appetite going. But tell me about yourself. I know you live in Palm Lakes, but are you married?"

"No, not for a long time. Can't seem to find a guy I can live with," Lydia teased.

"There aren't a lot of single guys in Palm Lakes," observed Jean.

"That's true, but I don't mind being on my own." Lydia's brown eyes twinkled.

Something about Lydia made Jean feel she could tell her anything and not be judged. "I think I wouldn't like being single. I hated dating as a teenager, and the thought of going back to it horrifies me."

Lydia gave her a strange, penetrating stare. "I'd rather be alone than with the wrong man."

Jean gulped at the insight. "I agree. Lately, my husband looks at me like I'm a witch, and it's bothering me. But he doesn't want to discuss it. I can tell he thinks the things I'm interested in are New Age nonsense at best, black magic at worst. I've only recently pursued them; maybe he figures I'm getting senile." She laughed self-consciously. What was it about Lydia that caused her to share so much?

"It can be hard when one person changes and the other doesn't," said Lydia sagely.

Jean felt flat all of a sudden, but the waitress came with their salads, and she turned her thoughts away from troubling topics. "So I bet you have no trouble getting dates. I'm envious of your curves. Guys didn't begin to notice me until I was 18 or 19. I bet you had to beat them off with a stick in high school."

A sad look flashed across Lydia's face. "Being 'popular' wasn't that much fun. All teenage boys want is sex. I had to learn the hard way it wasn't me they were admiring. One guy memorably said he liked me because I was taller lying down than standing up."

Jean snorted at the image; she'd never realized she'd been fortunate. Before she had a chance to ask herself why she was baring her soul to her new friend, she blurted, "I'm short like you, but I developed very late and not as much as I wanted. It hadn't occurred to me that I might be lucky. I felt so left out and unloved as a teenager, but it sounds like you had it worse."

Lydia shook her head. "I didn't have it worse. It's awful being a teenager for most of us. I'm just grateful it's in the past." She smiled sadly.

Their entrees arrived, and they ate in silence for a while. Finally, Lydia broke the quiet. "I'm used to being different, and it isn't so bad. But there aren't a lot of people in Palm Lakes who think like I do." Lydia's intelligent gaze lingered on Jean, as if she could see into her soul. She continued, "I could use a friend. We had a blast today, didn't we? How about we do more things together? We could practice dowsing. I could show you about crystals—that's my passion, and you can show me about Reiki."

Lydia's demeanor revealed vulnerability, and Jean's heart went out to her. "That sounds great. I can certainly use a friend. I know it sounds trite, but I feel I've know you forever."

Lydia grinned as she reached for her water glass. "Me, too. So we should plan to get together a few times before the next dowsing class. We can wow Joe with our competence."

"I really liked him," said Jean. "He reminds me of Spencer Tracy, or maybe a leprechaun."

Lydia choked on her water. "Don't make me laugh when I'm swallowing. I thought the same exact thing."

By the time dessert came, Jean was sure she'd found her soul sister.

* * *

Tanya, 4:30pm

TANYA BALANCED PRECARIOUSLY on 3-inch platform sandals as she stood outside the salon admiring her manicure in the bright sunlight. She genuinely liked Ashley, who always asked her opinion about products and techniques and listened so respectfully. She obviously had a burning desire to be the best. She reminded Tanya of herself when she was a young nail technician.

Her time as a cosmetology professional while her husband was in law school was so far in the past that she grimaced. She didn't like to think of those days, and she liked even less that they were so long ago. At least now, she didn't have to scrimp and save. They'd retired to Palm Lakes, and she had a maid to come in and do the heavy housework every couple weeks. So much had changed. It didn't occur to her that she'd been happier in the past, in spite of the hard work and poverty.

Her husband was such a bore. Always playing golf. As if he didn't think she knew he was doing anything just to get out of the house. Good riddance, she said. The less she saw of him, the better. Her dissatisfaction registered (as always) as a powerful thirst, and she considered how she would slake it as she stepped off the curb and ambled to her car.

Summer had arrived fast and heavy, and the air-conditioner would be laboring 24/7 until late in September. She didn't mind the heat and blazing sunshine; it felt cleansing. Or maybe it was a pleasant reminder of her youthful sun-worshipping days.

Her vehicle had turned into an oven in spite of the reflective shades in the window, so she sat with the a/c on full blast for a few minutes, pondering her next move.

Her husband didn't expect dinner until 6pm. He'd gotten a late tee time and always had a beer afterwards at the club house with his buddies. She leaned towards the rear view mirror, touching up her lipstick and checking her hair, then started the car and headed out of Palm Lakes for a nearby hotel that she'd visited in the past. It would be fun to have a drink and maybe make a new friend, and she'd never seen another Palm Lakes resident there, so it was safe.

As she entered the dark bar, she noticed that in spite of the early hour, several lone men sat nursing drinks and listening to the Country Western music pumping out of the old style juke box. Through a doorway on the other side of the room was the entrance to the hotel dining room, which appeared deserted.

She sashayed nonchalantly to an empty seat at the bar next to a man who was drinking some kind of whiskey. She had a good side view of his face. He was maybe 45 or a bit older, in his prime, gray just silvering his temples, thick dark hair cut short, but not military short. He had broad shoulders and would be tall when standing. She did like a tall man. His suit jacket hung on the seat back, and his tie was loosened. Probably traveling on business. Perfect.

She slipped into hunting mode and seated herself, ordering a vodka tonic when the bartender came over. She pretended not to notice the man next to her, but surreptitiously snuck glances at him. He had a five-o-clock shadow, strong chin and beaked nose. She couldn't see his eyes. Then he turned her way and gave her an appraising look.

She focused on her drink, playing coy, avoiding direct contact with the dark eyes. The cool liquid was a lovely contrast to the heat outdoors and the warmth simmering through her as she contemplated her next move. In her day, she'd fielded plenty of looks like that. It made her tingle all over.

Figuring she'd been shy long enough, she swallowed the last of her drink and turned to her companion, who was no longer facing her. Damn.

He was feigning a lack of interest. She knew he couldn't have missed her cleavage, even in the dim light. Her blouse was cut low enough to show her augmented boobs to advantage. Uncertainty crept into her mind, but she'd already committed. She needed to get laid, and he was a likely candidate. Not old enough to live in Palm Lakes, but mature and fit.

"Buy a girl a drink?" she asked him. "I'm Tanya." She pitched him her take-me-to-bed smile and waited for the expected response.

When he turned her way, she saw surprise in his mahogany eyes. That and something else. She glanced quickly at his left hand. No ring and no tan line. But still, something wasn't right.

"Uh, no offense, but you're a little old for me." He had the grace to appear embarrassed, then turned away from her.

Her voice completely failed her. And that was a first. She had a sharp tongue and a quick temper, as her husband could attest. But it was as if she'd been dropped into another universe.

Too old? How could he think that? She knew she had more than ten years on him, but she looked young for her age, didn't she? No one had ever spoken to her this way, and she was mortified.

Grateful she'd finished her drink, she fished a ten dollar bill out of her wallet and tossed it on the counter. At least no one had overheard. Without acknowledging her target's comment, she rushed outside and drove home, shaking with anger and frustration.

Once safely home, she poured herself a triple vodka from the bottle in the freezer and consoled herself with justifications for the man's inexplicable behavior. Maybe he was gay. Sure, that was it. It wasn't her fault if a gay man turned her down, was it?

Sipping the cold liquid banked the fire of her injured pride. Him being gay was a rational explanation, but doubt seeped in. Her husband had rejected her more than once lately, using her drinking as the excuse. And it had been quite a while since her last affair. She downed the remaining vodka and poured herself another, and gradually her old confidence returned.

Her husband was a waste of space and time. What he thought didn't matter. She'd never had problems finding admirers, and she wasn't going to let retirement stop her. She just needed to find a guy who wasn't gay.

* * *

Serafina, 4:45pm

THE PHONE JANGLED, waking Serafina from her doze in the recliner. She'd started doing that more often lately, falling asleep watching TV. She grabbed the phone to keep it from ringing again and muted the TV using the remote.

"Ma? It's me."

Serafina sighed. Another chapter in her daughter's messed up life. "What's wrong now?"

Mary Beth let out a ragged breath, and Serafina could picture her smoking like a chimney. What a filthy habit.

"I lost my job. Remember I told you old man Watts died of a stroke last week? Turns out, the business can't go on without him, so I'm not only getting divorced; I have no job."

Shocked, Serafina struggled to respond. "What are you going to do?"

"I was thinking maybe I could come stay with you. Just for a little while. I've got almost no money and no job. Living here has become impossible. Jason's soon-to-be wife is pregnant. The man always told me he didn't want kids." Mary Beth sounded more depressed than last time they had talked, and Serafina was sorry for her, but it was her own fault. She'd made her bed and had to lie in it.

"I never liked that Jason. I told you he was a liar and a con artist." It felt good to have her opinion of her daughter's ex validated so spectacularly. "You know you can't visit here for longer than a vacation. The covenants won't allow it. You're way too young to live here. I could get in trouble."

"I know that, but where the hell am I supposed to go? I've been trying to get another job, but my skills won't get me anything decent. Old man Watts overpaid me for what I did. Jesus, Mom, I can't support myself flipping burgers."

"How many times do I have to ask you to watch your mouth? I don't like that kind of language."

"OK, OK. But can I come out there and stay with you for a little while? Just long enough to get on my feet."

Serafina had mixed feelings. She tried to love Mary Beth

unconditionally, but they'd never had the easy relationship her daughter had had with her Dad. Mary Beth was always one to go her own way, often stumbling into disasters Serafina had warned her against. But what could she do? "OK, but not for long. There's a spy on my street reporting people to the HOA. I think it's Mrs. Jameson across the way. She's always watching everything, like a spider. If you stay for long, she'll see."

The silence stretched a few moments. "Like what does she do?"

"The lady down the road put up a cute new mailbox, but it wasn't the approved kind. They made her remove it. And someone was flying a flag in an unapproved way, and the HOA made them take it down. That old biddy has nothing better to do than complain about people breaking the covenants. You living here would be a big thing to report."

More silence. Serafina held her breath. She felt conflicted. She didn't want trouble from the HOA. Mary Beth and she would probably go at it like cats and dogs. But the thought of not being alone was attractive.

Mary Beth finally spoke. "They'd have to give you notice, a warning. If it comes to that, I'll leave. OK?"

That would work. Surely, they wouldn't kick her out of Palm Lakes without warning. "When will you come?"

"Soon."

"OK. I'll fix up the guest room." That settled, she found herself almost looking forward to it. The decision was made, and she'd have Mary Beth around to help her. She'd never admit it, but she was beginning to feel overwhelmed at all she had to do each day; she just didn't have the strength anymore.

Almost as if she'd read Serafina's mind, Mary Beth said, "Mom, you work too hard. I can fix it up when I arrive."

Serafina didn't want to argue anymore. "Just let me know when to expect you. I can make some lasagna."

Her daughter's voice warmed. "That would be great. I'll call and let you know once I set a date for the move."

"Fine." After they said their goodbyes, Serafina hung up the phone and thought about how strange life was. Just last week, her doctor had told her she had heart problems. He said the chest pains and weakness were symptoms, and he gave her some pills and cautioned her to slow down, but she only knew one way to live. The house had to be kept clean. Food had to be cooked. Shopping needed doing. If she didn't do it, who would? Did he think she was made of money?

She had no intention of turning her home over to Mary Beth to run, but there might a sunny side to her daughter's life falling apart. It felt good knowing she wouldn't have to face this alone. She might even get a little help.

CHAPTER THREE

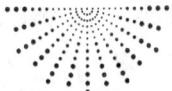

MONDAY, MAY 29, 1995

Helen, 11:00am

*H*elen heard the low rumble of the postman's truck as it stopped at her mailbox, then moved down her street to the next one. She wiped her hands and put the dish towel on the rack, pleased to have a distraction in her morning.

She stepped outside and was blinded by blazing sunlight as a wall of heat hit her. It was like being in a blast furnace. Memorial Day had dawned clear and bright, and it promised to be a typical desert scorcher. Not that most people in Palm Lakes Senior Community lingered outside this close to June; they were all cocooned in air-conditioned comfort.

As she tromped to the mailbox, she heard Barbara's door open and shut, and her next door neighbor strode down her sidewalk to pick up her mail. Helen waved shyly in recognition, then averted her gaze as she headed for her mailbox, but Barbara was not to be deterred by evasive tactics. "Helen, how are you?"

"I'm fine," she responded as she slowed down, unable to force herself to be rude. She wasn't really fine. But you couldn't tell people the truth, could you? They didn't really want to know.

Barbara came over and gave Helen a hug, which seemed an odd thing for a neighbor to do, but that was Barbara. She was the friendliest person Helen had ever met, and she seemed to be genuinely kind. Helen squirmed under her penetrating brown gaze, in spite of its warmth. "So, Helen, do you have any visitors for the holiday? Our kids managed to pry themselves away from their busy lives and come visit." She waved vaguely at the RV in her driveway and the strange car parked in front of her home. "We're having a barbecue later on. You and Lou are welcome to join us. We always have more than enough food." She reached up to push back a lock of auburn hair that had fallen across her eyes.

Helen was stymied by the unexpected invitation, though it wasn't the first. "Lou had to go out and run some errands, and I don't know what he has planned for later, so we'll have to pass. But thanks for inviting us."

Barbara reached over and patted her on the arm. She didn't seem put out by the rejection. "Another time, then."

Something furry rubbed against her bare legs, and Helen yelped and practically jumped out of her skin. Barbara recovered from Helen's screech and said calmly, "That's just Fluffy. You know her. She likes you."

Helen's eyes widened as she looked down at the long-haired, mostly white calico cat who was so enthusiastically rubbing against her. "She's lovely, but is it safe for her to be out here? And it's so hot today, too." Helen knew the neighbor on the other side of Barbara, Owen Schmidt, had been complaining about Barbara's pets running loose, because Barbara had mentioned it.

Barbara dismissed Helen's worries. "She never goes far. She's a real homebody. She doesn't like it when the house is full of strangers...Did I just call my kids and grandchildren 'strangers'?" She laughed, throwing her head back, and Helen found it impossible not to grin.

"But didn't he complain?" Helen pointed with her eyes towards Owen's house. "Couldn't he cause you trouble?"

Barbara waved her hand airily. "I think he was having a bad day and took it out on me. He threatened to report me to the HOA because our pets sometimes go in his yard. I don't let them out that often." She shrugged her shoulders and put her palms up in the air. "The right type of fence would cost too much. The covenants won't let you put up a chain link fence. We'll build a block wall someday, even though it will hit four figures. We don't want to have to put it on the credit card, so Jack and Fluffy will have to make do. They don't like being cooped up. We always let them roam back home, and frankly, it seems safer here."

Helen disagreed, but it was unlike her to argue. "I hope he won't report you."

"Don't worry about that, dear. We're just fine." Barbara looked down the row of graveled yards past Helen, her eyes shaded by her hand, her eyes squinting at the sun. "It's like Death Valley out here. This heat is draining me. I need to go back inside, and so do you. I'll see you later!" Barbara turned and got her mail out of her mailbox and jogged up the sidewalk, waving as she disappeared into the house.

Helen pulled the mail out of her box. A few bills and mostly junk mail. She wondered why she was always so eager to come check the mail, as if one day, there might actually be something interesting.

Samantha Taylor's pickup cruised down the street and pulled to a stop in front of her mother Maddie's house, just opposite Helen's. Samantha slipped out of the truck and waved at Helen, who waved back at her. Both of them headed into their houses.

As she opened her front door, Helen heard Maddie's dog, Beau, barking an alert that Samantha had arrived. It seemed everyone was having family celebrations today. She felt suddenly sad. Sad that she couldn't accept Barbara's generous invitations, which were tendered all too often. Sad that she wasn't having a family celebration this weekend. Sad that she had no one to be close to.

She sighed and went to dig her journal out of the cedar chest. Nestled with tens of other notebooks of varying sizes and colors under sweaters she hadn't used since leaving Wisconsin, her latest journal beckoned her to pour out her feelings. Lou hadn't said when he'd be back, but when he was in one of his moods, he was always gone for at least a few hours. And this morning, he'd been rumbling like Mt. St. Helens ready to erupt. After decades of marriage, she knew the signs. It didn't matter what she did. Sooner or later he'd take it out on her. So she was glad he was gone, and she'd steal some time to write in her journal.

She went out to the patio, even though it was stifling, just to feel she was getting away from the prison that was her home. She sat at the small table and opened the book, noting the date at the top of the next empty page using a Cross pen her kids had given her, one she saved for this purpose.

May 29, 1995

Memorial Day

I'm feeling sorry for myself again. Lou's off having a snit fit, and I know when he returns, nothing I do will prevent the explosion of his anger. At least he doesn't hit me anymore. It's been years since he got physical. His mother was right about that.

She paused in her writing, picturing that day years ago when her mother-in-law had made an unscheduled visit. It was about this time of year, and Helen was wearing a sleeveless shirt that did nothing to hide the huge black and purple bruises Lou had put on her upper arms. She was always careful to hide the bruises and never complained or said a word to her in-laws. She considered it her business and maybe her fault that he was like he was.

She'd run to answer the door when the bell rang, forgetting how she looked. Ethel's eyes had widened when she entered and saw the bruises, but she didn't immediately say anything. After a cup of coffee, she'd said without any preface, "It gets easier when they get older." Helen hadn't responded, because she couldn't quite comprehend. Did Ethel mean it was OK that Lou hit her? Obviously, she was a battered wife herself. Maybe growing up seeing that had warped Lou. She couldn't process how Ethel seemed to accept it as normal. But Ethel was right. As Lou aged, he became less physical in his abuse of her, but every time, she was still bruised. Just that now, you couldn't see the damage his anger wrought. Putting the pen on the page, she picked up the thread.

But the way he yells and gesticulates feels like he's hitting me. I've turned into a real coward. I don't really like myself, but I don't see how I can change things, so I just act small and quiet and hope things will blow over, and they do. But it's not a great way to live.

Barbara invited us over to a BBQ. She's so friendly and generous. She probably wonders what's wrong with me, with us. We never accept her invitations, and we never invite her over. Yet she continues to offer. She's the kind of person I wish I could be. Although I wouldn't let my cat wander outside. It's not only against the covenants; it's unsafe with all the coyotes and cars around here.

Just then the meowing started. Helen smiled and turned to see Sheba sitting inside the glass door, complaining that she couldn't be with her Mom. "I'll come back in, Precious. I didn't know you were awake. You know I love sitting with you." Helen picked up her journal and pen and slipped inside, reaching down to stroke Sheba's silky, long gray fur. She was rewarded with a deep barrage of purring. "Shall we go sit in the living room, Sheba?" Sheba looked at her as if she knew what she was saying. Maybe she did. Helen went to the couch and sat down. It wasn't a proper place to write, but she wouldn't be caught dead in Lou's office at his desk. He was so possessive of his territory.

Sheba jumped up next to Helen and settled in, pressing against Helen's leg in spite of the relative warmth of the day. Helen didn't mind. She continued her entry.

I hope that Fluffy and Jack stay safe. Barbara seems so confident, but I have doubts. And Owen Schmidt; I don't know why, but that man gives me the creeps. Maybe I've learned to recognize danger in a man. I certainly have had plenty of experience. Owen Schmidt seems reptilian —cold and alien— maybe I'm reading too much into it, but he scares me a little. I wouldn't cross him, but Barbara seems oblivious. I wonder who's right? I hope she is.

We don't get to see the kids and grandkids as often as I'd like, but then, I don't blame them for not wanting to visit us. Lou can be harsh, and they have lots of better things to do than visit us. Warren called yesterday to say hi. I haven't heard from Lena or Sally for weeks. Probably won't. Neither of them is the type for duty calls. I miss the kids, but they don't seem to miss me. I'm a little envious of Barbara and Maddie at times like this. I did the best I could with my kids, but they don't seem to have any affection for me.

I'd hoped living in Palm Lakes would be better. The desert is totally different from Wisconsin, but my life hasn't changed. I thought we'd have nicer weather here, but it turns out winters are cold enough to have the heat on, and the rest of the year, you're mostly locked inside your house in the air-conditioning. I had envisioned life here as closer to Nature, more outdoorsy. It's actually less so than Wisconsin.

And the neighborhood...Lou's thrilled not to cut grass or have children riding bikes up and down the sidewalk, screaming as they play, but I agree with Maddie. It's so quiet, it's like a mausoleum. I'd like to have a garden and be visited by my kids. This is supposed to be a fun retirement community. But Lou doesn't want me to participate in any clubs, and he won't accept invitations from the neighbors. So it hasn't been any fun.

Why don't I fight him? It isn't worth it. He might go back to hitting me. I'm so grateful I no longer have to put up with that.

Sheba reached out in her sleepy state, touching Helen's leg with her paw. Helen stopped and stroked the paw, and Sheba withdrew it. Then Helen petted Sheba's head, scratching her jaw. The purring ratcheted up a notch. "You like that, do you? You're my favorite person. I don't know what I'd do without you." Sheba continued purring in agreement. Thank heaven Lou never bothered Sheba. He seemed to instinctively know that Helen would not tolerate any violence towards her cat, just as she had made it clear she wouldn't tolerate violence towards her children. For some reason, he'd never challenged her on that, though he'd put her in the hospital twice and sent her to the doctor's more than once. Shaking her head at how strange life is, Helen decided to quit journaling. It wasn't helping her cast off her blues the way it usually did.

She returned the journal to its hiding place and wandered around the house doing laundry, dusting and vacuuming. Sheba made herself scarce when the vacuum came out. Poor thing. She didn't like the noise. Helen could relate. Loud noises scared her, too.

The afternoon sped by. She read a library book for a while, and then, seeing it was after 4pm, she decided she'd better make dinner. If Lou came home at 5pm on the dot, he'd expect it on the table and throw a tantrum if it wasn't. He was equally likely to berate her if he came home much later and the food was dried out and inedible. She couldn't win. But then, she never could with him, and she'd learned to take it in stride.

5:05 came and went, and she looked at the chili simmering on the stove. It wouldn't suffer for him being late. She better eat. He seemed to prefer not to eat with her when he was in one of his moods. She scooped out some chili and sat alone at the table, eating but not tasting it. Sheba sat glaring at her, telegraphing that it was time to feed her. Helen smiled. At least someone wanted and needed her. She finished her bowl of chili and then fed an appreciative Sheba her favorite tuna meal. By then it was approaching 6pm.

It was strange that Lou had been gone this long. When he went out, it was usually no more than 3 hours. Not that he ever told her where he went, and she never asked. Asking was a trigger for violence. He didn't feel answerable to anyone, and he wouldn't like her to challenge him with questions. He wasn't a social drinker, so he probably wasn't at a bar. He didn't run around, at least as far as she knew. But what did she really know about him? He was always disappearing, making it look like she'd made him mad. Maybe he had another family nearby. She shook her head at the incongruous thought, Lou pretending to be mad at her and running to be with another woman. What other woman would have him? He was such a jerk. Feeling a little guilty, she jumped when she heard the garage door go up. He was back. Instantly she was overcome with bone-deep fear, the premonition of something bad about to happen.

She looked about the room, as if checking to see it was in order, then she went into the kitchen and prepared to serve his meal. The chili looked fine, so he shouldn't complain about that. Well, he could and often did complain about things that weren't wrong. Why did she still expect even a vestige of rationality and fair play? Maybe like he said, she was the problem, not him.

He walked into the kitchen, his face sour and wrinkled. She could always tell by how his face looked that he was in one of his moods. Tense, rigid, practically simmering with rage, he seated himself at the table and dug into the bowl she put in front of him without a greeting or a word of explanation for his long absence. She said nothing.

She went over and got him a beer out of the refrigerator. He always liked to have a single beer with chili. She pulled a chilled glass out of the freezer and popped the top off the beer bottle, pouring the beer carefully to avoid too much foam. She placed the full glass, as pretty as any TV beer commercial, by his right side. He ignored her and kept wolfing down chili.

She had no illusions that the evening would go well, but she kept hoping. She always kept hoping. Maybe if she'd ever really given up, she would have left him. It was her infernal tendency to be hopeful that made it easier to stay with him than to leave. He hadn't even raised his eyes to her since he'd entered the room. She turned to leave. "Where do you think you're going?" he grumbled.

"I have some laundry to fold." He seemed to like it if she were working.

"Why didn't you do that while I was gone? What have you been doing all day? Shooting the breeze on the phone with your girlfriends?"

What a stupid question! He knew she had no friends. He made sure of it.

"Or were you watching soaps on the TV?" The sneer didn't bother her. It was the tightly held anger beneath the surface, glittering in his eyes, that scared her. He hadn't hit her in a long time, but there were no guarantees.

"I did all the housework and made dinner." Then, against her better judgment, she asked, "Is everything OK? You were gone a long time."

The flash in his eyes confirmed she had made a mistake. "What business is it of yours? I don't answer to you!" He stabbed at the chili with his spoon, then practically growled at her. "This chili stinks. Why can't you cook anything decent?"

So that was going to be the trigger this time. He'd always loved her chili, which was the very reason she'd made it, hoping to smooth things over. It seemed she'd spent her life trying to smooth his way, with very poor results. She said nothing, keeping her eyes cast down. He didn't like her to look straight at him when he was in this mood. Thank heaven Sheba was somewhere else. She had a sixth sense about avoiding Lou at times like this.

She heard rather than saw the dish crash against the edge of the counter, and the bowl shattered as it hit the floor, splashing chili everywhere. Helen cringed as she felt a few drops of chili and a small shard of glass hit her legs. Maybe he'd leave now that he'd broken something. Her eyes closed and cast down, she couldn't see what he did next, but she heard him rise abruptly, his chair hitting the wall, and stalk out of the kitchen. She took a deep breath, opened her eyes and surveyed the damage. She'd cleaned up worse.

She stepped around the mess and got a clean rag and the broom and dustpan out from under the sink. Paper towels would be wonderful at times like this, but Lou didn't like to spend money on anything like that. He wouldn't even let her buy Kleenex; he said toilet paper worked just fine for blowing your nose. You'd think he was still living through the Depression.

She picked the bigger pieces of glass up and threw them into the garbage can. Then she meticulously picked all the smaller fragments by hand and disposed of them as well. When she was pretty sure the glass was all collected, she wiped up the chili with the wet cloth. Afterwards, she took the broom and dustpan and swept the area at least five feet out from the point of impact. She couldn't have Sheba stepping in glass, and it always seemed at least one piece flew farther than you'd think. Ah, there it was, a good-sized chunk under the edge of the counter quite a distance from the point of impact. Satisfied that she had cleaned up the mess, she put everything away.

She could hear the TV blaring in the living room. Lou was getting deaf. Not that she minded. It was better than listening to him yell, and as long as he watched TV, he probably wouldn't attack her verbally. It appeared he wasn't going to make a bigger fuss tonight after all. Once again, she wondered where he'd been all day. He had nowhere else to go that she knew of.

She went into the laundry room and commenced folding the last load of clothes from the dryer. When she finished that, she would read her book. She planned to stay up reading until he went to bed and fell asleep. In spite of his antipathy towards her, he refused to let her move into the guest bedroom. Why, she didn't know. Who was she going to tell? Always, he'd been more afraid of how things looked to others than how it looked to her, but she didn't have the nerve to fight him. It took too much energy.

She petted Sheba, who was in the walk-in closet of the master bedroom hiding on a shelf behind Helen's clothes. Sheba seemed perfectly OK there. So she grabbed her library book and went out to the kitchen to read. She didn't want to be in the same room as Lou.

She got so engrossed in the romance novel that she lost track of time. At 9:05, she looked up and wondered why the TV was still blaring. He always went to bed at 9pm on the dot. She put the book down and crept to the doorway, looking out into the living room. She couldn't see anything but the top of Lou's head. His recliner faced the TV, away from her.

She stood in the doorway listening, as if she could discern what was going on with him by doing so. Nothing. Finally, she tiptoed into the living room, stopping every few steps to see if he reacted. Still nothing. When she got to the couch, she slowly sank into it, in case he woke up. She didn't want to appear to be looking at him. She could see his face in profile, and it appeared he had fallen asleep. That wasn't like him, but maybe the fight had taken more out of him than she realized. She gently kicked the coffee table, trying to wake him up without speaking to him. There was no reaction.

The room was fairly dark and she couldn't see a lot of detail, as the only light was that cast by the television. She was beginning to feel nervous. Something was wrong.

She stood up slowly and walked to the other side of his recliner and looked at him. His eyes were closed, and he looked more peaceful than she'd ever seen him. The tension had drained from his face. The corners of his lips were turned downward, but otherwise, he seemed relaxed.

Then she noticed. She couldn't see him breathing. She leaned closer, looking for the rise and fall of his chest or his ample belly. No movement that she could see. She looked for the telltale flicker of a pulse on the side of his neck, but there was nothing. Finally, she forced herself to reach over and touch his shoulder.

"Lou." Her whisper was ignored. She spoke a bit louder. "Lou!" He still didn't move. Not a flutter of an eyelash.

Something like fear gripped her, and she wondered why she was scared. She'd always thought he'd end up killing her, or at least, that she'd be the first to go. She grabbed his shoulder and shook it. "Lou, wake up!" She had disturbed the balance of his body, and it slumped forward. She gingerly reached to feel for the carotid artery, like they did on TV. No pulse, and not as warm as normal to the touch. He was dead.

She gazed on him as if from a distance for a few seconds, her mind skipping around the obvious fact, as if unwilling to grapple with it. She tottered over to the couch and sank into it, hands clasped, breathing shallowly, heart pumping as if fueled by adrenaline.

It was almost as if a wall had been flung up before her, hiding a future she didn't want to contemplate. The wall didn't prevent emotions from slowly seeping into her awareness. Fear came first, tied to the question, "What am I going to do?", a question for which she had no answer. Then guilt bit into her. She had wished him gone out of her life, even dead, more times than she wanted to admit, so did that mean she had any part in this event? Could you wish someone dead hard enough that they finally succumbed? No, that was ridiculous. She shoved the guilt aside, refused to acknowledge the fear, and that's when she got a glimmer, however faint, of light. Of happiness. Lou would never hurt her again. The prison sentence of her marriage had been commuted to a life sentence of being alone. Then she felt guilty all over again for being glad to be free.

Suddenly, she felt a chill in spite of the relative warmth of the room. If Lou's spirit were hanging around, which she hoped it wasn't, he'd be yelling at her for not having grabbed the phone immediately to call for help. That realization highlighted how different life would be from now on. No one was going to verbally abuse or control her ever again. She would have the right to choose what she did. She was ready to make the call.

She walked to the phone and dialed 911, then went to the door and waited for the EMTs. Not ten minutes later, they pulled up, lights flashing. One technician raced ahead to meet her while others got a stretcher out of the vehicle. It was a young woman with dark hair in a ponytail. "Did you place the call? Where's the patient?" Helen nodded and led the woman, whose name tag said Miller, into the living room. Ms. Miller crouched down, examined Lou and then looked at Helen with sympathy. "I'm sorry, but he's gone. We'll have to take him to the hospital morgue. You can follow us or come with us if you don't feel like driving."

Helen had known he was dead, but someone else saying it made it seem more real. She struggled to put words together. "I'll follow you in my car. Where should I go?"

"Just go to the hospital and ask at the desk. They'll direct you where to go. We'll need to get some information from you."

Helen shrank in on herself. What if they thought she had done something to Lou? Not that she hadn't wished him dead more than once. But she wasn't the type to kill a person. Panic seeped into her being, and she felt herself losing control. Beating it back, she forced herself to answer the woman. "Thank you. I'll do that. I won't be far behind." The other two team members loaded Lou's body onto the stretcher and carried it out in the dark to the ambulance.

Helen watched them drive away, their lights and sirens now thankfully off. The neighbors would be asking her tomorrow about what had happened. Not much got past them, and since this was a retirement community, incidents like this happened with a depressing frequency.

She got her purse and locked up the house and drove to the hospital. A good while later, she returned home to Sheba's protestations that she had abandoned her. Helen dropped her purse on the nearest table and crouched down to pick up Sheba. The clock said 11:23. She sank into an armchair, stroking the cat, wondering what to do next. It was too late to call the kids. She'd have to do that tomorrow. She dreaded it. It was almost as if she felt they'd blame her for Lou's death, or wish it were her, instead. Why did she feel that way? Was it just guilt, or was it something else?

She carried Sheba out to the kitchen. She knew she wouldn't sleep tonight. She hunted through the pantry and found a bottle of cheap red wine in the back. It had a screw top, so she didn't have to look for a corkscrew. She poured a healthy slug of wine into a juice glass. Sitting at the table, she spoke to Sheba, who sat on the adjacent chair. "It looks like I'm celebrating, but I'm not, really. I'm not sad. But I'm not happy, either. I don't know what I feel. Why did it never occur to me that something like this could happen?"

She sipped the wine, and a chill stole over her. She had a funeral to plan. At least he'd bought plots at the local cemetery, so she had a place to bury him. She had no idea about their finances. Lou had handled the bills and the money. She was going to have to learn all that. She didn't even know if he had life insurance. Her heart pounded in fear. She wasn't stupid, but she'd never been to college. She'd married him so young. She'd never been on her own before. Imagine. On her own at age 60 for the first time. She was scared.

She gulped more wine and looked at Sheba. "We'll manage fine without him." But her wavering voice betrayed her lack of conviction.

* * *

Alexander, 12:15pm

ALEXANDER SAVORED his cheeseburger as he sat alone at a wrought iron table in the retro diner's outdoor seating area, surrounded by shade trees and holiday makers taking advantage of the gorgeous summer weather. Located in Seligman, AZ on historic Route 66, the eatery, like so many in the small town, evoked another era before Interstate 40 had rerouted traffic away from many of the former locations where people once got their kicks.

Though the restaurant was more of an old style fast food place than a sit-down establishment, the hamburger was thick and juicy, made from local beef and paired with a rather nice cheddar cheese. The lettuce was not iceberg, thank heaven, and the tomato wasn't home grown, but at least was ripe, and they hadn't drowned the burger in condiments, a pet peeve of his. Why mask the flavor of good beef, cheese and fresh veggies? The fries, on the other hand, were greasy and rubbery. He wouldn't waste his appetite on them. The patter provided by the proprietor when he took the order made up for any deficiencies in the food, though. In spite of the hackneyed spiel, the middle-aged, bespectacled owner had a bright, enthusiastic delivery that forced a smile from you. He would recommend this place in his book. It was unique as hamburger joints went.

Alexander's microcassette recorder lay beside his plate, ready for his impressions. His latest book project was historic Route 66. As a travel and food writer, he had the opportunity to visit exotic places and eat delicious food in countries around the globe, and he'd made a fine living doing what he loved. When he'd first pitched this project to his publisher, he'd envisioned it as a break from his usual, more serious subjects of foreign travel and haute cuisine, a chance to have some fun and write a book that would appeal to a larger crowd. And it had the benefit of being close to home. For a change, he was traveling like an average tourist, sampling meals and being entertained on a budget.

He'd begun his journey in Chicago at one end of old Route 66 and worked westward, so he'd been on the road for some time before he arrived in Arizona a few days ago. As with other parts of the route, he found many of the smaller towns strung along the old road were dead or dying. Seligman was actually hopping, but he knew summer was the only time it was busy. Vacationers came in droves by car and bus, visiting the old diners, rock shops, gift stores and other tourist traps. The motel he was staying at, a refurbished 50s place, wasn't bad, just sad somehow.

The trip had failed to create the sense of discovery he usually had when he went exploring, and this place in particular had gotten to him. It was almost as if he were reviewing his life, and that wasn't a goal he'd had in mind for this trip.

Seligman had succeeded perhaps too well in throwing him back in time. Route 66's heyday was during his youth, when he was trying so hard to figure out who he was. He'd never been here before, but oldies music blasted everywhere he went, and everything from signs to cars to architecture plunged him decades into the past. He hadn't anticipated how it would affect him.

He fingered the recorder, then slipped it into his jacket pocket without saying anything. He'd record his observations later. He didn't want melancholia to tinge what he wrote. Maybe not so much because he felt it wouldn't go over well, but because it revealed too much. He realized that the written word of necessity exposed him to his readers, but he liked to limit how much he gave away. So he decided to enjoy the sunshine, the warmth and the juicy burger.

When he finished his meal, he tossed his trash into the bin and drove back to his motel. He dropped onto the bed—no fancy suite furniture here—and pondered what to do as traffic droned by beyond the parking lot. He was still feeling down.

He wasn't yet pressured by a deadline on his manuscript. Palm Lakes Senior Community, where he lived, was only a several hour drive away, and a scenic one at that, along fast interstates. Maybe he should go home and regroup. But he knew that he was kidding himself. This place had brought old wounds to the surface. It wasn't the location that was his problem. It was the past.

Seeing that old '49 Pontiac today, restored and painted bright yellow, had taken him back to his youth. His Dad had owned that exact car—painted black, of course—and he had vivid memories of it. It wasn't the most stylish ride, with the big seats, no seat belts, and windows that were hard for a kid to roll down, but every road trip had been an adventure for him, even though there hadn't been many. As a young teen, he had eagerly awaited the time when he could drive, and in fact, that Pontiac had been the very car he'd learned on. His Dad was a harsh teacher who tolerated no mistakes, but Alexander had been an apt pupil. He still enjoyed road trips.

Both his parents were gone now, had been for years, but his current surroundings had revived memories of unpleasant times, and they played in his head like old movies. He knew he couldn't change the past, and he very much wanted to move on, but some events haunted him, just waiting for a trigger, no matter how hard he tried to put them away for good.

Like the time his mother had told him, when he'd shared his 12-year-old's dream of becoming a writer, that he couldn't make a living that way and needed to choose something else. His dad had overheard the conversation and raged about him getting above himself. Asked him how he thought he'd pay for college. Dad had shouted that he couldn't and wouldn't pay for such nonsense. It was almost as if he felt Alexander was judging his father for being a lowly mechanic.

Ever after that day, Dad would rag on him after he'd had a few drinks, which happened more and more frequently as he aged. His favorite theme was how Alexander would never amount to anything. Mom had tried to balance his father's nastiness by praising him for doing well in school, but she couldn't erase the effects of his father's constant judgment.

Alexander didn't please his Dad by growing into a tall, handsome teenager any more than he had by being smart. His looks and his interest in school, writing and fashion both mystified and mortified Dad. One time when drunk, Dad had said he didn't know who Alexander's father was, but it obviously wasn't him. Funny how it had hurt at the time, yet with the wisdom of years, Alexander could see it was Dad's insecurity talking. But still, he wished it could have been different.

It seemed all through his teenage years, Alexander struggled to figure out where he belonged. A scholarship to ASU had been his ticket out of Chicago and into a whole new world, a world where he found acceptance and approval for the first time. He even began to accept he was a magnet for babes, even though dating wasn't his first priority. The looks his Dad criticized could have opened doors in Hollywood, but Alexander stuck to his plan of becoming a writer with a rare degree of focus.

Too bad his big breakthrough had come after he had lost both parents. It had taken him years after college to finally get published, and some years after that before he had a bestseller. Not that he had illusions his Dad would have been proud. Mom, maybe. But he'd burned too many bridges with them over the years. They'd hated his friends, his choices and had even blown up when he'd foolishly told them he'd fallen in love.

He rubbed his eyes in an effort to stop the replay of his past. He had to admit they'd been right about Leslie, but that was all over years ago. Serially unfaithful Leslie, whom he had forgiven and nursed through a long, ugly decline into death. He no longer looked for a happy ever after. Wasn't even sure he believed it existed.

He'd created a solid, predictable and successful life alone, and that's what he intended to stick with. Yet at times like this, he felt an aching emptiness that cried to be filled, not with money or success or adulation, but with warmth and easy companionship. He grimaced at his wallowing. This line of thought was stupid. He had friends, after all, and a cat who adored him, or at least liked having him as a servant. That was enough.

Coming here had stirred up the pain and rejection of the past, but wallowing in self-pity was pointless. He shook his head. He'd learned long ago that what he focused on expanded. He needed to look at the good things in his life, not those sorry childhood years. He suddenly laughed out loud at the picture of himself as some kind of victim.

He was a successful food and travel writer. Successful? No, he was more than that. He'd written over 20 books, five of them New York Times bestsellers, and he had more money than he could ever spend. His golf course mansion in Palm Lakes was furnished in a tasteful and expensive style that reminded him of his many trips exploring world cuisine and his status as a well-known travel writer, as well as showcasing valuable keepsakes from those trips. He also had his health, and even though it meant little to him, he had his looks.

Being handsome was something he regarded as a handicap. As a bachelor in Palm Lakes, he was vastly outnumbered by women desperate to find a mate, and the last thing he needed was romance. He was done with that, but no one could imagine him choosing to be alone, simply because of his looks.

He'd developed strategies for avoiding the many tuna casseroles and invitations to dinner and more by screening his calls and not socializing much. Barbara, whose husband Ben was a favorite golfing buddy, was a consummate hostess and extrovert who continued to try and set him up, but he skillfully turned down invitations to dinner to meet new people. He attended her parties, but he wasn't going on any more blind dates.

He was comfortable on his own, but still, he liked good company. That's one reason he'd joined the cooking club at Palm Lakes. It was a safe way to socialize without making sticky connections. He'd met a gay couple, Ray and Alan, in the last class, and he suspected they might become friends, but he was taking things slow. He was content to have his Siamese cat Fido as his closest confidante and friend. Fido never made demands on him other than expecting good service from his human servant.

So why was he in a funk? Thinking of the past made him feel lonely, because it highlighted his failure with his family and with 'true love.' Tired of the self-analysis, he determined to get out and hit a couple shops before going to get a steak at the biggest restaurant in town. He wasn't going to be dragged down this negative vortex. If anything could get him back on track, it was a good meal. Maybe they'd even have a nice vintage of cabernet sauvignon.

CHAPTER FOUR

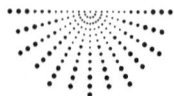

THURSDAY, JUNE 22, 1995

Maddie, 7:10am

$\mathcal{L}$ast night's monsoon storm had stripped the heat from the air, but Maddie knew the moisture would only add humidity to triple-digit temperatures by afternoon. At least right now, it was pleasant enough to sit on the back patio with her morning coffee watching the wildlife.

She delighted in seeing the quail families troop through the yard, pausing at the quail block for a snack. The hummers were noisily jockeying for position at the feeder that dangled just yards away, and their iridescent splendor never ceased to raise her spirits. But most of all, she loved the bunnies. The plethora of desert cottontails in Palm Lakes was regarded by some residents as a scourge, but to Maddie, they were charming friends. She leaned down and offered a small piece of lettuce to the adult rabbit she'd named Jeremiah. Her husband Stanley scoffed at her for naming the rabbits, not believing it was possible to tell one from another, but that was only because he didn't spend as much time watching them as she did.

"Come on, Jeremiah. You'll love this."

The rabbit had become bolder over the summer but still exercised caution. Beau, her big yellow Lab, was indoors, and he never harmed the animals, but the rabbits were understandably afraid of him.

"Beau's inside. You're safe."

Finally, Jeremiah hopped close enough to grab the green leaf, which he carried under the orange tree and munched happily, so close that even with her old ears, Maddie could hear the crunching.

Jeremiah might be a girl, of course; Maddie couldn't tell a rabbit's gender, but she'd decided Jeremiah was a boy because he was so brave and bold.

When her mug was empty, Maddie heaved herself from the chair, ignoring the joint and back pain that was becoming more insistent every day. Her daughter Samantha had been campaigning for her to see a doctor, and in spite of not wanting too, she'd given in. Her appointment was coming up in several days. It probably wouldn't do any good, but at least she'd get Samantha off her back by going. You'd think at age 72, she could be allowed to do as she pleased. She grunted with displeasure as she left her patio oasis.

Inside, she could tell that Stanley had eaten his breakfast by the dishes on the counter. He always had dry cereal and tea for breakfast, which gave her a break from cooking. Seemed like all she did was cook, and she hated it. She gave some thought to frying up some bacon and eggs for herself, but her appetite wasn't enough to overcome her aversion to cooking. Maybe she'd eat something later. She paused to load the dishwasher— Stanley emptied it every morning and put away the clean dishes, but never loaded it—and refilled her mug with coffee, then headed for the dining room table.

Flicking on the study lamp that sat in the middle of the table in the dim room—the curtains were closed to keep out the scalding summer sunshine —Maddie sank into a chair and reached for her jeweler's magnifying glasses, setting the contraption on her head like a miner's lamp.

The rectangular table was piled high on both ends with boxes of her jewelry supplies, leaving a clear, brightly-lit square in front of her in which to work. Thank heaven they only used the formal dining area for family dinners and special occasions. Unlike Stanley, who had a snug office with custom bookshelves in the converted laundry room, Maddie had no work area of her own. This had to do.

In front of her lay a nearly-completed necklace of graded, round tiger eye beads with gold findings, gold spacer beads and fresh water pearls for contrast. She was pleased with how it had turned out. Helen would like it, poor dear. Or maybe she wasn't a poor dear. Maddie had never really like Lou. Maybe Helen was better off without him. Sometimes she felt she'd be better off alone, but then, she hated the idea of being alone, so she didn't know what to wish for. Anyway, it was wrong to wish anyone dead, and she wouldn't do that.

Beau leaped from his spot near her chair, barking as he raced to the front door. Maddie's daughter Samantha walked in without knocking and leaned over to pet the dog, who wagged his whole body in welcome. Samantha was dressed for work—not that differently from everyday, but somehow less casual, even in shorts and sandals, so it must be a work day. Darned if Maddie knew what day of the week it was. They all seemed alike, except Sundays, when Samantha and her husband Arthur would come for a visit or a meal or drop off shopping items.

"Hey, Mom. Whatcha working on?" Samantha strode over and examined the necklace over Maddie's shoulder. "That's nice tiger eye. Who's it for?"

"Helen. Her husband died on Memorial Day, and we didn't go to the funeral. I can't do funerals ever since I was a kid and they made me kiss my dead aunt—the one I'm named after."

"Yuck! That's a horrible thing to do to a kid. How old were you?"

"I'm not sure. Maybe four or five."

"I can't understand why anyone would do that to a child!" She leaned over and brushed her fingers gently across the tiger eye beads. "Helen seems nice. I'm sure she'll understand."

Easy for her to say. It seemed to Maddie that no one ever understood her. "Well, I made this for her instead. She likes my jewelry, so I thought it would...show my sympathy. Not that I liked Lou. He was so gruff. Always scowling."

"It's kind of you to do this."

Maddie shrugged off the compliment. "I enjoy making jewelry, so it's no big deal."

Samantha patted Maddie's shoulder. "It is to those of us who get such beautiful gifts. You're very talented."

"Why the visit?" Maddie changed the subject to hide her discomfort at Samantha's kindness.

"I have an appointment on Echo Lane soon—a redo of a yard. Someone just moved in, and they want to make changes. I thought I'd stop by and say hi and see if you need anything from Price Club. We're going this weekend."

Maddie struggled to answer, not sure what they might need and unable to focus her mind away from not wanting her daughter to shop for her. Not that she liked to shop herself. She hated it. But she was uncomfortable being waited on. Samantha was so busy working and taking care of her own yard, and she still found time to bake, invite them to dinner and do things in Maddie's yard. Maddie knew she should be grateful, but it only seemed to highlight how incompetent she was, so she resented it.

"I'm not sure what we need, if anything," Maddie finally blurted.

"I can at least check your toilet paper stock," said Samantha, heading for the large hall closet they used as a storage area. After a minute, "No, you've got plenty," came Samantha's muffled voice from the closet.

When Samantha returned, Maddie said, "I think we're OK. I'll call you if I can think of something." Making lists was Stanley's strong suit, not hers, but she was pretty sure they didn't need anything.

"Then I'll head out," answered Samantha agreeably.

"Say hello to Dad first."

"OK." Samantha trooped off to Stanley's office with an air of reluctance. Maddie wasn't sure what that was about. She was perpetually mad at Stanley, but she'd never seen Samantha out of sorts with her father.

When Samantha left a short while later, Maddie was nearly finished the necklace and was thinking about the matching earrings. She'd already designed them and chosen materials. The end was in sight. This set was perfect for Helen's coloring. She was going to love it. At least, she hoped she would.

* * *

Barbara, 12:15pm

"THIS IS DELICIOUS!" Ben smacked his lips in exaggerated appreciation.

Barbara smiled at her husband's compliment. He was such an appreciative audience for a cook. "It's just chicken salad," she protested.

"But the...what do you call it, dressing? It's really good." He closed his eyes as he chewed, as if being transported to heaven.

What a hoot he was. "It's a Thai-style dressing with peanuts, lime juice, chopped fresh serrano pepper, things like that. I wanted a cold lunch, but I'm tired of the same old chicken salad recipe. Glad you approve." She tasted hers, nodding in agreement with him. This recipe was a keeper.

"This is restaurant quality. I hope you make it again."

His enjoyment pleased her. "Count on it. It did turn out rather well. So how was your golf game this morning?"

"Steven and I agree it's just too blasted hot to play. Even with the early tee time, it was horrible and sticky by the end of the game."

Barbara couldn't resist commenting, "You never had that problem back in California."

Ben shot her a sharp, blue-eyed look. "Are you not happy here? I know I was the one who wanted to move the most, but..."

Swamped with sudden guilt, Barbara shook her head. "I'm just a little down. The Homeowners Association sent us a letter about Fluffy and Jack. Owen must have complained, though they aren't naming names. I was really upset at first by their threats, but I've calmed down. Mostly." She chewed in troubled silence, then reached for her iced tea. When she put the glass down, her eyes met Ben's compassionate stare.

"I'm sorry, but it looks like we need to make more of an effort to keep them inside." He raised his hand before she could object. "I know, you hate doing that, and so do I, but what choice do we have? There isn't a fence we could erect that would contain Fluffy. Anyway, I'd like to postpone that expense."

Barbara sighed. "I can't imagine them kicking us out of Palm Lakes for something so small."

Ben chuckled. "They're just flexing their muscles, but let's try a bit harder to comply. What do you say?" He raised his iced tea in salute and sipped it.

"OK. But if they aren't serious about putting a lien on our house, it doesn't motivate me to put Jack and Fluffy in jail forever." She knew she was being stubborn, but this problem highlighted why she'd been happier in California.

Ben shook his head knowingly and drawled, "If you want to move back to California, let's just do it."

She knew she'd crossed an invisible line. Ben loved Palm Lakes and would hate to leave. Fact was, she was finding more to like every day. Changing the subject, she said, "I started a yoga class today. The teacher is excellent, and I met two nice ladies there. Jean and Lydia and I are going to have lunch regularly." That put the sparkle back in Ben's blue eyes. A flash of white teeth when he smiled and laugh lines crinkling in his tanned face assured her the crisis had passed. She rushed to reassure him. "I do like Palm Lakes. It's just when something like this happens, it's hard not to feel hemmed in. And summer is pretty brutal."

"Why not throw a party in August? It might relieve the monsoon blues."

Barbara grinned. "I do like a party."

"You always enjoy bringing people together. Speaking of which, are you matchmaking for anyone new at the moment?" He finished off his salad and tossed her a sly look.

"No one. Not really. But I have been thinking about Helen."

Ben harrumphed. "She's recently widowed."

"I know that, but I always had the feeling they weren't happy. In fact, she gives off an abused vibe, so afraid to speak up for herself."

Ben stood and started gathering the dishes, eyes unfocused as he processed what she'd said. "She does have a fragile air about her. Maybe you're right. We never got to know Lou more than to nod hello. Who are you planning to sacrifice on Cupid's altar?"

Barbara stood and put her hands on her hips. "Stop that!" It was pointless to even pretend annoyance. He knew her so well. "I was thinking of Alexander, but he's so slippery, I can't imagine how to even introduce them."

"I'm sure you'll find a way." Ben kissed her as he passed, hands full of dishes. She grabbed the remaining silverware and his glass and followed him into the kitchen. He started rinsing dishes and loaded the dishwasher. "They'd make a handsome couple, I'll give you that, but if you don't quit trying to hustle Alexander, I might lose him as a golfing buddy."

"I promise not to push too hard."

Ben's skepticism was palpable. After a poorly executed stern look, he said, "Just no more inviting him to dinner to meet someone. It's clear he's on to that ploy."

"I promise," she reassured him. She wasn't entirely certain about Helen, so it made sense to think about it some more. She'd figure a way.

* * *

Mary Beth, 4:30pm

MARY BETH HAD BEEN PUTTING off the decision for weeks, but the time had come. Her severance package had allowed her to hang around town, but the divorce was now final, and all her efforts to find a new job had failed. Her back was playing hell with her, and her cigarette habit had ballooned. Worse yet, she'd put on a few pounds because sweets had become her comfort food. Mom wasn't going to allow her to smoke indoors and had the eyes of an eagle and wasn't afraid to criticize, so she knew she was in for it.

Well, no time like the present. She'd decided to pull the plug, so she might as well inform Mom. She picked up the phone and dialed, half hoping she'd get no answer, but luck wasn't with her.

"Hello?"

"Mom, it's me."

A short silence was followed by her Mom's sharp voice. "So when are you coming out here, or was that just something you were saying? I thought you had money problems."

"Yeah, Mom. I do, but I was hoping I could find something here rather than impose on you. But there's nothing. And my severance package was OK, but it's dwindling, and I need money to rent a storage space and move. And the divorce is final. I'm ready to set a date and come out. If I can hold out to the end of July, I won't have to break my lease, and I'll get the security deposit back. Is early August OK for you?" She knew Mom would say yes but liked being asked.

A sigh from Mom confused her. "Whenever you want to is fine. Your room is ready." Why did Mom sound wistful? Or was she imagining it?

"Is everything all right?" She couldn't picture Mom being anything except totally fine, but something didn't sound normal.

"Of course, I am," Mom snapped.

Maybe she was just feeling paranoid because of all that had happened. "I'm going to look into storage units near Palm Lakes. Do you have one to recommend?"

"The U-Haul place is fairly new and close by. Their units are supposedly air-conditioned."

"That sounds perfect. I'll give them a call once I'm clear on how much space I need. It won't be large. Could you give me their phone number?" She was depressed to think how little stuff she had. On the other hand, maybe it was time to get rid of the old life completely. Suddenly, she craved a cigarette. "I'll let you know the exact date when I expect to arrive, but it will be early in August for sure."

"Whenever you get here, I'm ready. Maybe you can find a job out here. Hold on while I get the number for you."

She stared at the phone in astonished silence. Mom wanted her to stay? Well, Mary Beth was game to live in Arizona, just not with Mom forever. That would be a terrible mistake.

Finally, Mom returned with the phone number, and after she wrote it down, Mary Beth said, "Sure, Mom, I'll look for a job out there. I wouldn't mind living in Arizona. I like the sun."

"Good." The finality in Mom's voice signaled approbation. It was rare to hear approval from Mom. She wondered why Mom was glad to have her coming to live there when she'd expressed concerns. Well, that didn't matter.

Mary Beth signed off and immediately lit up a cigarette. Her life was too confusing now for her to toss another worry onto the heap. Mom sounded weird, but she needed to take her at her word. She had a few weeks to sort out the move and storage space, so she'd be busy. Certainly she'd be getting rid of a bunch of stuff rather than pay to store it. At this point, she could have walked away from it all without feeling anything. She was so numb from the events of the past months.

She crushed her cigarette in the ash tray and went to the tiny kitchen in her rented apartment to cook a frozen pizza. As the pizza heated, she pulled a beer out of the refrigerator and popped the top. Heineken. She didn't have much money, but good beer was a treat she was allowing herself. She rarely had more than two in an evening, and surely she deserved some kind of joy in her life. That would be another thing Mom would comment on. She would have to make sure she didn't drink more than Mom felt was appropriate. And she couldn't cuss. Dammit, what had she signed up for? All her vices were verboten at Mom's place. She was probably going to go batshit crazy living with Mom. Or they'd kill each other.

A sigh escaped her as she sank into a chair at the small dining table. She had no choice, in fact was lucky to have a fallback position. She'd manage somehow. It wouldn't be for long.

CHAPTER FIVE

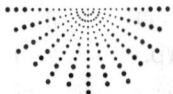

SATURDAY, JULY 1, 1995

Red, 5:50am

*T*he radio pierced the silence in Red's cruiser. "Who's closest to Sunset Drive?"

Red reached for the radio. "I am. What's up?"

"We've got a woman in distress, sounds like a possible heart attack. She didn't want to call 911. I called them anyway. 20146 Sunset Drive. Get over there and try to talk her into letting the ambulance take her to the hospital."

"Roger that." Red hung the radio back up on the dashboard and made his way as swiftly as possible to the address, noting that there was no sign of an ambulance. Great. He sure hoped the old lady didn't croak on him.

He pulled into the driveway, wondering if the woman had a husband. Probably not. If so, she'd have made him drive her to the hospital. The front door opened before he even had a chance to knock. A diminutive, gray-haired woman confronted him with a scowl. "You took long enough to get here," she panted, waving him inside.

Being dressed down was the last thing he'd expected. He entered and regarded her for signs of heart problems. She had a hand on her chest, and her wrinkled face was gray, but brown eyes pierced him with incredible focus. "I don't believe I should drive, the way I feel." She paused to catch her breath.

Talk about understatement. "How long have you felt this way?" Red was afraid she might collapse before the EMTs arrived.

"Since about 4am. But it's a little better. I have medicine, but it didn't help much. I have no one to drive me. Will you please?"

"The ambulance is on its way. We should wait for it."

Her eyes widened and anger flared in them. "I don't want to go in an ambulance. I made that very clear."

Riling her might be counterproductive at this point. Where was the ambulance, anyway? He made a snap decision. "OK, let's go. Do you have your ID, Medicare and insurance cards, things you'll need?"

She patted the large purse hanging on her arm. "I'm ready."

He escorted her to the car and got her seated, scanning the street for the ambulance, but there was nothing. He climbed in and started the car. Then he reached for the radio. "Base, it's Red. I'm taking...what's your name, ma'am?"

"Serafina Costello."

"I'm taking Ms. Costello to the hospital. The ambulance hasn't shown up, and she's having chest pains. I think I can get her there quicker, and she insists I take her. You better call off the EMTs." He hoped there wouldn't be liability issues.

"Ooookay," said dispatch. "Drive carefully."

"Roger that." He backed out of the driveway and sped to the hospital, a quick five minute drive. He kept glancing in the rear view mirror to the back seat where she rested quietly, her arms around her massive purse. "Are you buckled in?"

Her eyes, which had been half shut, snapped wide open. She snorted. "It's only a five minute drive, and you aren't going to crash."

He suppressed the urge to bark at her. He should have made her buckle up before he left her driveway, but decided not to turn it into a fight. "How's the pain?"

Her eyes drifted half shut again. "Not as bad as before, but still there. It's not easy to breathe."

"Hang on. I'll have you there in no time." Three minutes later, he pulled into the hospital parking lot and headed for the emergency

entrance. He yanked on the parking brake, lit up his hazard lights and
went around to get his passenger out. She took his hand. She must be in
worse shape than she let on. He had to help her out; she was a real
lightweight. Concerned about her, he walked her through the door with his
arm under her elbow. "Are you OK? Should I ask for a wheelchair?"

"I can make it." It seemed to take all the energy she had to stay on her
feet and walk, but he gave in to her demand.

He slowly led her to the admission area and helped her to a seat at a
window, behind which sat a large, middle-aged woman with curly red
hair. The woman looked up, saw his uniform and the elderly woman and
nodded knowingly. "I'll be right with you."

Red considered his next move. "Ms. Costello, do you have anyone I
should call? Someone who can come and be with you?"

She shrugged in resignation. "I'm a widow. But my daughter is coming
to visit in a few weeks. Can you wait and take me back home?"

Red sighed. It would probably be hours, and his shift ended at 7:00. But
there was such a plaintive note in her voice. Sure, she could call a cab, but
really, what else did he have to do? "I can wait for a while and see. If it
goes too long, I'll have to leave, but I'll try to stay. I need to go park my
cruiser, then I'll be back." Her brown eyes were birdlike and sharply
focused, but they softened briefly, and he could see the young girl she had
once been. It made him feel good about his decision. "I'll be back soon, and
I'll wait out here. I don't think they'll let me come in with you."

The frown returned. "Why not? Except if they want to examine me, it
should be fine. You're an officer of the law. I have no one, and it would feel
better to have someone there with me while I wait."

He shook his head. He had a tendency to get drawn into things,
especially with damsels in distress. Bad habit, but he didn't know how to
beat it. "Fine, if they let me…"

The redhead had been listening knowingly. Most of their patients came
from Palm Lakes and other retirement communities. She flashed a warm
smile at Red. He'd made points with her, keeping the old girl calm and
happy. Eventually, he'd get home to some food and sleep.

It hit him then. He thought of her as an old lady, but he lived in the
same retirement community. When had he gotten so old? For some reason,
his age seemed to have frozen at about 40. He was still strong and

vigorous, no obvious aches or pains, but Serafina Costello wasn't that much older than he was.

He hadn't ever thought much about his future. Was this what he had to look forward to? Being sick and alone? He didn't even have kids. He hoped when it came to it, someone would be there for him. All the more reason to help her, even if it wasn't in his job description.

He parked his car, and after about ten minutes of filling out forms, they were escorted to the waiting area by a nurse and put in a small examining/waiting spot surrounded by blue curtains. He took a seat next to the bed, uncomfortable in his role of…whatever it was.

Despite the relative emptiness of the emergency area, they were left alone for what seemed a long time. The quiet was punctuated occasionally by the loudspeaker calling a doctor. Serafina seemed calmer and even had a little color in her cheeks now as she lay on the bed. He wasn't sure what to say; at least she seemed over the worst of it.

Abruptly, she broke the silence. "My daughter Mary Beth got divorced recently. And then she lost her job. She was married to a real nothing of a man. I told her so, but she wouldn't listen to her mother. So now she has no husband and no job, and she says she's going to come here for a visit."

She paused, and a look of anxiety crossed her face. She took a deep breath. It seemed her physical distress had lessened. "I know she isn't supposed to stay long. You won't tell anyone, will you?" she whispered.

He reached over and patted her bony, wrinkled hand. "Don't you worry. My job has nothing to do with enforcing the covenants. I think they're too strict. Don't quote me on that, though." He gave her his best bad boy grin followed by a wink.

She melted and squeezed his hand. "I knew I could trust you. You're so…big and strong…and handsome," she added.

He grinned at her. "Thank you, ma'am. It's my pleasure to be of assistance."

"Do you live in Palm Lakes?"

"Yes, ma'am. As a matter of fact, just down the road from you."

"Well, I never. What a coincidence! I'm so lucky you responded to my call. I didn't want the ambulance coming to my house. That old lady across the way is a real busybody. I don't like people knowing my business. It was just an episode, after all."

"Is that what you call it?" He shook his head, mystified. Maybe it wasn't a full-out heart attack. He hoped so, for her sake.

"That's what the doctor called it. He told me I might have one now and then, and if the medicine didn't help, I should go to the Emergency Room. Which I did. But I don't see why everyone on the street has to know my personal problems." She harrumphed.

Red smiled at her spunk; the old gal was a pistol. "Well, what do you think they're gonna figure I was doing at your house before 6am on a Saturday?"

Her eyes widened. She hadn't thought of that. "Oh, dear, I hope they don't think I did anything illegal."

He'd made his point. No need to rub it in. "I'm sure no one even saw me. I didn't use the siren or lights."

"Mrs. Jameson might have seen. I was too distracted to check her window."

"Well, Mrs. Jameson will just have to wonder, won't she?"

Serafina smiled. "That's right. She can just wonder. Maybe she didn't see. But she'll probably see when you take me home."

"If she does, you can tell her you're helping with an ongoing investigation."

Serafina sputtered with laughter. "Wouldn't that just get her goat? She'd be green with envy. But we don't talk, really. She'll just have to speculate." Her wind was definitely improving. She was no longer pausing for a breath.

Just then, the doctor came in, and Red vacated the area while he did his thing. An hour later, relieved at how quick it had been, he dropped Serafina at her home, walking her to the door and making sure she got inside. She explained she had a new prescription—no, they'd given her some free samples, so she could wait to fill it—and she hadn't had a heart attack. It seemed that her spirits was higher since she got that diagnosis.

She invited him to come in for coffee, but by then, he was really bushed, so he declined. Hopefully, the old lady would be fine until her daughter showed up. He wasn't sure he'd want to be in the daughter's shoes. Serafina Costello was a force of nature.

* * *

Owen, 9:30am

IT WAS SO ANNOYING, the layer of dust on the coffee table. In fact, all surfaces gathered dust as if by magnetism. Owen shook his head. He loved Palm Lakes, really he did. The desert had a clean vibe he liked. Yet dust seeped into the house even when it was closed up tight all summer in the air-conditioning. It was a strange paradox about the desert he hadn't yet figured out, clean but dirty.

He grunted as he finished polishing the last piece of furniture. He was free now to either work out or spend time on his model train set. He loved creating his own orderly little world. He got to play God and create the scenery, the train's route, the town, the people, everything. So it would be simply perfect. But he also loved working out. His body was hard and strong. Godlike, even. So much freedom to choose how to spend his day. Retired life gave him more control and power than he'd ever imagined, even in his extracurricular activities outside Palm Lakes.

As he reflected on this, he noticed movement in the back yard. It was that damn cat from next door. Adrenaline pumped through him as he raced to the sliding glass door. He unlocked it and wrenched it open, ready to curse, but the cat streaked back into its own yard. Must be smarter than it looked. He stood in the doorway, unspent anger coursing through him.

His heart was pounding in his ears, and he had a death grip on the door handle. He was so sick of those damn animals messing his yard. It was obvious his complaint to the HOA hadn't done any good. Had they even notified Barbara? Bunch of fucking incompetents. If he wanted something done, he was going to have to do it himself. It was high time that cat learned a lesson.

He was pondering how to snatch the fucking feline when a voice spoke behind him. "Junior, you can't be serious! It would attract the wrong kind of attention."

Turning towards the voice, he snarled, "Oh, shut up, Mother. I don't care what you think. I've followed all the rules. I asked her nicely to lock up her pets. I yelled at her. I threatened to tell the HOA. Then I did. They said they'd send her a warning letter. It didn't do any good, if they even followed through. I'm fed up. It's her I'd like to deal with, not the stupid cat. She's laughing at me. I just know it." He slid the door shut and locked it, his hands fisting and opening, his jaw clenched. Then he walked into the kitchen and drew a glass of water from the tap; he noticed a slight tremor in his hands. Too much adrenaline. He hoped Mother would just be quiet. But she had more to say, as usual.

"You're going to get caught if you don't stop thinking like this. You can't harm a neighbor, or even a neighbor's cat, and expect not to attract attention. Do you want that? Do you want someone looking in your closet?"

"Damn it, Mother, they'd need a search warrant to do that, and they'd need probable cause to get a warrant. I wouldn't do anything to Barbara. I'm not stupid, in spite of what you think. I was just enjoying thinking about it. She isn't my type anyway. She's too buttoned up. Thinks the sun shines out her ass. Miss Perfect, who doesn't have to follow the rules, assuming everyone will just go along with what she wants, because she makes nice. I hate her. But I wouldn't do anything to her."

Mother's sigh reeked of long-suffering impatience. "You shouldn't even be thinking about it. Sooner or later, you'll do something, and everything will fall apart. You're losing control."

Quivering with rage, he slammed the empty glass on the counter. Then he stalked down the hall to his weight room. Once inside, blessed silence enveloped him. Mother never followed him into this room. It was his only haven from her in all the world. He sank to the bench and breathed deeply for a few minutes as his pulse calmed. That decided it. He'd work out. Anything for peace and quiet.

Forty-five minutes later, he'd worked up a sweat and felt loose and ready to tackle anything, even Mother. He took a shower, grateful to still be wrapped in silence, then dressed and grabbed his grocery list.

As he drove down the block, he noticed Tanya Cooper pulling the mail from her mailbox. He'd need to check his when he got back. She glanced up and gave him a look as he drove by, and he tossed one back at her. Now, she *was* his type, he mused as he stopped at the corner.

In spite of the early hour, she was dressed for streetwalking or some kind of trouble that got his blood flowing. She had on tights and a low-cut blouse that was cinched at the waist in a wide leather belt, showcasing tits that couldn't be real, but who cared if they were fake? They were riveting. The scarlet of the blouse was a nice contrast to the leopard skin print of the tights. Her tall sandals made her legs and ass look terrific, and her hair was blonde, probably bleached, but still, he liked that shade. As he rolled down the street, he smiled to himself. Tanya was something else, though he'd never talked to her. He could tell just by looking at her.

"Junior, you're at it again. Thinking about a neighbor."

Owen turned his head to the back seat in astonishment. Of course, no one was there. "Shut up! I have a right to think whatever I want!"

"Sure, big man. You don't even have the nerve to talk to a woman. You have to work yourself up to a frenzy before you do anything. You're afraid of women. Always have been. That's why you do what you do to them. You know you're small and worthless. They see right through you, just like I did." Her sneer raked his senses.

"So who got the last word, Mother? Me. No one laughs at me anymore and gets away with it. Not even you."

That shut her up. Finally.

* * *

Tanya, 11:15am

TANYA PAUSED in the denser heat that had accumulated under the overhang by the front door, speculating about Owen Schmidt. He'd never looked at her that way before; in fact, she couldn't recall him ever noticing her. His stare had been one of appraisal, and it was obvious he'd liked what he'd seen.

It had been too long since she'd been looked at that way. She let herself into the house, which was dark and cool in contrast to the brutal heat outside. Her husband was out playing golf—again—so she was free for a few hours. She'd put some chicken gumbo in the crock pot for dinner. It was one of her favorites and easy to make. What she needed right now was to think about what had just happened.

She stalked into the bedroom and slipped out of her sandals, relieved to be out of them. She sat on the bed and turned her feet in circles, trying to release the discomfort. She couldn't make herself go outside in an unfit state, but it was getting harder and harder to balance on high heels. She'd keep wearing them as long as she could. She knew they made her look younger, and she needed all the help she could get.

Speaking of help, she padded down the hall to the kitchen and poured herself a slug of vodka. Sinking onto the sofa in the living room and tucking her feet under her, she sipped the ice cold liquid and thought again about Owen.

She'd never had a chance to talk to Owen. He never came to Barbara's little dos. Word was, he had a war going with her over her pets running loose.

She only saw him rarely. Mostly, she'd see him driving down the road, but occasionally, she saw him at his mailbox, and once, she had spotted him in Safeway. He was short, maybe 5'8", with receding brown hair and brown eyes, but what he lacked in height and looks, he had in spades when it came to physique. He favored wife beater t-shirts and tank tops that revealed his muscular chest, shoulders and arms. He must lift weights to look that buff. She bet he could lift her like a feather.

There was something about his eyes, something predatory or ferocious, as if he were always spoiling for a fight. Or else she'd only seen him when he was angry. Whatever the cause, it gave him an air of alpha male, and she loved that. Maybe he was the kind of man who liked rough sex. She always fancied hooking up with someone like that, but never had. The thought of it gave her a pleasant tingle.

That made her think of her husband. What a waste of space he was. Mister missionary and always so courteous. Such a wimp. Though lately he'd become angry a few times about her drinking. She kind of liked it when he got steamed. It might actually be fun if they had sex when he was in a bad mood with her. God knows, she needed something to perk up her life. It was so boring in Palm Lakes.

He was always after her to join a club, but what did she know or care about quilting or making jewelry or writing a book? And sports were never her thing; they just made you sweaty. Swimming turned her hair green from the chlorine, and she couldn't have that. Shopping and drinking were really the only two things left. That and trolling for company at the local bars. Not that she'd had any luck lately.

She finished her vodka and got up for a refill. Maybe what she ought to do was seduce her husband tonight. It had been ages. He slept in the guest room now, and she was annoyed at the message that sent. They might as well be divorced if this continued. Divorce. If she could get enough in the settlement, it might be the way to go. But he was a retired lawyer, so it would be harder to take him to the cleaners. No, what she'd do is plan a quiet evening of seduction. And if it included him getting mad at her and finally showing he had a spine, all the better. Anything was better than the constant nothing in her life.

* * *

Barbara, 12:15pm

EVERY TABLE WAS full at the Jade Dragon restaurant, probably because it was the best Oriental eatery for miles around. Barbara looked up from a menu the size of a novel, or at least a novella, at Lydia and Jean, who were also contemplating the many exotic choices for lunch.

"I feel stupid if I always order the same thing, but it's hard for me to get anything else. I like their Szechuan pork so much," murmured Jean. "Maybe I lack imagination."

"Nonsense. You should order what you like. Why don't we share. If we each order something different, that gives us a lot of variety," suggested Barbara.

Lydia and Jean quickly concurred. "I'll have the General Tso's chicken," said Lydia, after closing the menu and setting it on the table beside her place setting.

"And I'll have the beef with broccoli," said Barbara. "That way, we have three different meats and lots of flavors. "Shall we order an appetizer? Won tons? Egg rolls?"

Lydia sighed dramatically. "Now you've done it. I dare not have another course. It goes straight to my hips when I pig out."

Jean slanted a look at Lydia. "Really, Lydia. Don't be so silly. You look great. Guys don't all want women built like boys."

Lydia, chuckled. "Well, they won't get that with me."

Lydia didn't appear upset, but Barbara didn't want to promote something that would lead to guilt or regret. "I'm not sure I could eat much more than the main course, to be honest. It just all looks so good, my eyes are bigger than my stomach."

Jean grinned. "I know what you mean. I'm ravenous, but I think the main course will do me today, too."

"Good," said Lydia. She regarded her companions with intelligent brown eyes that seemed to miss nothing.

"So what are you ladies doing outside of yoga?" asked Barbara. For some reason, Lydia's inspection made her eager for distraction.

"We pal around a lot, going to classes for New Age types. Jean is into Reiki, and I'm studying crystal healing. It's out there, but we enjoy it, don't we?" Lydia turned to Jean, who nodded enthusiastically.

"I'm so grateful to have met up with Lydia. And with you, too, Barbara. I love the yoga." Jean hesitated, biting her lower lip. She seemed on the brink of a revelation. "Richard has been treating me differently since I embarked on a study of metaphysical subjects, and it's such a relief not to feel alone. I may be a freak, but at least now, I have you two." Jean slumped as if the effort of sharing had taken a lot out of her.

Lydia responded warmly as she fingered the large turquoise beads in her silver necklace. "I feel the same way. I'm used to being seen as a woo-woo Californian, so it's nice to find someone with similar interests." She reached for her ice water and took a sip. "I'm really enjoying life in Palm Lakes these days, thanks to you ladies."

Barbara couldn't help but smile. The three of them were so different, yet they were so simpatico. Lydia looked like a well-to-do, aging hippie with her peasant blouses and long skirts; Jean with her slim blondness projected strong intellectual energy, like a retired teacher. Barbara wondered how she appeared to them, how she fit into the group. "You've made me appreciate living in Palm Lakes more. I was homesick, I have to admit, and it took me a while to find my feet. Ben adapted practically overnight. Of course, dry weather and golf were all he needed to be happy."

Lydia gave her a piercing gaze. "What did it take for you?"

Barbara paused to think. "I'm not sure I know, even now. Ben was the one who was gung-ho about moving. I wasn't sold, but I was willing to give it a try. I wasn't sure of the desert being right for me, and I was reluctant to put so much distance between us and Amelia; that's our daughter. She's divorced with children, and I like to think I was a help to her. Plus I miss our other grandchildren." Then she peered into her friends' eyes. She sensed support and compassion. "I feel like a plant that's been transplanted into a whole new life zone. At first, I was in shock. Ben was worried I wouldn't adapt. Now I'm finding things that I really like. Yoga is one. Making special friends like you two is another." Then she remembered. "And I almost forgot. I love throwing a party. And we're going to have one next month."

"Oh, that sounds wonderful," chirped Jean. "It will beat the summer doldrums."

Lydia nodded in agreement. "Just let us know how we can help."

Barbara waved them off. "I'm good at this, and I love doing it. It's no trouble. I was thinking of inviting everyone on our street and all of our various friends, Ben's golf buddies and you ladies—at least the ones who aren't snow birds. It should be a big crowd."

The server arrived and took their orders, and the rest of the meal passed swiftly in warm camaraderie. Barbara truly was feeling a part of Palm Lakes now.

When she returned home, Ben kissed her and asked, "How did your yoga group's lunch go?"

"Just wonderful! I really like Jean and Lydia. They're not conventional, but they're smart; they're nice; best yet, they're interesting. Being with them makes me think in new ways. And before you ask, I am really beginning to enjoy life in Palm Lakes, in spite of hiccups like Owen Schmidt. I can see possibilities for new friends and learning new things that I hadn't anticipated."

"Good." He drew her into a warm hug, and she thought again how grateful she was to have such a husband.

"Jean was saying her husband is looking at her funny since she started her new pursuits. You aren't going to feel that way about me, are you?"

"What new pursuits are you thinking of?" He looked at her quizzically.

Barbara laughed and drew him into the kitchen, where she reached into the refrigerator and pulled out the pitcher of iced tea. "How about a drink?"

"Sure. But what's this about weird looks?"

She filled two glasses with ice, less for herself than for Ben, then poured the tea. She pinched a few leaves off the mint plant in the pot in the kitchen window and crushed them before adding them to the tea. Then she stirred a spoonful of sugar into each glass. "Jean and Lydia are New Age types. I know we come from California, but we're pretty conventional. Lydia is into energy healing and crystals and such. And Jean does Reiki, some strange energy healing method. It's all Greek to me, but in spite of how strange it is, they're both so down-to-earth, I can't dismiss them entirely. It seems unfortunate that Jean's husband is giving her weird looks."

"Maybe Jean's just paranoid." Ben grinned.

"I don't think so. And she made some throwaway comment she didn't explain about him seeming to hide things from her lately, whatever that was about." She reached over and stroked his face, enjoying the scratchiness of his beard, which had grown out since he shaved that morning. "I can't picture you being like that to me, and I'm glad of it."

Ben leaned in and kissed her neck and whispered against her skin. "That's because I'm the perfect husband."

A chuckle bubbled out of her. "Yes, you are. We're a good match. Speaking of matches, I meant to tell you last night, but I forgot. I've figured out how to introduce Alexander to Helen without making them come to dinner here."

Ben scowled in a teasing way. "What great subterfuge do you have planned for trapping the poor man?"

"He mentioned last night at dinner that he's taking the cooking class in September. Just recently, Helen told me she's experimenting with exotic cooking. Apparently, Lou didn't like foreign food, and she's always wanted to try it. I'm going to call and suggest that she enroll in the class." She smiled smugly at him.

"What if she doesn't bite?"

Deflated, Barbara rejoined, "Well, I hadn't thought of that. My powers of persuasion are usually pretty good."

"I won't argue that, in spite of recent evidence to the contrary."

She raised her eyebrows at him and ran her fingers through his lush graying hair, enjoying the silky feel of it. She was glad he kept it just a little bit long. "No need to remind me of Owen. I admit I've failed miserably there."

"No one's perfect." Ben grinned, showing white, even teeth.

"I'm lucky to have you. It's going to be fun throwing the party."

"You *will* make your famous crab dip, I hope. That's all I ask."

"As long as I can find crab meat in the middle of a landlocked desert, of course I will." She loved making and eating the crab dip, and she genuinely enjoyed making things he liked.

He squeezed her bottom and kissed her again. "Good. Shall we go out on the patio and drink our tea? The mister is working great."

"Let's."

* * *

Jean, 2:10pm

JEAN PULLED into the garage and grabbed her purse off the passenger seat, eager to get into the cool of the house. The garage was stiflingly hot and close. She plunged through the utility room door into their converted study before the garage door closed completely and nearly bumped into Richard, whose chair was pushed back from the computer as if he had just decided to rise.

"Hi. Back so soon?" Richard's blue eyes darted around as he stood up. There was a tone of falseness in his question. But the minute she registered that, she questioned herself. Why did she think that? Certainly, his voice was lighter than usual, and it felt like he was covering something up. But was she imagining things?

"It's not that early. We met for lunch around noon." Jean peered at her husband, trying to find something to explain her concern, her suspicion that something wasn't quite right. He smiled at her scrutiny, showing uneven teeth yellowed from decades of smoking in his youth and a terrible aversion to dentists which he had never overcome. It hit her suddenly that he looked old. It felt unfair to pick on him like this.

He reached over and pecked her on the cheek. "I must have lost track of time."

"What have you been doing?" she asked, thinking to smooth things over with a neutral topic.

He looked around. Was that panic she saw as his eyes searched upward, as if to find an acceptable answer? He smiled weakly and turned and walked out of the computer room. "I'm thirsty. How about a drink? I'm going to have a beer." He strode to the kitchen assuming she would follow, so she was pulled along in his wake.

He bent into the refrigerator and grabbed a bottle of Michelob. "Want one?" He didn't even turn and look at her. It was as if he didn't want her to see his eyes. What in heaven's name was going on? Or was she losing it?

"No, I had a big lunch, and we drank a ton of tea. I'll pass." She waited to see if he was ever going to answer her question. He popped the top off the bottle and took a swig. Then he asked, "Not to put you on the spot, but what's for dinner? I didn't have a fancy lunch like you; I made do with a peanut butter sandwich."

She'd already planned dinner, so it was easy to say, "We're having the leftover lamb stew you like so much. I figured you could have more than me. I won't be that hungry."

"I love that stew," he gushed, a bit more than she felt was called for. Why was she hearing false notes in everything he said? Was it her, or was something up? And what could it possibly be? Richard wasn't a runaround; she was sure of that. At least, she always had been. But why would she be so sure? Was it simply because she wanted to see him as faithful? She shook her head as he stalked out to the living room and turned on the TV. He sank onto the sofa and flicked through stations.

She sighed, too tired of trying to sort out whether his odd behavior was real or not, and what it was about. She wanted to trust him, but he was acting guilty. That was it. He seemed guilty. Yet what would he have to hide here in their house? She couldn't puzzle it out.

He'd quickly tuned to a baseball game, and she knew he wouldn't want to be disturbed. That was the end of their conversation until dinner.

Jean went back to the master bedroom and changed into more casual clothes. She didn't wear shorts when she went out; she was too aware of the signs of age on her skin, but God, it was hot even in the air-conditioning, so she slipped into an old pair of baggie shorts and a soft cotton shirt and walked barefoot back into the kitchen. She stared out the window and wondered what to do now.

Dinner only required reheating. It hit her then. She'd been on such a high after lunch with Barbara and Lydia, and now she felt totally deflated. With the girls, she had lively conversations and felt life was filled with possibilities. Richard and she had nothing in common. They hadn't for years; she hadn't really noticed before. But now, it bothered her. He made fun of her interests and spurned socializing with her friends, and now it seemed he was hiding something.

She wasn't sure where to take this niggling feeling. It was so insubstantial, and Richard wasn't the type you hit head on. He was masterful at obfuscating, maybe because he had once practiced law.

If this continued, at some point, she'd have to ask him directly, but she hated confrontation, and she still wasn't sure her concerns weren't the fruit of an overactive imagination. She knew she'd get mad if he accused her of imagining things, and that would only make things worse.

She had a book on Reiki she'd been wanting to read. She walked back to the spare bedroom and pulled it off the bookshelf. That would restore her good mood.

* * *

Maddie, 2:55pm

MADDIE SAT in the chair in front of the doctor's desk waiting for her sentence. He was a mature, gray-haired man, maybe in his fifties (which made him seem young to her), stern-looking in his steel-rimmed glasses, his brow furrowed as he looked over her file. His white lab coat disguised his extra weight somewhat, but his fleshy face and red nose didn't speak of good health. You'd think a doctor would make more of an effort to be a good example to his patients. Her judgment helped boost her courage as he continued to scan test results.

He cleared his throat and looked up at her, an unreadable look on his face. Her heart began to constrict. What was he going to say? She knew she had some problems, but she couldn't imagine it was anything life-threatening.

"Mrs. O'Neill, your lab tests and your symptoms indicate you have osteoporosis, which means you are losing bone mass." His gray eyes conveyed authority, but no compassion. Typical doctor, she thought. "I'd like to prescribe a drug we've found to be useful in such cases."

She shook her head adamantly. Then she looked directly at him. "Will it reverse my condition?"

"No, but I believe it will delay the bone loss and help you avoid breaking bones if you fall, which is our main concern. You don't want to end up in the hospital with a broken hip." He pinned her with a challenging stare.

No, she didn't. He'd played that card well. Everyone knew a trip to the hospital with a broken hip was often one-way. But yet, she hated taking pills. She always seemed to have some reaction, and they never worked well. But what harm was there in filling the prescription? It would avoid a lot of conflict. "Okay." Things would go better if she could make him think she was compliant. She'd never been to this doctor before; Stanley had picked him based on his credentials, as always. Not on his bedside manner; that meant nothing to Stanley. If she could just get home, she'd figure this all out. She smiled faintly at the doctor, and he reached for his prescription pad and scribbled something down.

"You can call my office if you have any questions."

She nodded her head, then realized he couldn't see her, because he was still writing. "I will."

He handed her the prescription. "I'd like you to make a followup appointment for after you finish the first round of medication in about a month; I want to monitor your progress. See the receptionist and pick a good date on your way out."

She nodded at him and left his office and walked past the receptionist without stopping and out to the parking lot and got into her car, which was like an oven. Suddenly, she felt too weak to do anything. The constant pain in her joints and whole body were now explained, but knowing why didn't help. That's one reason she'd put this off for so long. It seemed having a doctor say something like that made it more real, as if ignoring it gave it a chance to go away, and now she was stuck with the diagnosis.

She leaned forward and put her hands on the steering wheel to support herself, then jerked back. The steering wheel was burning hot in spite of her having used the shades to protect it. Tears filled her eyes. She was so glad she hadn't let Samantha accompany her. It was kind of her to offer, but Samantha would want her to accept the doctor's guidance, and she knew she wasn't going to do that, so it was easier having no witnesses. She wouldn't lie about what he'd said, but she could soft-pedal it now.

By the time she'd stopped at the store to fill her prescription and arrived home, she'd forgotten a lot of what the doctor had told her. The details weren't worth remembering anyway, and she certainly didn't want to have to repeat them over and over. She swept them aside, as if into a room in her mind she never visited, with all the other unthinkable things. It was best not to think about bad things, especially when they couldn't be changed.

By the time she pulled into her cluttered garage, it was time to start planning dinner. She paused at the dining room table and sat, weary from the stress of the day. Stanley must be in his office. He hadn't even come out to see her and ask what she'd found out, but he was hard of hearing and probably didn't know she'd returned. Or maybe he had. Their marriage had become so thorny since they left Moab, she barely could speak to him without feeling anger well up from deep inside. The dinner menu had slipped from her mind as she got worked up about leaving her beloved home in red rock heaven.

She reached over and flicked on the study light, illuminating her latest project. Helen was really going to like this set. The tiger eye seemed to capture the light and warm it, bouncing it around in golden highlights. She had time to call now and give it to her. Helen was such a sweet girl and loved to get a present. Before she could change her mind, she carefully wound the necklace into a circle and set it in a gold gift box and laid the earrings in the center. She hauled herself out of the chair, ignoring the pain, and dialed Helen's number and listened to it ring a few times.

"Hello?" Helen's voice was tentative, as if she wasn't used to getting calls.

"It's me, Maddie. Is this a good time?"

"Yes, I was just cleaning. Nothing I can't stop."

Maddie laughed. Helen knew cleaning wasn't Maddie's thing. "I have something for you. Shall I bring it over?"

"No, I'll come over. Is now OK?"

"Sure."

"I'll be right there." Helen hung up, and Maddie placed the phone back into the base. She sat down creakily at the dining room table, then wondered if the front door was unlocked. It usually was during the day. Well, she'd wait and see. Helen knew to come right in.

Sure enough, Helen knocked a few minutes later, then opened the door. The bright sunlight poured into the darkened entryway and living room, backlighting her. She spotted Maddie at the dining room table, not a hard guess to make, even in the relative darkness compared to outside. "There you are!"

Helen was dressed in beige slacks and a short-sleeved lime green top that had faded from many washings. She was wearing flip-flops that slapped noisily as she walked across the living room carpet to get to Maddie. She paused at the table and swept a hand through her ragged strawberry blonde hair, pushing it back, a tentative look on her face. She was like Maddie, not one to easily accept gifts, though it was obvious she liked them. She smiled at Maddie, who handed her the gold box.

"I'm sorry I didn't come to the funeral. I couldn't. I never go to funerals. I've been thinking of you, though. I hope you like this." Maddie felt a sudden fear of judgment and rejection. People tended not to understand or accept her.

Helen's eyes widened when she opened the box and saw the tiger eye set. "Ooooh. This is beautiful. You shouldn't have done this. I don't deserve it."

"Nonsense. You've been through a lot. I love making jewelry, and when I thought of you, this design for tiger eye jumped into my head."

"It's perfect," she cooed. She put the open box on the table and immediately fastened the necklace and reached for the earrings. As she slipped them on, she said, "Do you mind if I look in the mirror?"

Pleased, Maddie, said, "The nearest bathroom is over there. She pointed across the living room to the hallway that led to the bedrooms. Helen scurried eagerly across the room and disappeared into the bathroom for a brief time, then returned with a wide smile. "This is absolutely gorgeous. I wish I had somewhere to wear them."

"You can wear them any time you like. I do. I always feel better somehow when I have my jewelry on. The stones seem to commune with me." Surprised at her own eloquence, Maddie shut up.

"I know what you mean. I've never felt this way about jewelry, but what you make seems to talk to me. Thank you so much for this." She stroked the stones in the necklace.

"If you need anything, I'm here. Let me know." Maddie hardly knew where that came from. She felt so broken down and incompetent, she couldn't imagine what Helen might need her for. But her heart went out to poor girl. She seemed so innocent and young, in spite of not being that much younger than she was. If she'd weathered a hard time with Lou, it hadn't left her embittered. Maddie wondered how she managed that. Not that she'd ever ask.

Before she could contemplate that deep thought further, Helen reached over and hugged her. The sudden pain caused Maddie to yelp. Helen pulled back, a regretful look in her eyes. "I'm sorry."

"I have osteoporosis. Or so the doctor told me today. He says that's why I hurt. It isn't your fault. I can't control my reaction."

Helen frowned. "I'm sorry to hear that. If I can do anything to help you, please let me. I enjoy your company, and I love your jewelry. I'm trying to learn how to do things on my own for the first time ever. I'm not used to having help or asking for it. Maybe you know what I mean. But if there's anything I can do, please ask me." She reached over and gently stroked Maddie's shoulder.

The kindness brought tears to Maddie's eyes. Somehow, Helen's offer didn't have the same effect as her daughter's, which always triggered a resistance in her. "Thanks, Helen. I'll let you know." She had no intention of imposing on Helen, but the offer warmed her heart.

Helen nodded and took her leave. It was past time to think about dinner. What did she have thawed? She couldn't remember. She was pretty sure there was some hamburger, but couldn't quite picture it. The thought of getting up and scrounging through the refrigerator was anathema, but she couldn't put it off much longer. Especially if it turned out nothing was thawed. She struggled to rise, biting back a cry of pain, and shuffled into the kitchen.

* * *

Helen, 3:15pm

HELEN STOOD in the master bathroom, admiring the lovely necklace that hung around her neck, fingering beads that glowed in the light as if alive. Who would have thought brown could look so good? Lou had never bought her jewelry, so she had very little, and what Maddie made was as good as anything from a jewelry store. Thanks to Maddie, she now had several lovely necklaces and matching earrings. They were all beautiful, but this was her new favorite.

She hadn't expected Maddie to come to the funeral. Barbara and Ben had come, but she hadn't wanted to invite many people. None of the neighbors really knew Lou. It had been a small ceremony dominated by her children, who breezed in and out of town as if blown by a hot desert wind. They didn't linger after the funeral, and she didn't ask them to. But it had hurt that all of them had been too busy to spend a little time helping her adjust to being alone.

Maddie's compassion overshadowed her children's lack of attention, and just thinking about it brought tears to her eyes. Maddie was one of the most generous people she'd ever met. She wondered how someone reached that age without being so scarred as to be unable to give. Maddie was eccentric, sure, but somehow, the innocence of a child radiated from her, especially when she talked about jewelry.

Helen caught a glimpse of her own anxious look above the new tiger eye necklace. Dark circles underlined her eyes. Her hair, one of her nicer features, was overly long and dull. She knew she'd been eating poorly. And drinking more than was healthy, but no more than a couple of glasses of wine a night. Or so. The nightmares were too much. She didn't understand why she was having all these dreams of past violence. Reliving those events was so exhausting, sometimes she was tempted just to stay up all night. On the nights she didn't relive past terror, she had weird dreams. Last night, a T. rex had been marauding through Palm Lakes, and she was all alone. There were plenty of houses to hide in, but the menace and solitude chilled her. She'd woken up in a cold sweat.

She unlatched the necklace and put it and the earrings back into the gold gift box, then carried it to her closet and placed it next to her jewelry box with the other gifts from Maddie. She really did wish she had places to go, things to do that would call for lovely jewelry. Of course, she didn't have any nice clothes, so that was a silly thought.

Sheba startled her out of her reverie by rubbing against her leg. She reached down and picked up the soft, furry critter and nuzzled her long gray fur. "I love you, Princess." Sheba purred loudly. She cradled the cat and ambled into the spare room that had been Lou's office. She sat at his desk, feeling a tinge of guilt, almost expecting to hear him roar for her to get away from his desk, as if it were off limits. She glanced at the pile of bills that sat on the corner and sighed. Soon she'd get up the courage to pay them. Not now.

The phone jangled, and she listlessly got up to answer it, placing Sheba carefully on the floor on the way to the phone.

"Helen? It's Barbara."

Helen smiled. "It's good to hear from you."

"What are you up to?"

"I just got back from Maddie's. She made me a lovely tiger eye necklace and earrings. She said it was to make up for not coming to the funeral."

"Wasn't that nice of her?" Barbara always saw the best in everyone, and Helen liked that about her.

"She's such a talented and generous person. She says she and Stanley simply don't go out at all." She knew how that felt. She wondered if Maddie minded it like she did.

"Speaking of which, I got a real brainstorm I wanted to share with you. There's a gourmet cooking club that has a class at the Recreation Center every so often. One is starting in September. I haven't taken it, but I know people who have, and they rave about it. You make exotic foods and get to take them home. It sounded like just what you've said you were looking for."

Barbara's enthusiasm was genuine, but Helen felt pressured. She was so resistant to mingling. "That was nice of you to think of me. I really am interested in cooking something different. But I'm not sure about doing a class." She couldn't think of an excuse not to, though.

"They only charge a small fee to cover the ingredients, and you can use what you make as a meal. I hope you'll consider doing it. I so enjoy the classes I've taken. It would do you good to get out and meet people."

That's what she was afraid of. She didn't really want to meet people. She liked the idea of having friends, but who would want to be friends with her? And she didn't really know how to make friends. She couldn't even force herself to accept Barbara's dinner invitations except on rare occasions so she wouldn't think she was an ingrate. "I promise to think about it. You're right. I know it's the best way to learn, and it might be fun."

She could hear Barbara's smile in her voice. "We'll talk more about it later. You should think about yoga, too. We'd love to have you in our class." Helen shrank at the thought of wearing skimpy clothes and trying to bend into impossible poses. "I don't think I'm ready for that yet."

"No worries, then. I'll ask again later." Barbara didn't seem surprised that she turned that one down flat.

She didn't really want to turn down all of Barbara's suggestions. She had been so supportive, and she really did enjoy both her and Ben. "I'll do the cooking class. You're right. It will get me out of the house and let me focus on something fun. I could use a distraction."

"Excellent," said Barbara. "I'll get the details for you and drop them off tomorrow."

They hung up, and Helen wondered how she'd managed to get talked into that. But it could be fun, and she did want to try new recipes. How hard could it be?

Sheba meowed at her feet, and Helen leaned down to pick her up again. "It looks like I'll be taking a cooking class. Not that you care, because you'll still be getting your favorite foods." She carried her feline friend into the living room and sat on the sofa. A book lay on the end table. It was a romance novel from the Palm Lakes library, and she was halfway through it.

She'd been spending a lot of time reading since Lou died. It carried her into other worlds where life wasn't so unpleasant and she had no cares. The escape was delicious, as was the thought that maybe life could be happy. Well, maybe not for her. It was too late for her. But surely other people were happy. Maddie wasn't; she was sure of that. She and Stanley seemed always to be prickly and at odds. But Ben and Barbara were a commercial for marital bliss. Was it possible they were only like that when others were present? Maybe they fought like cats and dogs in private. She chuckled at the thought. No, Barbara and Ben had the real deal.

If one person could do it, that meant it was possible for others. She stroked Sheba absentmindedly, dreaming how life would be if someone loved her the way Ben loved Barbara. Wouldn't it be wonderful to be able to talk with your husband, to touch him and be touched with love?

Ah well, it was too late for her. But she could enjoy reading about it. Maybe tonight she would have good dreams. She reached for the novel and buried her nose in it.

DO YOU CRAVE HAPPY ENDINGS TO STORIES?

The main theme in the *Autumn in the Desert* series is that life always offers you second chances for happiness, even in the autumn of your life. Helen, the main character in *Death in Autumn*, hasn't been dealt the best hand in life, but her luck is about to change.

The following free preview of the first five chapters of *Renaissance*, the next book in the series, will allow you to watch Helen's life take a major turn for the better. It will also introduce you to a variety of other residents of Palm Lakes who are rewriting their life stories.

Most of their stories have happy endings.

RENAISSANCE: CHAPTER 1

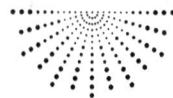

SATURDAY, JULY 22, 1995

Helen, 9:00am

*H*is ice blue eyes betrayed his intent, but she was paralyzed like a fly in amber. Pain bloomed through her skull when his hand struck her head, knocking her sideways. She recovered her balance and clumsily ran for the front door, her only thought to put as much distance between them as possible.

She grabbed for the doorknob, compensating when it appeared to swim to the right as if the house were swaying in an earthquake. As she threw the door open, she glanced back, relieved to see him rooted to the floor in the living room.

Until now, he'd only hit her where it didn't show. She wasn't sure if his loss of control signaled a new phase in his ongoing abusiveness, or if it meant this would be the day she would die. She wasn't going to wait around to find out.

Stumbling down the front steps like a drunk, she ran across the yard towards the street, tripping when she lost the battle with the rolling side-to-side motion. As she fled through the pines in the filtered moonlight, she berated herself for pushing his buttons; if only she would be properly submissive, this wouldn't happen.

The effort of thinking while running proved too much for her, and she paused, cursing herself for a fool. There was nowhere to go. She needed a car to escape, and no way could she drive in her condition, even if she could get around him.

The crunching of pine needles and twigs signaled his pursuit, and she took off *again in a jagged run, but the determination she had briefly felt transformed into a familiar feeling of resignation. She would never get away.*

He caught up with her and grabbed her arm roughly. "Where do you think you're going?"

"Anywhere but here," she snapped. She knew she was inviting more violence but couldn't help it.

"Don't be stupid! Get back in the house. How would it look if someone saw you wandering around at this time of night?"

"I don't care," she said weakly, but in truth, she did. Reason was returning. She couldn't leave the kids. What if he started hurting them? He'd made it clear she'd never take them away from him.

She turned in defeat and slowly trudged back to the house, her heart pounding from the adrenaline rush. In addition to the pain and dizziness, her ears were ringing. The persistent noise got louder and louder, finally blocking out the pain...

She shot into a sitting position, her hand over her pounding heart, trying to salvage some calm. *It's just the phone!* Instinctively her eyes sought the clock on her nightstand. 9:02am. *Warren, of course.*

Grateful that having the phone handy saved her the embarrassment of admitting she'd been asleep, Helen cleared her throat and picked up the handset.

"Mom. Hope I didn't disturb you. I wanted to touch base before I head out. How are you doing?"

"You don't need to call me every day anymore, Warren. I'm OK." She looked down at her hand, which was shaking slightly, no doubt an aftereffect of the nightmare. Good thing he couldn't see.

"You've never been on your own, Mom. It's a big shock, not having Dad to do things. And it's a big change being alone."

"I'm adjusting fine, Warren." She didn't sound convincing, even to herself. How could she prove to him that she was OK when being numb or asleep was the best part of her day?

"It's just that there were a lot of things Dad always did that are being forced on you now, and that's a lot of responsibility at a time like this."

"Warren, we've been through this before. Just because your Dad took care of finances doesn't mean I can't balance a checkbook, live on a budget or pay bills."

"It's not that I think you're incompetent, Mom. But why should you have to learn all that stuff and be alone when you have family you can rely on?"

She didn't hide her sigh as she anxiously bunched a handful of nightgown. She wasn't up to having this argument again. "If you're going to ask me to move back to Wisconsin, I've already told you a hundred times that I'll think about it, but it's too big a decision for me to make right now."

His sigh was nearly as big as hers. "Mom, we'd just feel so much better if we knew you were safe. You're out in the middle of the desert."

Exasperated at his total lack of empathy, she snapped at him. "Oh, for heaven's sake, Warren, it's not like there's a serial killer living down the street. This is a gated retirement community. We have additional security in the Posse. The crime rate is virtually zero. I'm safer here than I would be living with you in Wisconsin. And the winters are so much nicer." It was exhausting covering this ground over and over, especially since she wasn't really sure *what* she wanted, other than to have some peace and quiet.

"Lena and I both feel that at your age, with your health concerns, it would be better for everyone if you came back here to live. If you insist, you could live on your own near one of us. But you need to be near your family."

"I'll thank you not to refer to me as if I'm an invalid or cripple just because I had cancer several years ago. I'm probably healthier than you are."

She couldn't tell if his gusty sigh was a sign of relenting or annoyance. "OK, Mom, just remember we're concerned and think you'd be better off here. You know I can easily set up an apartment for you here at the old place. You'd have enough independence, but we'd be right here to help."

"You've made this generous offer many times in the past several weeks, Warren, and I appreciate it. But I'm not deciding now. You have a busy day, so I'll let you go." She'd run out of the patience required to deal with him, so before he could object, she pressed the 'off' button and shakily set the phone down.

She walked into the kitchen as if dragging a boulder behind her. She was so tired. She just wanted some peace. She stood looking around aimlessly while smoothing the shiny, worn surface of the nightgown as if soothing her ruffled feelings.

Her eyes fell on the half-empty bottle of wine stoppered on the counter. Too bad it was too early for that. And as much as she needed to wake up, her scrambled nerves just couldn't handle caffeine, so she poured a glass of orange juice, added an ice cube and walked out to the small patio, flicking the switch for the ceiling fan as she went through the door. It was hot outside (it was July in the desert, after all), but her patio was sheltered by a large citrus tree, so it was shady in spite of being hotter than she liked. The fan helped a bit, even though the moving air felt like it was escaping from an oven.

No one could see her, but she could see bits of sky and watch the hummingbirds come to the feeder. Before sitting down, she stepped beyond the edge of the patio and looked left and right. No walls surrounded her neighbors' back yards, so she had a clear view across them in both directions to the streets beyond. Not a person in sight, which was not surprising on a July day.

Her next door neighbor's calico cat Fluffy was walking into the yard two lots down. That wasn't good. Barbara had mentioned that Owen had lodged a complaint with the Homeowners' Association about her pets roaming. And that was *after* he had said a few nasty things directly to Barbara. Helen wondered why Barbara couldn't see that man was a very angry character. Should she call Barbara? No, Barbara had to have let the cat out. *Mind your own business, Helen...but what about the cat?*

Helen pushed the worry aside and sat in the padded chair as if she'd been on her feet for hours, wondering at the long sigh that escaped her lips. Why was she so tired? Not getting any answer, she sipped her cool juice and listened to the buzzing of the hummingbirds as they jockeyed for position at the feeder. Angry little dive bombers, they zipped back and forth from the patio to the tree. The occasional 'wahhhnn' of a quail punctuated the stillness. No other sounds marred the peace. The only breeze came from the ceiling fan.

A random thought invaded, as she recalled that a Saturday like this, back in Wisconsin, you'd hear someone mowing his lawn or working on a motorcycle in his driveway, revving the engine. Kids would be screaming as they ran wild through the neighborhood. The sounds of summer were so different here, if you could even call them sounds. Maddie, her neighbor across the street, had once said Palm Lakes was like a mausoleum. Maybe she was right. It sure was quiet.

Some minutes later, her glass empty, she was just beginning to feel comfortable when she heard the phone ringing. It couldn't be Warren; he never called back, and he had said he had somewhere to go. Nerves jangling, she reluctantly got up and went to the kitchen.

"Hi, Helen. It's Barbara. I tried to call sooner, but you must have been on the phone. How are you?"

"Sorry, Barbara. I should get call waiting with all the calls I've been having. I was talking with Warren. He calls every day. Nights during the week, but mornings on weekends."

"Isn't that considerate of him!"

Helen responded drily, "I think he has other motives."

After a brief silence, Barbara said, "What makes you say that?"

Regretting her impetuous comment, she forced herself to reply. "He wants me to come back to Wisconsin and live with him and let him run my life. He doesn't think I'm competent, safe or healthy enough to stay here without Lou. And he won't take 'no' for an answer. I don't want to go, not yet anyway, but I don't know what to do." She blurted the rest out without thinking. "I don't have enough money to stay in this house much longer anyway, now that Lou's gone."

She was horrified at herself. Barbara wasn't an intimate friend (not that she had *any* friends), and she probably didn't want to be bothered with such drama. Helen distractedly began to twist a handful of nightgown, hoping Barbara wouldn't think she was a whiner.

"Look, Helen, if you want to stay in Palm Lakes, maybe you can. You ought to talk to a realtor. I can refer you to a good one. Her name is Shari Lopez, and she's a real pro. The housing market is doing well. If you sell your home, you can move into a condo here in Palm Lakes. It's much less expensive, especially for utilities. And they take care of your landscaping as part of the fee. Would you like Shari's business card?"

Stunned at the suggestion, Helen brightened up. "Thank you, Barbara. Yes, please give me her card. I hadn't even thought of that option."

"I know the time often comes when people choose to go back 'home' and live with family. But if you don't want to, there's no reason you can't find a way to stay. We'd hate to lose you."

Helen wondered why Barbara would pay her such a compliment. "That's kind of you. You've done so much for me since Lou passed, and all I've ever been is the hermit next door. You've kept me going since the funeral. All those invitations to Sunday dinner and the casseroles you've brought to divert me from a diet of Twinkies and boxed wine. How will I ever repay you?"

Barbara laughed as if she didn't believe Helen would choose such a demented eating plan. "You haven't come over more than three times in seven weeks. That hardly constitutes a debt you need to repay. You shouldn't be alone all the time. We're here to help."

"I appreciate your suggesting the realtor. My mind hasn't been firing on all cylinders lately." It chilled her to realize how frighteningly true that statement was.

"Glad to help. How about coming to our place for dinner tomorrow? We're having fettucini alfredo. And I can give you Shari's card then."

"Thanks, I would like that very much. What time?"

"5:30 will be about right."

"Can I bring dessert or wine or something?"

"A bottle of wine would be lovely. Or a box." Her joke coaxed a small laugh from Helen. "See you then!"

As Helen placed the phone back in the base, Sheba came walking through the kitchen door, meowing for her meal. Helen picked her up and crooned at her.

"Hello, Princess! Did you sleep well? I love you so much." She snuggled in the long gray fur, feeling the soothing rumble of Sheba's loud purr.

Sheba quietly accepted the obeisance that was her due, but her pinned back ears said she was hungry and running out of patience.

"Mama's little treasure wants dinner? OK, I'll fix it for you."

Putting her down, Helen got Sheba's bowl and opened a can of her favorite cat chow. She placed it ceremoniously on the mat beside Sheba's crockery water bowl. "Here, Your Majesty. Your dinner is served."

Sheba began to chow down without further comment. Helen went to collect the empty glass from the patio table. As she returned to the kitchen, she reflected that Sheba seemed to be losing weight.

"Sheba, are you feeling OK? I know you're older and don't like to jump now, but are you hurting?"

Sheba stopped gulping food long enough to look at Helen with pale green eyes that glittered with an uncanny intelligence, but gave no answer beyond one meow.

The rest of the day played out like all the others since Lou died. She couldn't sit still long enough to read or watch TV. Nothing seemed interesting, yet she wanted to be distracted. She didn't feel like doing housework. She wasn't hungry, so she didn't eat. Life had become frustrating and confusing, like trying to eat soup with a fork. All hard work and no nourishment. At least she managed to shower and dress, though she put on no makeup or jewelry.

Early in the evening, Helen sat at the desk in the small office, staring at the pile of bills and other correspondence, annoyed at herself for ignoring them. There were more condolence letters and cards to answer. It was amazing how many people had written in support, and even more surprising how many had said nice things about Lou, given that he was an abusive bastard. Not that she'd ever told anyone, so what could she expect? It made it so hard to reply sincerely.

She looked at the to-do list on the note pad. She'd been looking at the same list for weeks, but once a month the bills *had* to get paid. Maybe she could focus long enough to get it done. She grabbed the checkbook, looked at the anemic total and felt the familiar clenching in her stomach. The savings account had a bit in it, but not a lot. How long could she put off making a decision about what to do with her life? She sighed and started writing checks.

It didn't take as long as she had feared. She put the last check into the proper envelope and stamped all of them. She carried the envelopes to the front room and put them into the little basket near the door so she'd remember to put them in the mailbox next time she went out. At least one onerous task was done. After a day without food, hunger was finally clawing its way into her consciousness, so she went to the kitchen to see what she could throw together.

The inside of the refrigerator was a nearly-empty white cavern. She'd finished the last of Barbara's most recent casserole two days ago. Some condiments, a container of half-and-half and a butter dish dominated the landscape. There was a partial pack of hot dogs, so she decided to fry some up and have some scrambled eggs with them.

She'd lost weight since Lou died, and she knew she needed to snap out of it, whatever 'it' was, but she felt so tired all the time. As much as she loved cooking, doing it for one seemed pointless, especially since she had no appetite. But she hadn't eaten all day, so she forced herself to go through the motions.

Not tasting a thing, she ate her dinner in front of the television while an old movie played in black and white, a reflection of her colorless mood. A few glasses of wine cloaked her in a welcome numbness. At some point, she realized the movie was over and got up and rinsed the dishes and put them in the dishwasher. It took a few days to fill it up enough to justify running it, but she didn't have the energy to hand wash them, even though that made the most sense. At least there was no one around to criticize her. Except herself.

Wrapped in a wine-fueled softness, she wandered into the office to journal before bed. For most of her marriage, journaling had been her therapy, keeping her sane when life threatened to spin out of control. Now it was the one spot of routine in the shifting landscape of her life. But the changing landscape had diminished her compulsion to write, so she'd sit and stare at an empty page wondering how to fill it. It was as if Lou had been her only inspiration, and now that he was gone, she had nothing to say. No, it felt worse than that. It was like by dying, he'd stolen from her the one thing that gave her joy. Which seemed just the opposite of how she should feel. Not that anything made sense anymore.

Sitting at her father-in-law's antique oak desk, she gazed at all the books she'd used for journals, which now held a place of honor on a nearby shelf. She ran her fingers along their spines, reminiscing about the escape they had offered from an existence that was close to incarceration, a sentence that had ended seven weeks ago when Lou died suddenly of a heart attack. Twenty-seven of them lined the shelf, a riot of sizes, colors and textures. There were bound journals, spiral notebooks and thick diaries. Some were gifts from her children, who knew she liked to write. Others were leftover school notebooks the kids hadn't used.

These books were the truest friends she ever had (besides Sheba), and it gave her a pang to admit that. At her age, she should have some human friends, but Lou hadn't wanted her to socialize, and she hadn't cared enough to fight him about it.

She pulled out the journal that was covered in cloth that looked like zebra skin and thumbed through its pages. That was the year Sally was born, and the book held stories of fear, pain and then, the wonder and joy of her youngest child's birth. It was hard to believe that was thirty years ago. She slipped the old journal back among the others and pulled out the thick purple book from the end.

She used to love writing in her journal, could hardly wait to pour her heart out. Now she felt nothing. Disturbed by her lack of motivation, she picked up the pen anyway and dated the next blank page.

July 22, 1995

I dreamt last night about the time Lou hit me in the head so hard I was dizzy for over a year. It was so long ago. Why dream about it now? It's not as if he'd been hitting me lately. He actually mellowed these last 10 years, as if he didn't have the energy to get physical.

I used to think he'd end up killing me. But I didn't see any way out when the kids were small, and by the time all of them were gone, he'd gotten a lot better. There were times I wished him dead, but I never really thought he'd die before me. I couldn't even picture being on my own.

It's been nearly two months, and I have no idea what to do with my life. I never made any plans. It would be easy to give in to Warren and put all the decisions on him. He'd be so pleased. I couldn't live with Lena, but maybe I could force myself to live with him.

And yet...I'm not eager to put myself under another man's thumb. I want to do what I want to do...but I don't know what that is.

It comes down to money. The house and car are paid for, but with Lou's retirement gone and so little savings, I know I can't go on living here much longer. He didn't make any plans for me to survive him. And it never occurred to me to ask.

Barbara made a kind suggestion, and it might be worth looking into. And maybe I should consider getting a part-time job. The one thing I have plenty of is time and the freedom to spend it however I wish. Now that I'm on my own, maybe I should participate in some of the clubs or courses they have here. It's strange to be able to choose...It's overwhelming.

Why do I feel so stuck now that I'm finally free? Why do I have to force myself to write? I was more functional when Lou was alive. Now I can barely eat, sleep or clean house. Or even take proper care of Sheba.

Feeling disgusted with herself, Helen put the pen down and closed the journal. Replacing the book on the shelf, she decided to turn in for the night. It was past midnight again, and tomorrow she needed to go to Barbara's for dinner.

A cricket chirped loudly from the master bedroom. *How do they get in, anyway?* Most of the time, you couldn't find them to remove them. Lou had hated the noise, but she found they made her feel less alone, especially at night, when the emptiness, which should have comforted her, was an aching, menacing presence that reminded her how alone and confused she was.

She carried Sheba into the master suite and laid her on the queen-sized bed. Sheba barely stirred (it was past her bedtime), but the purr was loud and soothing to Helen's nerves.

She dressed in her nightgown and climbed into bed and snuggled up beside Sheba. Between Sheba's purrs and loud chirps from Mr. Cricket, Helen drifted off to sleep in spite of her unanswered questions about the future.

* * *

Tanya, 9:06am

IGNORING the pounding headache that demanded her attention, Tanya scrutinized her reflection in the bathroom mirror. She ran a hand through her bleached hair, noting it could use another treatment. Suppressing both pain and annoyance, she wondered yet again why the skimpy black negligee had not done the trick last night.

She stepped back from the mirror to appraise her assets. The distance made her vision just hazy enough to take ten years off her age. Her skin was weathered from years of sun-worshipping, but her legs were shapely, and she had boobs that turned men's minds to mush. What real man would reject a body like hers, especially gift-wrapped in such an enticing negligee? She ran her hands down the silky fabric, unable to solve the puzzle.

Could he have a lover? The thought was ridiculous; he didn't have the balls. Unlike her. She wasn't afraid to go after what she wanted. Maybe it was time to go on the hunt again. If he didn't want her, she'd find someone who did.

Slipping into in her red silk robe, she headed to the kitchen, past the closed door of the guest bedroom where her husband always slept. She could hear him moving around as he got ready to go play golf. What a bore! It was all he ever did.

After filling a large mug with orange juice and a generous splash of vodka (she really needed to take the edge off after last night's rejection), she sat on the faux leopardskin couch in the living room ready to pounce on him when he came through.

She was primed and aching for a fight. Not that they ever really fought. She pictured a fight as being more aggressive, with a clear victor and passionate makeup sex afterwards. All they ever did was replay the same tedious arguments over and over, neither of them actually winning, and sex had become a rarity.

Sipping her drink and pumping herself up by replaying last night's drama in her head, she didn't have to wait long for him to appear. He tiptoed around the corner on his way to the garage door, unaware that she sat on the couch behind him. He looked like a skinny gray scarecrow in his unfashionable clothes.

"You coward! Were you going to slink out of the house without even apologizing for last night?"

He stopped and turned around, pulling himself to his full six feet of height, a surprising hint of disdain in his eyes. "I was unaware that I had done anything that called for an apology, Tanya."

She loathed it when he took that superior tone with her. "I dressed special for you, and you rejected me out of hand."

"I'd hardly call it special when you were three sheets to the wind from drinking. You know how I feel about your over-imbibing. It's unattractive."

His criticism stung her more than she wanted to admit. "I'm tired of you judging me, using fancy words to make me feel like you're better than me. I may not have gone to college, but I put you through law school so you could become a big-shot lawyer, and you owe me."

"I'm tired of the same old arguments. How many years will I have to suffer because you worked to put me through law school? I've never cheated on you. I've stayed with you through everything. God knows why." Disgust hung on him like an old jacket, a bedraggled but perfect fit. "I owe you nothing. I'm sick of your drinking and your abusive behavior."

Enraged at his judgment, she shrieked at him. "You spineless wimp! Go ahead and run off to your golf game. Or your whore. You think I'm stupid? You aren't interested in sex with me, so you must be getting it elsewhere. I'll find out and divorce you!"

Anger flashed across his face, but instead of responding to her taunts, he turned and walked out the door, slamming it behind him. Tanya slumped and reached for her drink. Drained but still thrumming with anger, she decided she deserved to be pampered for the way things had turned out last night. She'd go get a manicure. That always raised her spirits.

At the salon an hour later, her favorite tech Ashley worked on her nails, blonde head bent over Tanya's hands in concentration. "You know, Mrs. Cooper, seeing as how you're a professional, you know all the tricks of the nail trade, so I have to stay on my toes with you." Her blue eyes glanced up at Tanya, a hint of laughter in them.

Reminded of herself at that age, Tanya replied with uncharacteristic kindness, "You always do a good job, Ashley."

Smiling at the compliment, Ashley turned around and selected a bottle of scarlet nail polish, then placed it on the table in front of Tanya. "What do you think of this color?"

Nodding in approval, Tanya commented, "Actually, that reminds me of my first nail varnish. It was my favorite color."

Back at work and head bent, Ashley said, "Lots of people are doing nontraditional colors now, but I think the classics suit you best."

"I've always loved that shade of red. My old man wasn't too keen on it, though. He found me painting my nails, threw a fit and scraped it off with a pocket knife."

Ashley raised her head, her widened eyes searching Tanya's face sympathetically. "Why'd he do that?"

"He was a religious nut and called me a whore for painting my nails. I was 15."

Ashley bit her lower lip, obviously shocked. "That was harsh."

"It was the last straw for me. I got married as soon as I could and ended up working in a nail salon. He's probably turning over in his grave at how my life turned out. At least I hope he is." Tanya harrumphed in emphasis.

Tanya returned home from her outing in a good mood. By mid-afternoon, she had a pretty good buzz on, but she'd nearly run out of vodka. She poured the last bit of it into her travel mug and added some coffee to get her through her shopping trip.

Stiletto heels were a challenge to wear when she was tipsy, but she wasn't going to sacrifice fashion for comfort or safety. Her ensemble of lacy, low-cut black top and leopardskin tights showcased her figure. Not for the first time, she was done with trying to make her marriage work. Maybe she'd find a handsome man and leave her husband, or at least have an affair.

During the drive to the supermarket, she found it hard to focus on the road, and she nearly ran over an elderly woman who jaywalked in front of her. She yelled at the old bat and tried to steady her hands on the wheel. The near miss scared her sober, and worry suddenly overcame her. She had too many citations as it was, and another would be ammunition for her husband.

At the next stop light, she drank her vodka-laced coffee and gave herself a pep talk. *Stay focused!*

With no further incidents, she arrived and parked (pretty well) and wove her way into the market and took a cart; it was excellent support.

She'd gotten most of what she needed, including more vodka, and was perusing the items on a sale shelf when Owen Schmidt from down the street nearly ran into her with his cart, bringing a bit of sunshine into her gloomy thoughts. What a hunk he was. Not as tall as she'd like, but a beautifully sculpted body. "Owen! Fancy meeting you here!"

His reaction confused her. She gave him a good look at her boobs, and he couldn't take his eyes off them, which sent pleasure shooting through her. Then he acted tongue-tied and raced off. All she'd done was touch his arm. Was he shy or playing hard to get?

Owen's sudden exit did not deter Tanya's alcohol-fueled fantasy. She would seduce him. It would serve her husband right if she found another man, a real man who would appreciate her. She could picture it now, Owen's muscled, naked body wrapped around hers in a passionate embrace. She could tell he was a man who knew what to do with a woman.

* * *

Owen, 9:10am

THE AIR-CONDITIONING WAS BLASTING full force in Owen's new BMW M3 but wasn't making a dent in the accumulated heat of the past week. Not for the first time, he wished they had covered parking at the lot where he stored his RV, but it was the closest one to his home, so he wouldn't complain.

He watched the desert scenery fly by as the car effortlessly ate the road. The temperature outside was 95, headed to triple digits on a day when yet again, there wasn't a cloud in the sky.

Owen turned off the main road at the entrance to Palm Lakes, "Senior Living At Its Best," and slowed to pass through the entrance. His car's sticker showed he was a resident, and the bored uniform in the guardhouse waved him through. Some people's idea of security was pretty stupid, but that wasn't his problem. In fact, it usually was to his advantage.

The palm-tree-lined road wound sinuously around the edge of the golf course that was at the heart of the community. In most of Palm Lakes, all you could see were the nearest stuccoed homes, but along this stretch of road, you could see acres of well-tended grass with sparkling lakes interspersed, the whole thing framed by tall palms against a backdrop of purple mountains in the hazy distance. Golf carts zipped along the paths, making the scene look like a brochure for a happy retirement. Owen had no interest in golf, but anywhere that had palm trees said 'paradise' to him.

Keeping to the speed limit, he passed street after street of houses that looked alike. Sure, there were different models, but the styles and range of colors didn't vary enough to create dissonance. Palm Lakes had a uniformity that appealed to his sense of order.

The roads and yards were deserted, but it was July. The wimps who couldn't take the heat had fled to second homes up north and the Canadian snow birds had returned to their mother country. Everyone else was locked inside their homes with the air-conditioning on. And that was fine with him. He rather liked the post-Armageddon feeling he got from driving along the deserted summer streets.

After pulling into his garage, he entered his home through the laundry room, placing his travel bag on top of the drier, aligning it with the front edge. In the living room, light streamed through the transom windows above closed curtains. His favorite design feature of the house, they allowed total privacy while filling the room with light. It felt good to be home.

Opening the refrigerator, he grabbed a bottle of Coke. As he disposed of the cap in the covered trash bin, he noticed with disgust that the cover was dirty.

A flash of paranoia ripped through him, the hair on the back of his neck standing to attention. Had someone been in the house? He'd only been gone a week. There were no signs of forced entry, and no one else had a key. He forced himself to calm down and take a deep breath. No one knew. He had just overlooked it in his rush to get on the road.

Feeling calmer, he put his Coke down and reached for the rubber gloves that lay across the dish drain. Squirting some green washing liquid onto the new sponge, he began to scrub the soiled area as if he were preparing an operating room for surgery. Finally, he judged it to be clean enough.

Task completed, he reached for his cold drink, noting that the chill was pleasant on his bandaged right hand. The injury was still tender, but he had treated it properly, so he knew it wouldn't become infected.

"You really did it this time, Junior!" He flinched as the familiar voice stabbed at him.

"Oh, shut up, Mother!" Why couldn't she just leave him alone?

"How dare you address me in that fashion? You will not use such language when speaking to me!" He could picture her pointing an index finger at him and shaking it.

"What are you going to do, wash my mouth out with soap? You're dead! You've been dead for years! So shut up!" He slammed his half-empty Coke on the counter, and some liquid sloshed out. Immediately he grabbed his cleaning supplies and tried to ignore his mother's armor-piercing voice as he scrubbed away.

"You need to quit making stupid mistakes."

His ire rose a notch at her criticism. "What are you going to do? Put me in the closet like you used to? You can't touch me anymore!" Though his anger was threatening to spin out of control, he managed to push it back down.

He did feel bad, though, because she was right; he had made a mistake this time. When he wielded the knife, he cut himself as he cut the woman, and he surely left his own blood behind, and that was bad. He didn't fully understand the whole DNA thing, but he was pretty sure he had left some. At least the body was well disposed of. His mother had gone quiet. Thank heaven for small favors.

He went into the master bathroom and took a long, hot shower. Though traveling by RV gave him some anonymity and privacy, the shower in it left a lot to be desired. Steam wrapped around him in a warm embrace, filling his nostrils with the citrusy scent of the soap, taking the edge off his anxiety and washing away any lingering evidence of his recent activities, but there was still a bony finger of concern plucking at his nerves as he toweled himself dry.

He knew what would help. He had to put the house in order. After starting a load of laundry, he went into the living room and surveyed it. He'd been gone a week, so there was a thin layer of dust on the furniture, and he knew the carpet was equally filthy. His books and CDs filled shelves in orderly, alphabetized rows, but the haze of dust irritated him. He attacked the chores with relish, anticipating the relief he'd feel when the room was clean.

While he was meticulously vacuuming the living room carpet, a motion caught his eye. Through the curtains he'd opened in order to shed more light on the rug, he saw an animal creeping stealthily across his yard.

Barbara's cat was once again pissing or shitting on his property. He fumed while the cat dug through the fine gravel, pooped and then covered it up half-heartedly. Before the cat could finish, he impulsively slid the glass door open and said, "Come here, kitty." Surprisingly, the cat came in. He quickly closed the door and scanned the yard. The mature landscaping screened his back door from the neighbors, so no one could have seen him let the cat in. Finally, he could do whatever he wanted with her.

He knew it was a female because it was calico. Females of all species deserved judgment. This one had a lot to answer for. She'd been trespassing in his yard for a long time, and the stupid bitch owner ignored his polite requests. The HOA didn't have the teeth to do anything except warn her. A fat lot of good that had done.

Well, he could fix the problem for good now. Scooping the cat up, he took her into the spare bedroom and put her in the empty closet. He'd deal with her...he just needed to set things up so cleanup would be easy.

His mother's voice intruded, laced with atypical fear. "Junior, you can't do that. You mustn't ever do that here."

"It's a cat, Mother. This is way better than complaining over and over to the Home Owners' Association. Those morons didn't do anything."

"You're the moron, Junior. Who do you suppose they'll suspect when the cat goes missing? After the number of complaints you've filed, they'll come knocking on your door. Do you really want to get caught over a cat?"

"They won't send police out looking for clues about a lost cat. I know how to clean up. Do you always have to criticize me?"

Her lack of response caused him to smile. Barbara would wonder what happened to her cat, but she would never know. Served her right.

The afternoon sped by. It was always like that when he was doing one of his projects. The house had been cleaned spotless, the laundry was drying and the remains of the cat were in a trash bag that he would take to a dumpster after dark. It had really been quite easy and invigorating once he figured out how to keep her quiet. It made him feel so invincible that he was tempted to find ways to continue relieving the neighborhood of wayward pets.

The refrigerator needed restocking, so he made a grocery list and drove to the market just outside the entrance to Palm Lakes. Pushing his cart down the aisles and grabbing each item on his list, he had to dodge old farts standing in the middle of the narrow aisles, staring at the labels on canned goods as if they were discovering the mysteries of life. They irritated the hell out of him.

He rounded the end of the aisle and nearly plowed into Tanya from up the street. Like the other old farts, she was blocking his way, staring at stock on the end of the shelf. But unlike the typical grandmotherly residents of Palm Lakes, Tanya dressed provocatively. Leopardskin tights, low-cut black top and sparkly stiletto heels showed off a figure that owed a lot either to great genes or to plastic surgery. Large sunglasses and bleached blonde hair added an exotic aura as if she were a celebrity slumming at the Safeway.

Her gaze drifted to him. "Owen! Fancy meeting you here!" Through the lenses of her sunglasses, she eyed him like a hungry predator.

Temporarily paralyzed, he held still as she leaned towards him, the fragrances of perfume and alcohol wrapping around him like invisible chains. His eyes were riveted on the view down her top. She had on a bra, but there wasn't much to the top half of it, and he basked in the glow of her nearly naked, perfectly-shaped tits just inches from his face. A chorus of conflicting emotions clamored for his attention. A coherent reaction was impossible. He tried to take his eyes off her tits without success.

"Owen, you look stronger every time I see you. You must work out a lot to be so buff! Here, let me feel your biceps." She squeezed his arm and then stroked it seductively. Beginning to sweat in spite of the air-conditioning, he mumbled an excuse and fled towards the next aisle without looking back.

In spite of the pandemonium raging within him, Owen completed his shopping and drove home, obeying the speed limit and making a full stop at all stop signs. By the time he arrived home, he had pushed all the conflicting feelings aside.

He unloaded the bags and put his groceries away. Satisfied that everything was lined up neatly and alphabetically, he decided to spend some time with his model train set. It made him feel like the Creator, designing and engineering his own miniature world. The feelings of order and control soothed him, though lately, the effect wasn't lasting as long as it used to.

He walked back to the second bedroom, his hobby room. He paused in the doorway to admire the order and beauty of what he had spent a year creating. There was no furniture here except his ergonomic chair and the small table at which he did some of the finer work of modeling. The floor space was mostly taken up with a scale model of a village and steam railway, including mountains, tunnels and bridges. Lakes with Canada geese and forests with a few deer added to the natural beauty.

Truly at peace for the first time since returning from his trip, he knelt down to continue working on the village. He was adding some new businesses to the small Main Street. He began to hum tunelessly as he sank into an almost meditative state, all the events of the day forgotten.

RENAISSANCE: CHAPTER 2

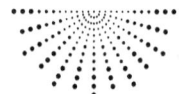

SATURDAY, AUGUST 12, 1995

Samantha , 9:00am

*S*amantha pulled up in front of Owen Schmidt's house for her 9am appointment. His large mesquite tree lay on its side, bare roots reaching for the sky like giant, alien fingers. It was another casualty of the monsoon storm that had ripped through town last night, taking off roofs and downing trees. If it was like most she'd seen today (she'd already had three appointments), there was no hope of propping it back up. But they always hated to hear that. They didn't believe the tree couldn't heal, no matter what she said. They told her things like "I don't have enough years left to start over." As if that would change the facts. Cruel Mother Nature had done her worst last night, and Samantha Taylor of Palo Verde Landscaping had to be the bearer of bad tidings.

She reached for her broad-brimmed straw hat and got out of the car, hoping this guy wouldn't shoot the messenger. His door opened not five seconds after she rang the bell. He didn't look happy.

She'd seen him from a distance a few times when visiting her parents across the street, but they'd never been introduced. "Mr. Schmidt, I'm Samantha from Palo Verde Landscaping. Shall we take a look at your tree?"

She turned and walked back to the tree without watching to see if he followed. Lots of these older guys weren't too keen on taking advice from a woman, especially one her age, and it seemed to help if she just took charge.

They stood on opposite sides of the gouged earth. The subtle message didn't escape her notice. She knew immediately the tree was a goner, but she'd learned not to pass that information on too quickly. So she squatted down on the edge of the hole, examining the mangled roots.

She glanced up at Owen, who stood watching with slitted eyes. He obviously wasn't an outdoors type, because he had no tan to speak of, in spite of his dark hair and brown eyes. Though his skin was pasty, his tank top revealed serious upper body sculpting. Maybe he lifted weights, possibly as compensation for his shorter-than-average height.

She brushed the dirt off her hands and stood up. He had a creepy vibe, but she wouldn't let him intimidate her. "Mr. Schmidt, this tree cannot be saved. I'm sorry."

Before she had a chance to explain anything, he cut her off. "Why can't you just prop it up. I see people do that all the time. I don't want to have to start over." He glared at her with mistrust.

Samantha suppressed a sigh and tried to be diplomatic. "Mr. Schmidt, there are some companies which would let you pay to prop this tree back up. It might not die. It has some roots still attached on one side. But very few, and propping it up won't regrow the roots that have been damaged. It will never be strong, and it won't take much of a wind to knock it over again. You're better off taking it out now and starting over. I can give you an estimate on a replacement, or I can make suggestions about other types of trees. The mesquite trees are quite prone to be damaged this way. I could suggest something sturdier if you like." She tried to smile but felt it turn to a grimace and chided herself for letting him get to her. The day was only starting; she needed to be thicker-skinned.

"Why did it happen to my tree, and not theirs?" He pointed diagonally across the street to her parents' gorgeous mesquite, apparently unaware of her relationship with his neighbors.

"Mr. Schmidt, there's no telling why the wind touched down here and not there. I can see that your tree hasn't been watered to encourage it to grow deep roots. If we plant a new tree for you, I can tell you how to water it properly. Also, mesquites grow fast. They get top-heavy and need frequent pruning, or the canopy acts as a sail to the wind. If you go around town, you'll see that mesquites are about 75% of the downed trees, and I can guarantee you that over 90% of them haven't been properly watered and pruned."

He wasn't paying any attention to what she said. His mouth was an angry slash, and he made a dismissive sound and walked toward the house. "Come on in and give me an estimate."

Owen didn't wait for her or hold the door, but she didn't mind. At least they were still talking. The air-conditioning hit her like a breath of the arctic as she entered the house, which was meticulously clean and neat. This man was no hoarder like Mom. She saw no sign of a wife, but that didn't mean anything. She'd have to ask her parents. She didn't know many men who were such good housekeepers.

"Your home is lovely, Mr. Schmidt." She continued to notice impressive little details, like the total lack of dust and the shelf with alphabetically organized videotapes.

He looked surprised at the compliment but recovered quickly. "Thank you."

They discussed the particulars of planting the new tree. He was parsimonious with words, so it didn't take long. When they finished, Samantha got into her truck and drove the few feet to her parents' house, parking in their driveway. She couldn't say what it was, but something about Owen Schmidt made the hair on the back of her neck stand up.

She surveyed her parents' beautiful front yard as she got out of the truck. No storm damage was evident, but their mesquite tree needed pruning. She'd have to urge Mom to hire someone. At least it was being watered correctly, so that helped. The roof looked fine. Her boots crunched on the gravel as she walked along the side of the house to the back gate. The wrought iron fence was a lovely shade of brown that contrasted nicely with the cream stucco of the house. The hummingbird pattern on the gate always cheered her. Like her mother, she was fond of the hummers.

The gate creaked open and then latched shut behind her with a metallic clang. The back yard was in good order, the two citrus trees loaded with little fruitlets. The harvest would be good this winter. No damage that she could see.

Her Dad had designed the yard, and it was beautiful. She'd never thought of him as artistic, and it felt weird that he had done such a good job, never having shown any previous interest in gardening. Perhaps just as strange, he showed no interest in the maintenance of the yard once the plants were put in, leaving the details of that to her mother.

The heavy wrought iron screen door opened with a tug, and she let herself into the kitchen. She announced herself to avoid scaring her mother. "Mom, it's me." No one answered, but her folks were getting hard of hearing these days. She cruised through the kitchen into the small dining alcove then through the living room, patting Beau as he came to greet her, tail wagging. She finally found her mother in the guest bedroom sorting through jewelry supplies on the bed.

The room was packed tightly with furniture and assorted boxes of stuff lying against the walls. Every square inch of the bed was covered with the bits and pieces of her mother's jewelry hobby. Curtains covered the window, and the only lamp had a weak bulb that barely cast enough light to avoid tripping over the many obstacles.

Maddie O'Neill looked up at her daughter. Her eyeglasses were barely hanging onto the end of her nose. Her dirty-blonde hair, miraculously free of gray even though she was in her seventies, gave her a wild look; she cut it herself, and it was uneven in a punk sort of style that had to be unintentional, as she had no interest in fashion. The smile in her faded blue eyes was genuine but short-lived. Her wrinkled face spoke of the wear and tear of a stressful and unhappy life. Samantha hoped she wouldn't look as worn out in 30 years, then felt ashamed for thinking it.

Going back to her search, Mom waved her over. "Bring your young eyes over here. I need help finding something."

"Gee, Mom, my eyes aren't that young anymore, and it's so dark in here, I can't see anything."

"They're younger than mine, so give me a hand."

Samantha walked over and looked into the shoebox her mother was scooping through. It was loaded with beads of all colors, sizes and shapes. It wasn't going to be easy to find anything in that mess.

"Why are they are lumped together like this? You usually sort them and put them in boxes according to type. What exactly are you trying to find?"

Mom looked up briefly at the implied criticism and then went back to sifting through the beads. "These are the odd ones I don't have enough of to do anything with and that I don't intend to reorder, so I throw them in here. But it's getting so full, I can't find anything. My eyes don't distinguish as well as they used to. I'm looking for a 5/8 inch center-drilled bead of glass, shaped like a lizard and the color of red wine. Can you see anything like that?"

"Let me have the box, and I'll see if I can find it. But don't get your hopes up." Samantha smiled at her mother's reluctance to surrender the box to her. "Can we go out into the dining room where the light is better? I can't stay long, but I'll try to find it for you."

In the dining room, Samantha turned on the study light that sat on the table which was covered with jewelry supplies, partially finished projects and boxes of beads. They each took a seat. "Why don't I spill them out and we'll look together?"

Springing into action, Mom grabbed an old white tea towel and unfolded it on the table top. "Here, pour them on this cloth. The color contrast is helpful, and it might keep them from rolling onto the floor. We don't want Beau to eat them. You know he's not too discriminating."

The yellow lab in question padded quietly into the dining room and sat beside Samantha, who stroked him while pushing the beads apart with her other hand.

"I'm glad to see your yard and roof are OK. It's pretty bad around town."

"I saw on the news how much damage there was all over this side of the valley. There hasn't been a storm this bad in years." Mom continued to sort through the beads with her usual laser focus.

"Mom, even though you're watering your mesquite properly, it needs pruning. A storm like this could still blow it over. How about I set up an appointment for the guys to come by and do it?"

"You know I don't like them. They're too expensive. I'll do it myself."

"The tree is getting too big for you to do it. I wouldn't even undertake that job. Please don't try and do it yourself." Samantha shook her head, worried that she'd done more harm than good. Now Mom would try to prune the tree herself.

A flash of rebellion in her eyes, Mom said, "Never mind about the tree. Help me find the bead." They continued to spread the beads apart but didn't find what she wanted.

"How's Dad? I didn't see him when I came in. Is he home?"

"He may be in his study. You should go by and say hi before you leave."

"I will. I have an appointment soon. The brothers don't mind me visiting you during working hours, but I don't want to take advantage of their good will. I just wanted to see how you were doing after that bad storm."

"We're OK. Wait...I think I found it!" Mom held up a wine red lizard-shaped bead. It was very pretty.

"What are you using it for?"

"I'm replacing an earring that Barbara lost."

"You're so generous. The women around here are almost as loaded up with your jewelry as I am. That would make a pretty earring."

"I only had a few of these, and when I discovered how good they looked, there weren't any more for sale. I'm sorry I didn't make you a pair."

"You make me plenty of jewelry. I wasn't hinting or complaining."

"You never do. Go see your Dad before you leave." Mom had already started sweeping the other beads back into the box. There was no more time for small talk.

Samantha hugged her, petted Beau and went into her Dad's little office. The walls were lined floor to ceiling with bookshelves Mom had made to hold all of Dad's books, and in the center, there was just enough room for his desk and chair. Dad looked up. "I didn't hear you come in."

"I let myself in the back. I figured the front door was still locked, but you let Beau out, so the back would be open."

"Lots of trees down around town?" It was a rhetorical question, like so many of the scripted conversations she had with her parents, but that was OK, because she preferred staying on topics that didn't lead to conflict.

"Yes, it's pretty bad. We'll be busy for a while cleaning up and replacing trees. I'm glad you weren't affected. The yard looks good."

"It's doing OK. I need to talk with you about finances."

Not again. Has he forgotten he just went over this a week ago? "I can't stay now. I have an appointment. I just wanted to make sure you were all right after the storm. I had an appointment with your neighbor whose tree is down. Mr. Schmidt."

"Don't know much about him. He's quiet and lives alone. Keeps his yard clean. Doesn't make trouble, although Mom told me he complained to the HOA about Barbara's cat running free. He's right. She's an idiot for letting those animals out, with the coyotes around. Serve her right if it got eaten."

Samantha winced. "I'm sorry for the cat. She didn't mean anyone any harm."

"So when can you sit down with me for a few minutes?"

"We'll be over tomorrow afternoon."

"Fine." He went back to reading the book that lay open on the desk. She was dismissed and left to stare at the top of his head. His wavy hair was still thick, even though it was white. Stanley O'Neill was rather proud of having all his hair and teeth at nearly 84 years of age.

It struck her as strange to suddenly realize her parents were *old*. Of course they were, but she never thought of them as elderly in spite of their age. That was probably one reason she hated these little talks. She didn't want to think about either of them dying.

There was nothing else to say, so she turned and left, not looking forward to tomorrow. It had become a nearly weekly ritual for him to harangue her about how Mom was probably going to outlive him, and she wasn't fit to handle the money, and there wouldn't be very much, anyway. She didn't enjoy being in the middle of the decades-long war of her parents' marriage, nor did she like to contemplate having a mess to deal with after Dad died. She couldn't imagine her mother managing the practicalities of life without Dad, especially if money was scarce.

Thinking about their finances as she slipped out the back door, Samantha reflected on the alarm she felt every time he showed her the numbers. How had he let it get away from him so badly? Is was so contrary to his controlling personality to have so little savings, but she didn't dare ask him. He wanted an audience, not advice.

She started the truck, slid back into work mode and tried to let go of the nagging worry.

* * *

Jean, 9:53am

JEAN SAT at the stop light waiting for it to turn green, the air-conditioning blasting cool air in her face as she drifted back to what she had learned this morning. She was in shock. Sure, she and Richard had grown apart, but that hadn't seemed so terrible. They each had their interests, and she didn't begrudge him his golf or cards with the boys, and he never complained about her "New Age" pursuits and all the courses she was taking, even though she could tell he thought it was hogwash.

The sound of a car horn pierced her fog, bringing her back to present time. She forced herself to focus on the road and drove the rest of the way to class, fighting to break out of the miasma of sadness and confusion.

As she turned into the Community College's parking lot, she saw Lydia's car. She usually looked forward to being with Lydia. Lydia was so knowledgeable and enthusiastic, and just a bit eccentric, which made her even more interesting.

But today, she didn't feel like facing Lydia. She didn't believe in complaining about her spouse, but she was so down, she knew she'd never be able to hide it. Lydia would read her like a book and demand to know what was going on. (Sometimes she wondered if Lydia was psychic, but she'd never had the nerve to ask.) She didn't want to lie to her best friend, but she didn't know what to say, either.

She grabbed her purse and notebook, locked the car and walked reluctantly into the building. Stepping into the ladies' room, she applied new lipstick with a shaky hand, finger-combed her short, blonde hair and tried to calm her heart. It had been beating so fast for so long, she thought it might burst. What was she going to do? Obviously, nothing right now. She needed to focus on the class, Lydia, and having a good time. She'd figure out what to do about Richard later. Straightening her shoulders and putting on a faint smile, she went down the hall to the classroom.

The crystal healing course was being taught by a lovely woman in her 30s. Considering that retirees were mostly conservative types not interested in healing and metaphysics, the room was surprisingly full. Most of the 35 students were women.

Lydia had saved a seat for her, so she slipped along the back of the classroom and sat next to her, nodding a good morning. Lydia was dressed as usual in a flamboyant aging-hippie style, her sandals and long purple skirt topped by a tie-dyed blouse with a scooped neck that showed her ample cleavage to advantage. A necklace of shells clattered as she leaned down to get a pen out of her large cloth purse. Hooped gold earrings set off her olive skin and dark, curly hair, which cascaded lushly to her shoulders.

Jean fished in her purse for a pen, averting her gaze long enough to suppress the tears welling up in her eyes. It wouldn't do to cry in public. Then she'd have to explain for sure. The class hushed as the teacher began to speak. She'd have 50 minutes to compose herself. That should be enough.

It wasn't. When the class came to a close, she looked down at her notebook and wondered how she'd managed to take any notes. She had no recollection of what the teacher had said. The class had ended, and people were scrambling to collect their belongings and exit the classroom as if it were on fire. Lydia, typically atypical, was putting her belongings together slowly. They usually did a bit of shopping and then had lunch on class days. Jean didn't know if she could bear it today, but the idea of going home to Richard was even less attractive.

They walked in silence to the parking lot, and Lydia turned to her. "Let's take my car. You're too shook up to drive." Jean acquiesced with a nod and got into the passenger seat.

"Are you going to tell me, or are you going to make me beg?" The silence stretched as Jean tried to decide what was appropriate. The tears were welling up again, and as they began to spill over, she gave up trying to hold it all back.

"I had a shock today..."

"What sort of shock?"

"I found out Richard is into porn on the computer." Even though it was true, it didn't feel right telling anyone else. She didn't want sympathy. She just wanted to understand. Or maybe just get past it.

"Is that all? I thought maybe he was having an affair. I could tell you were really upset, but I knew it wasn't storm damage. You would have told me about that right off."

"I *am* really upset. It's bad enough we don't have a close relationship, but I don't like the idea of porn on our computer. It's disgusting. I would never have guessed he would do that." Jean bit her lower lip, wishing she hadn't said so much, but she knew Lydia wouldn't gossip. "I don't know what to do. I asked him not to do it anymore. He's an educated man. Why would he have to wallow in dirt like that? And what does it say about our marriage?"

"How did you discover this? Surely, he wasn't doing it in front of you?"

"Of course not. It was pure coincidence. There was an article in the paper today about clearing the browser history on your computer. I'm trying to become more savvy about it, and so I went and found what the History was...it shows what sites you've visited. And you can clear the record, but I never even knew about it. And Richard obviously didn't, either, because there were a bunch of porn sites listed. He's been visiting them frequently. I was stunned. I couldn't imagine him doing that. In fact, he never gave me the impression he knows much about the computer. When I confronted him, he acted guilty and ashamed. I asked him to stop doing it, and he promised that he would."

"So you believe he'll quit?" Lydia's tone implied she wouldn't make that assumption.

"Why would I mistrust him when he gave me his word? He knows I can forgive him this time, but lying to me would be unforgivable. We may not be that close anymore, but I can't imagine he'd lie to me."

Lydia reached over and patted her arm. "I hope you're right, honey. If he values you, he won't lie. I hope he realizes how lucky he is that you're forgiving him."

"It's not so much that I'm forgiving him. It's just that I don't want to dwell on what's wrong, and I'm hoping we can put things right. But I have to admit, I didn't have the nerve to ask him *why* he did it; how long he's been doing it; or whether it had anything to do with our marriage." She paused and shook her head as if trying to clear it. "Maybe I'm a fool. I was afraid to ask, I guess. And now I'm thinking I missed the opportunity." She put her hands over her face and started sobbing.

"Come on, Jean, honey. I'm taking you to an early lunch at the Mexican place. Double frozen margaritas for us both! You can't solve all the problems of life in one morning."

That's what Jean loved about Lydia. She always put things in perspective. They'd only known each other a few months, and they were so different, yet they were like sisters.

"Thanks, Lyd. I don't know what I'd do without you. I need to clear my head and not think about this." She let the cool air flow over her face as they trundled down the road to the restaurant.

After lunch, Lydia dropped Jean back at her car and she drove home, feeling much better for the companionship and compassion. But pulling into her garage in the stifling heat, she felt depression descend again, enervating her.

She was relieved to find the house empty. Richard's golf cart was in the garage, so a friend must have picked him up, or else he'd gone for a walk. There was no note saying where he was or when he'd be back. She wished he'd go away and never come back, then felt awful for having thought it. Her life had suddenly gotten so complicated. She wanted it to be as it was before. No conflicts. No fights. The freedom to learn new things.

Hoping to find a bit of peace, she poured herself a glass of cold, white wine and sat in the living room staring at the TV, even though it was off. Minutes or hours passed, she wasn't sure which. The glass was empty, and she couldn't find the energy to get up and refill it. It disturbed her to realize that when he came home, she wouldn't demand that they discuss what happened. She found she had somehow decided to give him a second chance, and so she would. They'd go on and try to get past this.

Tears welled in her eyes. She wasn't sure she could stand it, but it seemed the only choice. She heard the front door unlock and swiped her hands across her eyes. She didn't want Richard to see her crying.

* * *

Helen, 11:47am

HELEN OPENED ONE EYE, then the other, pushing through the pounding headache. The light peeking out around the edges of the curtains told her it was broad daylight. Turning over gingerly to check the bedside clock, she confirmed it was nearly noon. That wasn't nearly as big a surprise as her state of undress. She was lying naked on top of the covers, and that scared her. She always wore something to bed, but then, she didn't remember coming to bed last night. As her mind cast about for answers, panic seeped in. What had she done? She really couldn't remember.

Sheba lay sleeping soundly in her usual spot, and Helen reached over and petted her, trying to ground herself in normal reality. Sheba immediately began to purr loudly, which was very soothing to her frazzled nerves. Too bad she couldn't ask Sheba what had happened last night.

Finally she recalled that it was Saturday. Had Warren called, and she didn't even hear the phone ringing? She clutched her hands to her aching head. It just got worse and worse.

Taking care not to move too fast, she reached for the clothes that were strewn haphazardly across the foot of the bed, continuing to dig deep into her memory for what had happened last night. She remembered sitting and drinking a few glasses of wine with her movie as usual, but after that, it became a blank.

The best thing to do would be to get a shower and take a couple Tylenol. She pushed the crumpled clothes aside, got up and walked unsteadily into the bathroom. The shower washed away some of the bad feelings, brushing her teeth took the terrible taste out of her mouth and the Tylenol soon began to dim the headache. But she still couldn't remember last night, and that scared her.

After dressing in clean clothes, she went into the kitchen, followed by Sheba, who was protesting that it was way past feeding time. The meowing was hurtful in more ways than one, and she barked at Sheba. "Quit fussing. I'm moving as fast as I can!" She immediately felt guilty for being so unpleasant and bent down to pet Sheba in apology, but regretted it as a drumbeat hammered her fragile head.

She gingerly righted herself and turned towards the counter. A brief stab of paranoia and fear shot through her, but she quickly suppressed it. Of course no one had come into the house. She had the only key. So who had brought in those groceries that were lying on the counter? She picked up the tin of smoked oysters, then looked at the box of crackers that lay open on the counter, one sleeve partially empty with crumbs lying about. Turning towards the refrigerator, she opened the door and got slapped with shock again. The refrigerator was full. There were eggs, bacon, orange juice, meats and veggies. It was almost as if the good fairy had come and filled her fridge.

Not feeling like eating anything, she poured herself a large glass of orange juice and greedily drank it. Then she refilled it and set it on the counter, pausing long enough to feed Sheba. She grabbed the glass and went out to her spot on the patio, sinking into the chair. She'd forgotten to check the message machine. Oh well, she could do that later.

As she sipped her juice, she tried to reconstruct the previous evening. Try as she might, she couldn't remember a thing after the movie. She'd taken to drinking Sangria. It was cheap and tasty with ice, almost like drinking fruit juice. She never drank before 11am, and almost never drank much before 5 or 6pm. Most nights, it was 3 glasses of Sangria with a movie, then to bed. But yesterday, she'd had a glass at lunchtime...though no lunch; she hadn't been hungry (again). Then she had started drinking earlier than usual. By movie time, she was hungry, but there wasn't anything to eat (as usual). She remembered that much. She had watched the movie, but after that, it was blank.

Shame washed over her. She couldn't deny her drinking was a problem anymore. What was wrong with her? She'd never been a big drinker, and now she was acting like a lush. She finished her orange juice. Her head was still throbbing slightly, but she did feel somewhat stronger and more balanced. She got up and went into the house to check the message machine. She had one message. Punching the button, she listened to Warren's brief message. She'd call him later on when she felt better.

As she turned away from the machine, her gaze fell on the part of the living room she could see through the kitchen doorway. Her handbag and keys were sitting on the chair nearest the door to the garage. That's not where she usually left them.

It was all coming back to her now. She had been hungry for a snack, and she was frustrated there wasn't anything to eat, so she'd gone to the grocery store and stocked up...way more than she had intended. Now she had all the staples she could ask for and plenty of nice snacks, too. The problem was, she had no recollection, even now, of having gone to the store. She must have driven there in a drunken haze.

She was stunned and guilt-ridden. One thing she was sure of: she had to make a change, and she had to make it now. She'd also have to make sure she hadn't overdrawn her checking account; it was perilously low. Funny how her money fears, which had loomed so large, were now dwarfed by her concerns about the drinking. She stood there, shaking a bit with the realization that she could have killed herself or someone else.

The doorbell rang, adding another dissonant note to her day. *Who could that be?* She moved as fast as she dared towards the door to stop whoever it was from ringing the bell again. Not bothering to peer through the spy hole, she threw the door open with uncharacteristic carelessness.

A man stood framed in the door. He wasn't young, but he was tall and well-built. Very handsome in a Nordic way with his thinning gray-blonde hair and blue eyes. Obviously a Posse member, as he wore the uniform of the volunteer security personnel of Palm Lakes.

He held his ID up to the screen door. "Good afternoon, Mrs. Mueller. It is Mrs. Mueller, isn't it? I'm Red Johnson, with the Posse. Would it be possible for me to interview you about an incident that's been reported to us?"

Panic stabbed her in the chest, but she labored to hide it. "Certainly, Mr. Johnson. Yes, I'm Helen Mueller. I'll unlock the door." She reached for the key to the screen door which hung on a hook a couple feet from the door. Fortunately, it was out of his view, or he'd have seen how clumsy she was as she made two grabs for it. Could it be a mere coincidence for him to show up today? If only she could remember what had happened last night.

Unlocking the door with greater than usual deliberation, she ushered him in. "Would you like something to drink? Coffee? Tea? Water?" She was so nervous, she didn't know what to do. Even if he had come any other day, she'd still be nervous; she wasn't comfortable around strange men, especially big ones like this guy.

"Thanks, ma'am, but I'm fine. I just have a few questions to ask you." His voice was courteous and unthreatening, but she still couldn't calm down.

She preceded him into the living room and pointed him to a chair. Thank heaven the room was clean and tidy. It never got used, so aside from a bit of inevitable dust, it was fine for company. After he sat in the wing chair, she perched on the sofa, gathering her wits about her. "What can I help with, Mr. Johnson? Is everything okay in the neighborhood? I hope everyone is all right." Could he hear the guilt in her voice?

"Well, Mrs. Mueller, that was quite a storm last night, wasn't it?"

She tightened with fear at the non sequitur. Why was he asking that? She had no recollection of last night, including a storm. Her eyes darted left and right, and then she responded, "I haven't been out today or read the paper."

"Wow, you must be a heavy sleeper. There are trees down all over, even big ones. Parts of rooftops are torn off. Your neighbor down the street lost his tree. It's the biggest storm they've had in some years."

He looked searchingly at her, and she belatedly realized he was just making small talk. "I'm sorry; I'm just preoccupied today." She smiled weakly at him, hoping that would be enough.

"You're probably wondering why I'm here. I'm collecting information about a missing cat. Mrs. Blackstone's cat, to be exact; the one that went missing in late July. It's taken us a while to get around to it, but we'd like to see if we can give any closure to Mrs. Blackstone. Can you tell me anything that might help?"

Blessed relief washed over her. "Oh, dear, no. I know Fluffy went missing, but I guess we all assumed a coyote got her. Barbara told me the day after she disappeared. Coyotes seem to be a real hazard to pets here. I wish people wouldn't let their animals run loose...oh, please don't tell Barbara I said that. I'm not like Owen, all upset about Fluffy peeing in my yard." She had her wits about her enough to see his eyebrows shoot up when she mentioned Owen and immediately regretted it but pressed on. "I like animals. I have a cat of my own. I really never minded Fluffy coming into my yard. But I did always worry about her getting eaten by the coyotes or maybe getting hit by a car."

The officer wrote in his small notepad, then his blue eyes locked on her. "One reason we're following up on this lost cat is that there have been issues about it in the past. Your neighbor Owen Schmidt filed a complaint with the Homeowners' Association that Mrs. Blackstone's cat was running free, which is not only a violation of the law but against the covenants of Palm Lakes. This happened some months ago."

Uncomfortable with his scrutiny, she looked down. "Yes, Barbara told me that Owen was upset about Fluffy. She said he'd reported her to the HOA; that he had yelled at her once or twice about Fluffy before that."

"Yes, that's what I'm hearing from your neighbors. While it's most likely the cat was killed by predators, we have to rule out other causes. Would you have any reason to believe it could be anything else?"

She answered without even considering the ridiculous implication. "No. Of course not. I know Owen was upset, but I can't imagine he'd harm Fluffy...are you suggesting that?"

"No, ma'am. We just want to see if there's any reason to suspect foul play since there were obviously some bad feelings." He flashed her a Dennis Quaid smile with lots of wattage, and she felt herself relaxing.

Bringing her focus back, she suddenly remembered seeing Fluffy go into Owen's yard that morning long ago. When had Fluffy gone missing? It was just after that, wasn't it? But would it be fair to Owen to even mention that? She hesitated, wondering what she should do.

"Mrs. Mueller, did you remember something that might help my investigation?"

My, he is observant. "I'm not sure. I'm not convinced it will help, and I don't want to cause problems by saying something that might be meaningless."

He leaned forward a bit on the chair, obviously eager to hear what she had to say. "I respect your concern for keeping peace among the neighbors. But let me be the one to decide what's important. What you say will be kept confidential."

She took a deep breath and let it out. "OK. I remember the last time I saw Fluffy. It was a morning in late July, just before she disappeared. I was out on my patio, and I was enjoying looking around, and I saw her walk into Owen's yard. I remember thinking that he wouldn't be happy if he saw her because he had complained about her a number of times, not only to Barbara but to the HOA. I was wondering why Barbara let her loose. I even considered calling her, but I told myself, she must have let the cat out, and I didn't want to add to the judgment Owen had put on her. Now I'm wishing I had called her."

"It's not your fault, Mrs. Mueller. We don't know at this point what happened to the cat. We only know it disappeared after July 22nd. We're interviewing the neighbors to see if anyone saw the cat after that. So far, you seem to be the last person to see her alive."

"Have you learned anything from the other neighbors?"

"Not yet, but I still have some to interview."

"I imagine this is a pretty tame subject to be working on."

"I'd rather be doing this than investigating a homicide. Which is what I used to do." His disarming, boyish grin must be a deliberate attempt to soothe her into telling him everything he wanted to know. Well, it had worked.

She stood up in an attempt to end the interview. "I don't expect Fluffy will be found, and I feel bad for her and Barbara, but I suppose it was coyotes. They are everywhere, as you know. I wish people understood how dangerous they are."

He rose as she did, seemingly content with what she had told him. "You and me both. I've taken enough of your time. If you think of anything, here's my card. Just give me a call."

"Thanks, but I doubt I'll have anything to add. Good luck in the search. And thanks for helping." Locking the doors after he left, she went back into the kitchen and sank into a chair, exhausted from the feeling of having had a near miss.

By evening the hangover was largely gone and she was hungry for the first time in ages. For a change, there were all kinds of wonderful foods to work with. She fried up some bacon, then sautéed sliced shallots in the bacon grease and sliced an apple and put a couple pieces of chicken in the iron skillet with all the ingredients, threw in a few sprigs of thyme and put it all in the oven to roast. While it cooked, she mixed up a salad of greens, cucumber and tomatoes with some chopped fresh basil. She set the balsamic vinegar and olive oil out and went into her office to write in her journal while her dinner cooked.

Saturday, August 12, 1995

I lost some time last night. It wouldn't be so bad if I'd stayed home, but I went out to the grocery store when I was drunk. I've never been more ashamed in my life. The only good part is it appears no harm was done. Someone must have been watching over me. Even though the Posse guy showed up today, it wasn't to tell me I'd sideswiped a car or hit a pedestrian.

I guess the drinking started because I don't like being alone. The wine helped me sleep, kept me from listening to strange house noises or brooding in the middle of the night. But there must be other ways of getting a good night's sleep.

I commit to drinking responsibly from now on and spending time resolving how and where I'm going to live. And while I'm at it, I'm going to participate in some activities and accept invitations. I'm going to be so busy I won't feel alone anymore. The first class I'm going to take is the cooking class that starts next month. Maybe that will inspire me to eat more regularly.

Still weighed down by shame, she found she couldn't write any more.

But at least she'd made a promise to herself that she'd make changes, and she was determined to keep that vow.

Later, after enjoying dinner for the first time in weeks, she watched a movie and had no inclination to drink wine. It was a start.

* * *

Red, 12:25pm

RED WALKED BACK to his cruiser, plowing through the hazy heat. The monsoon was well under way, and the humidity was up to 45%. He chuckled to himself. Forty-five percent wasn't that much, but it sure felt like it in the desert. As he slid into the broiling hot seat, he was grateful he had his uniform pants on instead of the shorts he wore when he was off duty. The reflectors he put in the window did little to make the car habitable, but they did keep the steering wheel from giving him third degree burns.

He reached into the small cooler for a bottle of water. Coffee was his nonalcoholic drink of choice, but in this weather, he had to have water in the afternoons. He drained the bottle while pondering the progress on this 'case.' Hardly worth being called a case, but at least it provided some variety from the petty thefts he usually dealt with, most of them because residents forgot to put their garage doors down. Plus, it was less stressful to be looking for a lost pet than an elderly person who wandered off due to Alzheimer's. In any case, it beat his old job as a homicide detective for low stress.

He took the micro-recorder out of his pocket so he could add his impressions from the interview. Old habits die hard, and he was meticulous about laying the groundwork in a case, rent-a-cop or not. "Mrs. Mueller seems to be a contradiction. She has an unusual innocence and youth about her, but she was hiding something. I'm sure of it. It may not be related to the lost cat; she smelled of alcohol under the soap and perfume. She may still be grieving; her neighbor told me she's a recent widow. Her deer-in-the-headlights look and the way she twisted her pants leg while she talked made her look anxious, if not suspicious. Maybe I'm reading too much into it. She doesn't seem the type to kill a cat. I know I tend to read too much into things when I'm bored, and let's face it, this job may be low stress, but it's boring."

He paused for a few seconds, thinking about the pretty woman's apparent fear of her neighbor. "She was concerned about Mr. Schmidt. She's scared of him. She didn't want it getting back to him that she saw the cat in his yard. So far, it appears she was the last person to see the cat alive. That isn't good for Schmidt. And she's far more credible as a witness than her neighbor Tanya Cooper." That, and she was far better looking than Tanya. Helen had the aura of a delicate flower, albeit one that hinted at having steel underneath.

Tanya, on the other hand, was brass on the outside and who knew what on the inside? When he'd knocked on her door at 9:30 this morning, she'd greeted him in a flimsy negligee with a drink in hand, leering at him. Boy did she have a rack on her! She reminded him so much of his second ex that he'd almost been afraid to go into the house. But he managed to ask his questions and escape unscathed.

It was obvious that Tanya had a thing for Owen Schmidt, the way she defended him when he mentioned the shouting match about the cat. Maybe she was even sleeping with him. Palm Lakes was a desert version of Peyton Place, just with older players. People never ceased to amaze him. It didn't matter how old they got; they didn't get any smarter.

He sighed and pocketed the recorder. Retiring here had been a great idea, no matter what. Divorced three times, he could only afford a small condo, but he had golfing privileges and his Posse job kept him busy, if not entertained or challenged. Life was good, but sometimes he missed the chase. He'd been really good as a cop; lots of bad guys were locked up thanks to him. If only he'd been better at marriage. All three of his exes had the same complaint: he put work before them, working too many hours. Maybe if he'd hated his job, he'd still be married.

Tossing the empty plastic bottle into the small garbage bag that hung from the dashboard, he got out of the car and walked down to Owen Schmidt's house. This would be the most interesting interview for sure. Everyone he had talked to had mentioned that Owen didn't like the cat, and now the cat was missing and presumed dead. No one had anything bad to say about him, but no one had anything good to say, either; well, except for Tanya, and she didn't count. Was it a coincidence that the cat went missing? Or did Owen disappear the cat? He didn't really believe in coincidences, but he tried to keep an open mind.

He pressed the doorbell and waited for Schmidt to answer. The heat had accumulated in the southwest-facing alcove. His shirt was actually sticking to his back from the sweat.

The door opened to reveal a short, well-muscled man with thinning dark hair and brown eyes. He was obviously surprised to see Red, and a look of irritation flitted across his face before he could suppress it. "Can I help you, Officer?"

"Hi, I'm Red Johnson and I'm here to talk with Owen Schmidt. Is that you? I have a few questions."

"What's this about? Is everything all right?" For some reason, even though everyone asked him that question, it sounded different when Schmidt asked it, a bit too light, but at the same time concerned. Schmidt scanned the road outside as if he were waiting for someone.

Red asked, "Too bad about your tree. That was a hell of a storm last night."

Schmidt snorted briefly. "You got that right."

"I have a few routine questions I'm asking all the neighbors if you have time to answer them. I'd appreciate it, so I don't have to come back later." He didn't reveal further details. It sometimes was helpful to let subjects fill in the blanks on their own. This time, nothing happened, in spite of an awkward silence of ten seconds that seemed like years.

"Come on in, Officer. Get out of the heat." Schmidt finally opened the door and stepped back so Red could enter. It was amazing how cold 74 degrees felt when it was 110 outside. He never got over the contrast. With the sweat standing on his skin, it actually felt unpleasantly cold. He shrugged it off and followed the man into an impossibly clean living room. He thought *he* was a neat freak, but Schmidt had him outdone by a mile. He noticed CDs on the shelf by the stereo were arranged alphabetically, and there wasn't a speck of dust anywhere. Impressive. Maybe even pathological.

His short host sat in a recliner and watched with a hooded look as Red sat on the sofa and pulled out his notebook. It didn't escape Red's attention that he hadn't been offered any refreshments. Schmidt was at least a hostile witness, if not a perp. "I've been asking all the neighbors about a cat that was reported missing last month. Have you seen any cats wandering around lately?"

Schmidt appeared to be thinking. Finally, he spoke. "Well, I'm sure you know about the problem I had with my neighbor next door about her cat. In fact, both her pets are a nuisance. She lets them run free, and that's against the law, isn't it? There's a leash law in this county, right?"

"That is correct, Mr. Schmidt, but I'm not here to argue about whether it's legal for the cat to be running free. I just want to know if you have any information that might help us solve its disappearance. Do you remember how it looked?"

"Of course, it wasn't that long ago I saw it, but it was before the cat went missing. Barbara called me a couple days after and asked if I'd seen it. Must have been near the end of July." Schmidt's left bicep was twitching, and his mouth was clenched in a tight line that dipped down on the left side. No wonder Mrs. Mueller was scared of him. He was short, but his body said he pumped iron. He looked tightly wound and ready to explode.

Nodding and taking notes, Red continued,"Would you mind telling me the sequence of events leading to your altercation with Mrs. Blackstone about the cat?"

"I wouldn't call it an altercation exactly." Owen Schmidt's right hand reached up and swept back through his thinning hair in denial or exasperation. Maybe both.

Time to press him for details. "Well, Mrs. Blackstone said you raised your voice to her and threatened her about the cat messing in your yard. Do you deny that?"

Schmidt blinked, got up and went into the kitchen that bordered the living room. He got himself a glass of water, came back and sat down without offering Red anything. "I wouldn't say I threatened her. I told her I'd report her to the HOA because she was in violation of the covenants. I did report her the next time the cat came into my yard. But they didn't do anything besides tell her not to let the cat loose." He put his glass down and spread his hands apart as if asking what he could do. "She tried to tell me that she couldn't afford a fence, and the cat was used to roaming her property back wherever the hell she came from, and that she'd try to contain it, but she never did." He finished by clenching his jaw in a grimace.

Red gave him his complete attention. "When did you report her to the HOA?"

"A few months ago; I can't remember exactly. They keep records, don't they? Why don't you ask them?" The man's eyes dodged left and right, often a sign of prevarication or deflection.

Now was the time to apply even more pressure. "I'll do that, Mr. Schmidt. How did you feel about the cat continuing to roam free?" Red kept his voice light and smiled, hoping to disarm Schmidt or to trigger an outburst. Either one could help the case.

Schmidt paused and squirmed a bit. "No matter what I say, now that the cat is gone, it will look bad. Everyone knows I didn't like the cat coming into my yard and messing my property. But that doesn't mean I did anything to the cat. Probably a coyote got it. They're all over the place. The golf course is just a few blocks that way."

It was a reasonable assumption about the coyote, one that anyone would make, and the proximity to the golf course made it more likely. But Red wasn't buying it. Schmidt was hiding something. The question was, was he hiding something about the cat, or was he hiding something else, like Helen Mueller? Everyone had their secrets.

Red's cop antennae were tingling. Could he have killed the cat and disposed of its body? Anything was possible. But this late, it wouldn't be easy to find clues, and no one would bother with a search warrant without probable cause (especially for a missing cat), and pushing for that might make things worse between Schmidt and the neighbor lady.

"Well, that does it for me, Mr. Schmidt. Thanks for sharing your impressions. If you think of anything else, here's my card. Give me a call anytime." Holding the card like it was about to give him Ebola, Schmidt walked Red out to the door and sent him on his way.

Red sat in the car trying to put the pieces of the puzzle together. The timing of the complaints and the disappearance of the cat were circumstantial but highly suspicious. He took out his recorder. "Owen Schmidt appears to be a very fit individual who is repressing a lot of anger. While he has a right to be annoyed at his neighbor's unwillingness to keep her cat at home, he seems, in general, to be angrier than that alone would explain. He was also quite guarded when I interviewed him. Though many people are nervous when questioned by cops, it just felt wrong. His house was too clean. He doesn't have a wife, so it must be his preference to keep it so neat and tidy. I don't like him. He could have done it." He put the recorder away and looked at his watch. His shift was over in ninety minutes.

Sitting in the stuffy car, Red was already thinking of that first glass of scotch. The sound of the ice cubes dropping into the glass. The peaty taste. The air-conditioning cranked. Some Domino's pizza. A game he'd taped on the VCR. He had a nice evening ahead of him. He'd spend the rest of his shift cruising, letting the details of the case ferment in his mind. His intuition told him Schmidt bore watching, but gut feelings weren't enough. He needed some facts. And he knew just how he was going to get them.

After arriving home, he placed a call to an old friend at the Bureau. "Henry, how the hell are you? It's Red...Red Johnson."

"Why you old devil, what's up? I thought you'd retired."

Red laughed. "I did, but I'm doing a gig with the community patrol, and I have a favor to ask."

"Damn it, Red, you know the FBI doesn't do that kind of favor."

"I realize that, Henry, but we go back a long way. I could remind you of that case in '85."

"Don't you dare, you bastard! OK, what do you need?"

"I just want to check the background and record of a resident here. He gives me a bad vibe, but I have nothing on him and no access to records at this stage. If I give you a name and address, can you get back to me with information?"

"Sure, give me the details. I'll get back to you next week with what I can find. Just don't make a habit of this."

Later on, Red relaxed with his scotch. This investigation was stalled, but now that Schmidt was on his radar, he'd be swinging through his neighborhood more often. He didn't expect to find anything, but you never knew what following your intuition would lead to. And Henry might come up with something interesting to support or discount his feelings. Who knew where it would lead? Suddenly, retirement had just become a lot more interesting.

RENAISSANCE: CHAPTER 3

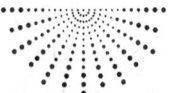

SATURDAY, AUGUST 19, 1995

Mary Beth, 10:35am

*D*ressing quickly in the clothes she had discarded the night
before, Mary Beth stumbled into the bathroom and prepared
herself to face another day. She looked in the mirror and winced. It was
obvious that she'd put on weight since the divorce. She'd never been thin,
but then again, she'd never been fat. The extra weight aged her, not that it
mattered much in Palm Lakes, where everyone was older than she was.
Her thick dark hair hadn't been cut in a couple of months due to lack of
funds. Her green eyes, always her best feature, had bags under them. "You
look like shit, girl."

She went and turned the water on in the shower, discarding her clothes
in the hamper. At times like this, she was glad her mother set the
thermostat at 85 degrees. It made sleeping a bitch, but when she stepped
out of the shower wet, it felt like the beach on a summer's day.

Trying to ignore her craving for a cigarette, Mary Beth stepped into the
shower and began to wash away the sweat from another night of tossing
and turning. She'd been a strange combination of restless and stuck ever
since Jason had divorced her, starting a domino effect that had demolished
her life.

Mom cautioned her through the closed door, "Mary Beth, don't use up all the hot water. I have to wash clothes."

"Okay, Mom." No doubt her mother was annoyed at her staying in bed until 10:30. Mom was always up at 5am doing something like cleaning or cooking.

Pursued by ever-present Catholic guilt, she hurried through her shower, then went back to her small bedroom. She could hear Mom vacuuming the living room. It was a wonder there was any carpet left.

This is what her life boiled down to...living with her mother in a 2-bedroom condo that was way too small for both of them. Her tiny room consisted of a twin bed and a dresser, but this was her only option after losing her job. It was like as her worth shrank, her world shrank. Now she was living in borrowed space, begrudged borrowed space at that. Dressing quickly, she steeled herself for her mother's verbal assault and went out to the kitchen. As she passed the living room, Mom paused the vacuum and said, "So you're finally up, lazy head?"

"Yeah, Mom. I'm up. Just going to grab some breakfast."

"It's almost lunch time. When are you going to get on a regular schedule?"

"Shit, Mom, I don't know. Give me a break."

"Watch your mouth, Mary Beth."

"Yeah, Mom. Sure..." Mary Beth rooted around the sparkling kitchen and found some cereal and milk, and there was even a cup of coffee left in the pot Mom had made earlier. After she finished her meal, she put the dishes in the dishwasher. Her lower back was killing her, but she hated to take the pills. It had been years since the accident, and it seemed her back was getting worse, not better.

"What do you have planned today, Mary Beth?" There was a challenge in her mother's voice as she stood in the kitchen doorway holding a dust cloth.

"Not much, Mom." Mary Beth knew what was coming next. *Jesus, I've got to get out of here. She's driving me batshit crazy.*

"When are you going to *do* something with yourself? You can't sit around eating me out of house and home forever! I can't afford to support you."

"I know that, Mom. I've only been here a couple of weeks. I've contributed what I can. I didn't get much except debt in the divorce."

"Just about what I'd expect. That no-account Jason dumped you and ran off with another woman. Of course, he wouldn't live up to his obligations. Why didn't you fight for more?" Sighing, Mom sat in the chair nearest her, apparently breathless from her outburst.

"Mom, I've told you over and over. I didn't want alimony, and all we really had together was debt. If I had pressed for alimony, he might have been able to prove that my job paid more than his business, and he could have sued *me* for alimony." She looked at her mother, pleading for understanding, then sighed. "I wasn't thinking straight at the time, but I still feel it was right. I needed a complete break from him." She'd never admit it, but lately, she'd been wondering if she should have fought for more.

"He wasn't supporting you like a real man, and then he goes off and gets some woman half your age pregnant? How could you let that happen?"

"Jesus, Mom, I trusted him. I thought we were happy. Sure, we had to struggle, but we didn't fight."

"I've asked you not to talk like that!" Before Mary Beth could reply, she raged on. "Your living here is in violation of the covenants, and if anyone reports me, I could get into trouble. You aren't supposed to be here for longer than a vacation. You don't meet the age requirements."

"Damn it, Mom, I am aware of that. Where do you want me to go? The divorce left me nothing, and I lost my job. I need to start over. I need a chance to get myself together."

"Then do it. Quit sitting around feeling sorry for yourself."

"I'm not feeling sorry for myself." Mary Beth swallowed the obvious lie. Of course, she was feeling sorry for herself.

"So your rotten husband left you for someone younger. It happens all the time. Why are you unwilling to move on?"

"I want to move on, Mom. But the divorce wiped me out financially. Now I have to start over. Give me some time, for Christ's sake. I won't stay forever."

"Don't take the Lord's name in vain! I'm trying to tell you that you *can't* stay forever, even if you wanted to. I can't violate the covenants, and besides, this place is too small for both of us."

"You got that right," mumbled Mary Beth.

Back in her bedroom with the door closed, Mary Beth took stock of things. She really didn't want to be here at all. But she had no job, no money and no prospect of income for the future. Her meager savings were nearly gone.

She was 45, had good job skills, but didn't know how to start over. Her back had been giving her more trouble over the years, and the pills only helped so much. She feared becoming addicted to them. She knew she was eating to fill the hole the divorce made, and her self-judgment at gaining ten pounds in the past few weeks only weighed her down further. If she gained more, she wouldn't fit into her clothes, and she couldn't afford new ones. To top it off, she was smoking more than ever.

Every time she thought about starting over, all she could see was a blank wall. It was as if her future were empty, which was how she felt these days. What had she done with her life? All she knew was that she couldn't stay here without making some changes, and she didn't know where to begin.

Mom knocked on her door. "Can I come in and clean your room now? I have other things I need to do soon."

"Sure, come in, Mom. I'll go into the living room." Mary Beth slunk out and settled herself on the couch. Everything smelled faintly of lemon furniture polish. There was no dust on any surface, a real accomplishment in the desert. She didn't know how Mom managed. She just knew she couldn't.

Mom was so different from Dad. Too bad he was gone. He was the one who had loved her unconditionally. If Dad were still around, things would be different. She wouldn't be criticized daily for the failure of her marriage or her lack of plans for the future. But Dad was gone, and this was the life she had. At least it was better than being homeless.

An idea came to her, and she yelled to the back of the condo, "Mom, do I have privileges at the exercise classes here?"

"I could get you a card, but it costs money. Can you contribute anything?"

"I don't have much money. I guess I'll wait. I was thinking of doing an exercise class or something to get fit."

"I think it's a good idea you want to lose weight. You've put weight on sitting around here all day feeling sorry for yourself. But you only need to quit eating so much if you want to lose weight. You don't have to join a class. Or maybe you could go out walking. Lots of people do that here."

Mary Beth considered the walking idea. It annoyed her to agree with her mother, but walking had its attraction. It would get her out of the house and help her get in shape.

Mom appeared in the doorway to the hall. "Walking is a good idea, but what are your plans for the future?" Her voice had taken on the lecturing tone again, and it grated on Mary Beth's nerves.

"How the fuck should I know?" she barked.

Mom's finger was pointed at her like a gun. "Mind your manners, or I'll have to wash your mouth out with soap. And don't think you're too old for me to do that."

"Really, Mom. Get a grip. I try to live by your rules, but you don't cut me any slack. I'm tired of being treated like a loser. And I'm not a teenager anymore. I'm an adult." She couldn't hide the whine in her voice, and she hated it.

"Maybe you feel that way because you *are* a loser. Have you considered that? You lost your marriage and your job and managed to walk away with nothing. Now you're coming back here looking to me, an old woman on a fixed income, to support you? Is that what you call normal?"

Mary Beth didn't answer. It was the same old argument day in and day out. She was too depressed to deal with it. She slouched out of the house and into the bright sunshine. As the door clicked shut behind her, she heard her mother's continuing protests and felt a great relief to be away from her, even if only for a little while.

It wasn't quite the hottest part of the year according to the weatherman, but you couldn't prove it by Mary Beth. Today it was going to be about 110 degrees. She probably should have taken a hat, but she just couldn't face her mother right now. To hell with it. So what if she got sunburn. The sun blazed in a clear blue sky that held no promise of monsoon rain. There was no breeze, and the street was as empty as the world after nuclear armageddon.

None of the sounds Mary Beth associated with summer could be heard. No cicadas. No lawn mowers. No children shrieking as they played in their yards or marauded up and down the sidewalks with skateboards and bikes. The covenants were the foundation of both the appeal and the emptiness of this place. No one under 55 could live here unless married to someone 55 or older. You rarely saw children, because children under 19 were not allowed to live here. She couldn't imagine getting used to this degree of silence. It was deathlike. Yet Mom loved it, as apparently did the other residents.

Mary Beth started walking aimlessly and ended up along the golf course, looking across the neatly groomed grass, seeing the golfers skim by in their carts, chasing their little white balls hither and yon. She had never understood the appeal of golf. But it sure made for lovely open spaces. Only along the golf course could you be guaranteed a view of the distant mountains. The palm trees that gave the development its name surrounded a large manmade oasis. She headed for a bench at the edge of the lake.

She sat for some time watching the pair of swans swimming to and fro like they owned the lake. She stared across the sun-dappled water at the mountains as the small fountain in the center of the lake stabbed into the sharp brilliance of the summer sky. A slight breeze wafted an occasional bit of mist from the fountain her way.

A family of quail crossed the grass in the distance, single file with an adult at the head and tail of the queue. The young ones were nearly full grown now. A plane flew over, shattering the harmony of the scene, and she found the energy to stand up and leave the lakeside.

The grocery store wasn't that far; it was just outside the community. She could extend her walk by going there to pick up items for dinner. Lucky she always had her wallet in her pocket, and she had enough cash for groceries. It was about time she did some cooking. That would get Mom off her back. Well, maybe for a little while.

As she plodded towards the gated entrance of the community, she pondered what she should make for dinner. Homemade spaghetti always hit the spot for Mom. She could afford a cheap bottle of chianti to go with it.

The trek was longer than she had anticipated, having based her judgment on how short a drive it was to the store. As she crossed through the open doorway of the Safeway 25 minutes later, she flinched at the cold shock wave of air that blew into the parking lot, causing her to wonder what their electric bill was. The temperature inside, like everywhere here, was frigid. Her mother would have a word to say about them jacking their prices up so they could air-condition the outdoors. She smiled at the thought.

Covered with goosebumps and having trouble adjusting to the relatively darker interior of the store (she'd forgotten her sunglasses), Mary Beth grabbed a basket and moved through the aisles as quickly as was possible with all the retirees standing in the middle of them. Jesus Christ, she hoped she never got that feebleminded.

She filled her basket with ground meat, pasta, onions, garlic, a bunch of fresh basil and a large can of tomato puree. She considered getting rolls or bread and decided against the extra calories, then chose a cheap bottle of chianti to complement the meal. If she weren't on foot, she might have added some sherbet for dessert, but it was just as well. She needed to cut back. She grabbed a copy of the local paper. She'd been here long enough that it was time she started looking for work. Steady income would be the first step back to freedom.

The clerk rang up her purchases, and as Mary Beth exited the store, she felt as if she'd stepped into an oversized oven, a shopping bag in each hand. Son of a bitch, the wind felt like a blast from hell. She was used to hot back home, but not the extreme, dry heat of the desert. How did anyone get used to it?

The walk back felt a lot longer, probably because of the weight of the groceries. She reaffirmed her commitment to get more exercise. She was too young to be this weak and worn out.

As she neared home, Mary Beth saw the curtain move in the window of the condo across the street. The nosy neighbor was at it again. Mrs. Jameson was a widow with few outside interests other than reporting her neighbors for infractions of the covenants, or so Mom had said. It was possible that the neighbor would report her if she stayed longer than a few weeks.

She toyed with the idea of flipping her the bird but instead got off the street as fast as possible. "Mom, I'm home. I took a long walk and got the fixings for a nice spaghetti dinner. I'm cooking tonight." The silence that greeted her felt wrong. "Mom?"

She dropped the bags where she stood and rushed through the condo, checking rooms and calling, worry growing with each step. When she got back to the master bedroom, she found her mother sitting on a chair, hunched over and clutching her chest, her gray face etched with pain.

"Mom, what's wrong? Do you need a pill? Should I call 911?"

Mom looked up weakly and whispered, "No, I'll be all right. The doctor gave me some medicine. It's just worse than usual. It will pass."

The strife between them forgotten, Mary Beth knelt down next to the chair and put her arm around her mother. "Can I get you a glass of water or anything?"

Mom shook her head and leaned into Mary Beth. "Glad you're here" was all she said.

* * *

Maddie, 1:00pm

MADDIE HAD GOTTEN some work done on the tree during the cooler morning hours. Now, after lunch, the sun was high and beating down on the yard like a hammer, reminding her that she wasn't as young as she used to be. Like she needed a reminder. As she stepped into the front yard and looked at the pruning equipment she'd left under the tree, she felt bone tired.

Crunching across the red gravel, she leaned down and picked up the pruning saw. She stood back and examined the tree, walking around and looking at it from all angles. Just lifting the pruning saw made her shoulder and back ache something awful. Ignoring the pain, she sawed off a small limb. Time was, this would have been a cakewalk. Now it was an ordeal.

She regretted having the mesquite, although it was gorgeous with its spreading 15-foot canopy. A good ten feet tall, it needed frequent pruning now that it was full grown, and she had to admit she just didn't have the energy to do it. There was no way she could wield the long pruning saw required to trim the higher branches. All she could handle was a small saw for the lower ones.

She didn't want to admit defeat to Samantha. The yard work was the only thing she enjoyed doing other than making jewelry. She hated cooking and housework, always had. It seemed wrong that something she got joy from was being taken from her simply because she was getting older. Pruning this tree had become an act of rebellion, but she wondered how long her body would be able to pay the price.

While she was pausing to get her breath, a Posse vehicle drove slowly down the street. As it passed, she saw it was that nice man, what was his name?...Red, that was his name, though there wasn't a red thing about him, all tall and Swedish-looking. He smiled and waved as he drove by. Maybe he was just doing rounds. But she'd seen him a number of times since the incident with Barbara's cat. Was she only noticing him now because she knew him, or was he driving by more frequently?

Maybe it was nothing, or maybe he suspected Owen of something. Word was that Owen had it in for that missing cat. She couldn't imagine anyone harming a helpless animal. Owen never did anything objectionable that she knew of. He never socialized, and he kept his yard neat. He was quiet. All the things she had told Red were true. Owen seemed like a fine neighbor, except for the fact that he went off on Barbara about the cat. But he had a point. Barbara was violating the covenants, and he had a right to complain.

Turning back to the task at hand, Maddie raised the pruning saw yet again and ignored the pain and muscle weakness, determined to get all the way around the lower branches today before quitting and cleaning up the debris. After removing just a few larger branches, she lopped off downward pointing branchlets and focused on a slow, steady rate of progress. Sweat trickled down her face, dripping off the end of her nose. Only in monsoon season did you get enough humidity for that to happen, and it was a deeply unpleasant sensation. She'd have prickly heat under her boobs for sure before the day was out. But she kept pushing on.

A tentative touch on her shoulder sent Maddie into orbit. Was her hearing going, or had she done that thing where she blocked everything out when she was focused on something? Helen was obviously taken aback by Maddie's screech of surprise.

"I'm so sorry I disturbed you, Maddie. I didn't mean to sneak up on you. I just saw you working so hard over here and thought I'd see how you were doing. This is such a lovely tree."

Maddie wiped the sweat from her forehead with her gloved hand, put the pruning saw down and straightened up slowly. She was relieved for the interruption in spite of the shock of it. "It is a real specimen. I just don't want it blowing over like Owen's did."

"Yes, that's a real shame. A lot of trees went down in that storm. Pruning this thing is a big job. I don't know how you do it. And you're out in this sun without a hat. Don't you sunburn?"

"I'm enough in the shade of the tree, and I won't be out here much longer."

"Well, you've sure done a great job."

Maddie was uncomfortable with compliments, so she ignored it. "Your hair looks lovely, Helen, but then, it always does. Are you on your way somewhere?"

"I'll be doing a few errands soon. I just got my mail and saw you and thought I'd say hi. Is there anything I can do to help? I have time on my hands."

"No, no, I'm fine. Why don't you come inside for a minute? I want to show you my latest creation."

Helen gave her a smile. "Sure, Maddie. I'd love to see it."

The pruning forgotten, Maddie led Helen into the house and walked over to the dining room table, which was buried in jewelry-making supplies and projects, and waved Helen over to a less cluttered part where pairs of earrings lay on a white cloth. She clicked the reading light on, illuminating them.

One design was antique gold lizards hanging from French earwires with a clear crystal bead just above the lizard. They were her particular favorites. Others featured carved Zuni bears made of semi-precious stones. Still other pairs were cloisonné beads in a variety of beautiful colors.

"Oh, Maddie, they are just so beautiful!" Helen picked up and examined the different designs. "What is the occasion? Will these be birthday or Christmas gifts?"

"I just like making them. I'll be giving some to Samantha, of course. But I have lots of extras. Take a pair. Take two pairs." Helen was one of the few people, along with Samantha, whom Maddie was convinced really appreciated her jewelry.

Helen seemed reluctant to respond. "You're too kind, Maddie. You've already given me so many lovely things. I shouldn't take anymore." She hesitated, but Maddie was sure she wanted to say 'yes.'

"Nonsense. I have more than enough for everyone. Please take a pair."

Helen reached out and picked a pair of the lizard earrings, looking closely at them. "These speak to me."

"Good choice. They're really special. You know I always put them by Martin's statue after I make them. He blesses them." Maddie pointed to the nearly three-foot-high statue of a black saint which sat on a small table in the corner of the dining room, votive lamp burning in front of it. Helen followed her pointed finger and nodded without saying anything. Maddie bent her head, already immersed in ideas for new earrings, having forgotten all about the pruning out front.

"Thanks so much, Maddie. I need to run. But I'm going home and putting on these earrings right away. Give Stanley my best." Helen patted Maddie on the arm and walked to the front door, waving as she left.

* * *

Helen, 1:40pm

HELEN STROLLED across the street towards her house. She heard the garage door go up at Owen's house, and his sleek BMW slid out. She paused, letting him pass her before crossing to her side of the road. He didn't acknowledge her wave. Following his progress down the street, she noticed Tanya tottering out to her mailbox on 4-inch heels. She seemed to sway a bit, but who wouldn't, wearing those shoes? Tanya arrived at her mailbox just as Owen was passing by. She hollered out to him and waved conspicuously as if trying to flag him down, but other than the briefest pause, he didn't stop. *What was that about?*

"It's not polite to spy," she murmured to herself. She didn't know much about what went on in the neighborhood. But Barbara *was* au courant with events. She'd probably know if there was any gossip about Tanya having an affair. Funny how she was interested in what was going on in the neighborhood now that she was on her own.

Letting herself into the cool house, Helen marched to the bathroom and switched her earrings. Putting on the earrings had a magical effect, like her fairy godmother had dressed her for the ball. Maybe there *was* something to Maddie's blessing ritual, in spite of how eerily Medieval it seemed.

Fact was, she could already see the effects of better eating, more sleep and less wine. Her eyes weren't puffy or bloodshot. Her hair needed a trim, but it was shiny and thick and felt good as she dragged her fingers through it. She must have good genes, as her skin looked years younger than her age.

She went into the bedroom to put her other earrings in her jewelry box and noticed that Sheba had thrown up. Fear stabbed at her when she saw that instead of the expected hairball, it was laced with bright red blood. Sheba had lost weight recently, and she was elderly. Maybe she should take her to the vet. As if she could afford that.

The doorbell rang, dragging her attention away from her worries. Dropping her earrings on the dresser, she ran to the front door. Peering through the peephole, she saw it was Barbara. She unlocked and pushed the heavy wrought iron door open and let Barbara slip through. "How nice of you to come by! How are you doing today?"

"Same old, same old, dear. Not a whole lot going on. Just have a bit of news for you. Thought you might enjoy some company for a few minutes." They walked together into the kitchen.

"Can I get you a cup of coffee or tea?"

"That would be so nice; coffee, please. Sugar and milk or whatever you have." Barbara's beatific smile highlighted a heart-shaped face which was framed by beautifully coifed short auburn hair. She was dressed in casual elegance, as always. Helen had never seen her in worn clothes or colors that were unflattering. Her makeup was perfect, just enough to soften the age lines and allow her to pass for 10 years younger than she was. Without a speck of envy, Helen wished she could be more like Barbara.

After brewing a new pot of coffee, Helen carried the mugs over to the small kitchen table and looked at Barbara expectantly.

Murmuring thanks for the coffee, Barbara dove right into the news. "I heard from the Posse guy, what's his name? Red Johnson? Why is his name

Red, anyway? He doesn't have red hair. Did he tell you why he's called Red?"

Helen smiled at the digression. "No, I didn't ask, and he didn't say. It must be a cop nickname. I bet there's a story there."

"Well, he called to apologize that they didn't have anything new to tell me about Fluffy's disappearance and that they thought she probably got taken by coyotes. It's so horrible to think that is what happened to her. He was quite thorough in his investigation. I would never have thought they'd go to that trouble for a cat. So many people told me he'd interviewed them. Not that anything came of it." Barbara paused for a minute, obviously overcome with emotion.

"I'm so sorry, Barbara. I know it's terrible. I'd be lost without Sheba. How is Jack doing?"

Barbara perked up at the change of subject. "Oh, that little rascal? He seems fine. He used to play with Fluffy, but he doesn't seem depressed without her." She paused for a second, shaking her head. "The main reason I came over was to invite you to our party next Saturday. I know you're not a party animal, but it'll be fun. A chance to see the neighbors in a happier setting than the last time we were all together. What do you think?"

"Lou and I never got out much, and I'm pretty shy in groups, but I wouldn't miss it for anything, as long as you don't mind me being a wallflower."

"You'll love it. Just don't let Bernie get anywhere near you. Once he's had a few, he turns into an octopus."

"I am forewarned. Thank you." Helen suppressed alarm and the obvious question.

Barbara flecked a bit of lint off her linen slacks, then focused dark brown eyes on Helen. "So have you had a chance to talk to Shari yet?"

Helen flinched in guilt. "No, I haven't." She contemplated not adding details but then felt an uncharacteristic need to unburden herself. "I keep going back and forth about what the best thing to do is. I want to stay here. I know that. But I've never been in charge of my life or finances, and I'm worried about making a poor choice and ending up having to cut and run after losing lots of money. I'd never hear the end of it from my kids...well, from two of them." She looked down and noticed she was twisting the fabric of her slacks. Forcing herself to stop, she looked directly at Barbara, which took more effort than she would have guessed.

Barbara took a sip of her coffee and paused as if thinking what to say. "Helen, there are no guarantees in life. Things can go either way for any of us. You have to do what feels right for you. If you think it would help, Ben is pretty good with numbers, even though he's only a doctor. I'm sure he'd be happy to look at things and offer an opinion, but in the end, it's your choice."

Something about Barbara's voice calmed Helen. "I think you're right. I'll let Ben look over things after I'm sure what I want to do. He could tell me if he sees any potential problems."

"That would seem to be a good compromise. Of course, he can't anticipate some things, but he could give you a second opinion on how it looks. That might give you some confidence."

"That would be so kind. I don't know what I'd do without you." The anxiety she'd carried around for so long drained away.

Barbara finished her coffee. "I need to run some errands now. I wanted to invite you for dinner tomorrow, but we have a commitment with some friends and won't be eating at home. Can I count on you next weekend for the party?"

"Sure, I'll be there with bells on. Let me know what to bring." Helen smiled and escorted Barbara to the front door.

In the bedroom, Sheba was fast asleep on the bed, and Helen joined her and cooed gently at her, telling her how much she loved and appreciated her. Then she cleaned up the now-dry mess, glancing around the room as she dabbed at the carpet, her eyes falling on Lou's clothes hanging in the walk-in closet. She had a sudden urge to clear it all out and went to survey the scope of the project. She could go by Goodwill when she did her errands. She felt a need to wipe all traces of him from the house.

Before she knew it, she had three large garbage bags full of clothes and shoes. Feeling like she was on a roll, she moved to the dresser. She filled another garbage bag with underwear, socks and t-shirts, then moved on to his 'junk drawer.' There were keys she had no clue about and slips of paper with cryptic notes on them, as well as his wallet (which she'd totally forgotten about). Opening the wallet, she saw it contained a stack of 20s. On counting them, she was shocked to discover they totaled $320.

She put the money on top of the dresser, relieved that this cash would pay for groceries over the next couple of months, but puzzled about the find. She felt like she was on a treasure hunt as she dug through the drawer further. She removed the odd cuff link that had no mate and a few paper clips and a comb that had seen better days. In the back of the drawer amongst bits of fluff and the odd hair, she found a bulging business-sized white envelope. Expecting some kind of document, she dragged the envelope out and opened the flap. She almost dropped the envelope in shock. There was a stack of bills in it. In a daze, she pulled the money out and flipped through it. It was a stack of crisp, new 100s. More money than she'd ever seen in one place in her life.

Her mind was filled with questions that would never be answered. Lou had been secretive, especially about money. Stranger still, he'd always acted like they were poor. How was it possible that he had so much cash lying around? She counted the bills and discovered she had a windfall of $5000. She was stunned. It wasn't enough to keep her in this house, but it would tide her over nicely while she made plans for the future. She could afford to move now, as long as she sold the house. Or, in the unlikely event she took Warren up on his offer, she had her own money she could keep to herself.

Where had this money come from? Lou had retired from an upper management position in a major hotel chain, but he'd started at the bottom and worked his way up, spending his early years as an inspector, which meant he was frequently on the road. She never quizzed him about his trips. And now it was too late.

Then it came to her. What if Lou had more secrets? What if there were other assets she was unaware of? She went back to the pile of stuff from the junk drawer and looked at the keys. Some were for luggage or belonged to things that were long gone. There were his regular keys on his chain; house, car, nothing strange there. Then she picked up a loose key that was shaped differently from the others. She had no recollection of what that was for.

She went and plopped down on the bed. It looked like a safe deposit box key, but to what bank? What was Lou hiding from her? Although part of her was hurt and even afraid at discovering this, another part felt intrigued. This was a mystery, and she was going to solve it.

Saturday, August 19, 1995

Today I found a pile of cash that Lou had hidden in a drawer. I have no clue what it was for or where it came from. I never showed much interest in our financial affairs, and maybe that was a mistake. But it never was a good idea to push Lou. I just left him alone as much as possible and hoped he'd do the same for me.

Lou obviously had secrets, but I'm not sure how to decode them. I found a key that looks like a safe deposit box key, but he never told me we had a safe deposit box. I wonder where it is and what's in it? I'll have to do some detective work to solve this mystery. I wonder if there's more cash or valuables in the box? Wouldn't that be exciting? What if it turned out I was a rich woman? Wouldn't that be a laugh?

She paused and thought about how her life would change if she found a lot of money. There would be no reason at all to consider going to live with Warren if she had financial security.

Just thinking about solving this puzzle has made me aware of how much I really want to stay in Palm Lakes. Life has turned into a big adventure, and it's getting more interesting all the time.

Sheba raked her with her paw, telling her she wanted to sit in her lap. She laid her pen down and picked Sheba up, snuggling her. "What do you suppose we're going to find in that safe deposit box, Sheba? Maybe we'll be rich!"

RENAISSANCE: CHAPTER 4

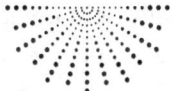

SATURDAY, AUGUST 26, 1995

Helen, 10:30am

"*J*'m pregnant." Sally looked directly into Helen's eyes as if challenging her to say something judgmental. Sally had arrived on the heels of a phone call the previous night. Helen had known the unexpected visit meant big news; she just hadn't expected something this big.

They sat at the breakfast table, two empty plates between them, having finished a sumptuous brunch celebrating Sally's surprise visit. The food now sat like wet cement in Helen's stomach.

Well, that explained the few extra pounds that looked so good on Sally. She'd always been rail thin and now looked perfect (at least to Helen). Her long blonde hair was caught up in a scrunchy instead of her usual braid, and she had a tan that hinted at time in the sun or maybe a tanning bed. She was always beautiful, but she looked positively radiant, in spite of the tension in her blue-gray eyes. Pregnancy suited her.

"Aren't you going to say anything, Mom?"

Now she wanted Helen to say something? Nothing Helen said would change anything. "I'm just trying to process the news. What does Rafael have to say about this? I'm assuming you didn't plan this?"

Sally frowned. "Of course, it was an accident! It's complicated. I got laid off a few weeks ago. I always made more than Rafael, and he wasn't happy with me not bringing in money. He left. Then I found out I was pregnant."

"So you haven't told him about the baby?"

"Like he'd want to come back to a pregnant, unemployed girlfriend?" Sally rolled her eyes and shook her head.

"Have you decided what you want to do?" Helen got up and started clearing off the table just to have something to do with her hands.

"I want to keep the baby." Sally held up her hands in protest as Helen opened her mouth. "I know you're going to say it's foolish. I know that a baby is a big commitment. But I want the baby."

Helen could see the sincerity in Sally's tear-filled eyes, but she wondered if she had any idea what she was in for.

"So what's next?" Helen started to rinse dishes and put them in the dishwasher.

"I was hoping I could stay with you for a while."

"You know the covenants won't allow you to stay for more than a brief visit because of your age. I'm happy for you to be here for a little while, but what are you going to do after that?"

"I thought it would be nice to live nearby. I need a clean break, and there are probably some job opportunities. I have good references and skills. I was hoping you could take care of the baby when she arrives, so I can work. We could get a place together somewhere else, since I can't live here."

Helen bit her tongue rather than ask Sally why none of her children seemed to think she might want a life of her own now that Lou was gone. Closing the door of the dishwasher and pushing the buttons to buy time, she tried to calm down and think. In the few seconds it took for her irritation to dissipate, she reflected that it would be nice to have Sally and the baby nearby. Maybe there was a way they could both have what they wanted. She screwed up her courage and turned to face Sally.

"I'd love it if you lived nearby. But I'm not leaving Palm Lakes, and I probably need to get a job myself, so what I can contribute will be limited." She took another breath and plunged on, feeling the tremor in her voice. "I'll help as best I can, but you won't be able to rely on me for regular day care. Why don't we make job- and apartment-hunting our project for the next couple of weeks? You can see how things develop and go from there."

Sally nodded slowly in affirmation, looking only a little bit disturbed. Helen was stupefied to have such quick resolution. "So when's the baby due?"

"Mid-March is what the doctor says."

"You have time to sort all this out, and I'll be here to help. Let's try to be positive. I'd like to celebrate my next grandchild. I'm going to call Barbara and see if she minds me bringing you to her party tonight. I'm sure she'll be glad to have you. You'll be the only young person there, but there will be food and drink -- wait a minute, you shouldn't drink alcohol -- but lots of good food, soft drinks and nice people. Let's go out shopping for something to wear. I haven't got a thing that's appropriate, and you could probably use a new dress. How's that?"

Sally brightened up immediately. "That would be terrific!" She jumped up and hugged Helen and then ran from the room to get ready to go shopping.

Helen let out a sigh and finished the dishes. She hoped she was up to the challenge of helping Sally without giving up on her own dreams.

* * *

Owen, 11:00am

OWEN PACED in his living room, rubbing sweaty palms on his jeans. Last time he'd seen her, Tanya had leaned over and given him an eyeful as she told him she hoped to see him at Barbara's party tonight. He never went to parties, and he wasn't used to being hit on by women. She was a drinker and a slut, yet he was strangely attracted to her. And there was something about Mother he couldn't quite place...

"Are you getting ready to do something stupid again?" Mother's shrill voice pierced the knot of confusion he was trying to unravel.

"Go away. I don't have time for you now. I'm trying to think."

"You're getting ready to do something stupid again, just like your father. Can't you use your head? Nothing good will come of going to that party."

"I have a right to make up my own mind. So shut up and leave me alone."

"Or what? What will you do if I don't? It's not like you can kill me again, Junior."

Owen pressed his hands to his temples. He had known that going to the party would upset her, but he had an itch about Tanya he wanted to scratch. He couldn't explain the attraction he felt; it shamed him and got him hot at the same time.

"What do you think that whore has in mind, Junior? She'd sleep with any man who wasn't dead. Just because she's coming on to you doesn't mean you're attractive."

"I don't need you to criticize me, Mother. You were as much a whore as Tanya is. So just let me think. I need to find out if Barbara is suspicious about her cat." The minute he said it, he knew it was a mistake.

"Of course, she is, you numbskull. You should never have killed that cat. You just don't exercise good judgment and foresight. You get that from your father. He was weak and stupid."

"So why did you marry him? Oh, yeah, let me guess. For his money. Quit distracting me."

He sighed and went into the spare bedroom, where he had his weights set up. A good workout would clear his head, and Mother never spoke to him in this room. It had never occurred to him to ask why, but it offered him much-needed peace. He stripped and put on the clean gym clothes that were neatly folded on a chair, then proceeded to do a punishing workout. By the end of it, he was sweating profusely. He loved the sensation of burning in his muscles and how he could block out everything while lifting weights.

When he finished, he grabbed the clothes he'd had on earlier and went into the master bathroom, threw them in the laundry hamper with his gym clothes and showered. Afterwards, he dried off with a big Egyptian cotton towel and wiped the steam off the mirror. Looking at himself critically, he turned this way and that, flexing his muscles. He'd made a decision. He was going to the party.

* * *

132

Red, 5:15pm

FOR THE PAST TEN DAYS, Red had taken to swinging through Owen Schmidt's neighborhood at least twice a day, often on his own time. Henry's report had been inconclusive but tantalizing. Schmidt had no criminal record, not even a juvenile one. But his mother had died in mysterious circumstances when he was 17.

The autopsy showed she had a blood-alcohol level that would have toppled a horse, and that was consistent with the boy's claim that she fell down the stairs while drunk. But there were some injuries that didn't quite match a fall; not enough that further investigation yielded charges against the boy, but clearly the coroner had questions. Schmidt had no record and there was no history of problems, though, so it had all gone away.

Since he was 17 at the time of his mother's death and had no other living relatives, he had to go into foster care, but it wasn't for long, and being the sole survivor, he inherited everything. It was a surprisingly large estate, built by the late father, who had apparently been quite an entrepreneur. The boy went on to college and a career that had no blemishes as far as Red could tell. Yet Red was still suspicious.

So he found himself prowling through Schmidt's neighborhood, looking for anything strange, unwilling to let go, but not having enough evidence to take action of any kind. As he turned the corner at Schmidt's street, putting the late afternoon sun behind him, he could see there was a party going on at Barbara Blackstone's house. She was the one who had lost the cat. Cars were parked up and down the street, and a trickle of guests entered the house. But what really surprised him was Owen Schmidt striding up the walk to Barbara's house. Schmidt was all eyes ahead and hadn't noticed the cop car. Why in God's name was he going to her party? Weren't they fighting?

Intrigued, he went around the block a few times, watching more partygoers arrive. The second time around, two women sauntered up the sidewalk, arm in arm, one a small blonde, the other a curvy brunette with a rich, sensuous laugh that penetrated his closed windows. She looked like the woman who lived down the street from him. He never spoke to any of his neighbors, so he didn't know her name. On his third pass, he saw Tanya and her husband walking up to Barbara's door. Tanya was tarted up as usual, tottering on spiked heels. The husband was a very unmemorable-looking guy. Red felt sorry for him. He wondered again if Tanya was having a fling with Schmidt. That could explain him going to the party. Or not.

He had to admit he couldn't watch Schmidt enough to catch him at anything except through pure luck, but it wasn't like he had anything more interesting to do. With that thought, he realized he'd slipped back into his old habits. It was always about the job for him. That's what ruined his marriages; his inability to leave work behind. He was supposed to be retired now. He needed to play golf and do things retired people do.

Maybe instead of cruising up and down Schmidt's street, he ought to go to Vegas and have some fun. Play a little black jack, maybe even win. Get laid. Wouldn't that be better than shadowing a potential perp? Why couldn't he just let it go? Tomorrow he'd consider taking some time off.

* * *

Jean, 5:15pm

JEAN PULLED up in front of Lydia's condo. The sun was creeping towards the horizon, but the air outside was still like an oven. The air-conditioning in the car valiantly blasted out cool air on the maximum setting, barely making a dent in the heat.

Lydia's door popped open, and she stepped out and waved at Jean, turning to lock the door behind her. She had on a long, flowing black skirt with a wide leather belt cinching the waist, white peasant blouse with scooped neck, and a beautiful squash blossom necklace. It complemented her coloring and personality perfectly but set her apart from most of the women in Palm Lakes, who dressed more conservatively. Lydia marched down the sidewalk, opened the passenger door and settled into the seat, buckling her seat belt. She must have just washed her hair, because it was slightly damp and curling madly.

"You have such beautiful hair, Lyd."

"And here I always thought my tits were my best feature."

Jean choked on a laugh. "I always feel good when I'm with you."

Lydia looked directly at her as Jean shifted into gear and pulled away from the curb. "How are things going at home?"

"No change. I'm going crazy. All I do is think and think. What should I do? What *can* I do? What's going to happen? I can't sleep. I have no appetite." She sighed and fell silent.

"Have you tried talking to Richard? Maybe suggest counseling?"

"I'd do it, but you know that won't fly with him. He doesn't talk. And he won't see a shrink. It would be admitting something's wrong with him."

"What about your marriage?"

"That's the thing. We've been living separate lives for a long time, but it wasn't until this porn thing that I realized what that meant. I thought we were doing okay because we didn't fight, but we have nothing in common anymore.

"What's worse is he thinks you're a bad influence on me. I was never interested in New Age stuff until we became friends, and now I'm rabid about it, so of course, it's your fault. As if I have no mind of my own. I can't talk to him about anything I love. He thinks yoga, crystals and energy work are for airheads, and even though he knows I'm level-headed, he treats me like I'm some vacuous blonde."

Lydia giggled. "That's the last word I'd use to describe you. I'm so sorry this is happening. Do you think it might take some pressure off if we took a break? Maybe if I weren't around, he'd calm down."

"Don't you dare suggest that! I don't know what I'd do if we couldn't talk and do things together. It's the only fun in my life right now, and it's keeping me sane. So don't mention that again, unless you're getting tired of listening to my complaints." Jean's voice drifted to a whisper at the end, as if she were afraid maybe Lydia *was* sick of being around her.

"What, and give up the best friend I've had in years? No way, José. Quit talking like that. And here I brought a surprise for tonight. We're going to par-tee!"

Jean's curiosity got the better of her. "What surprise? Of course, we're going to Barbara's party."

Lydia reached into her generous-sized handbag and pulled out a baggie of some kind of herb. "I got the best pot you can find in this area, and I'm going to share it with you. You need to mellow out, girlfriend, and this is just the way to do it."

Jean's fingers gripped the steering wheel harder as her eyes widened. "Are you kidding? You've got pot? Be careful! We don't want anyone to see that. What if I got pulled over?"

"Calm down, Jean. We're staying in Palm Lakes and you're a great driver. No one is going to pull us over, and they can't search without cause. Besides, it's only the rent-a-cops here, and they're useless."

Jean chose not to argue that point. "But I don't smoke, and I never have. I wouldn't know how. Plus where were you thinking of doing this?"

Lydia put the baggie back into her mini-suitcase. "We'll see how things go tonight. If necessary, we can go back to my place after the party and unwind. It'll do you good."

Jean shook her head skeptically. "I appreciate the thought, Lyd, but alcohol is my drug of choice, and I made myself a promise I'd enjoy myself tonight. So I'm going to have a good time, don't you worry. You just be careful with that. We don't know most of the people who are invited. One of them might even be in the Posse." She frowned as she said it, anticipating that the party might not be so much fun after all.

"I know you're shy, Jean, but don't worry. You won't have to do much. The alcohol will be flowing and people will ask lame questions like 'what's your sign?' and stuff their faces and get plowed. There will be shameless flirting, most of it harmless. Even though Barbara knows how to throw a party and keep it from derailing, there are bound to be a few cases of excess, and I'm looking forward to being a spectator. Who knows, I might even meet a handsome guy who'll sweep me off my feet."

"Yeah, right. With a 10 to 1 ratio of available women to men, that's not likely to happen anytime soon. No offense meant, but most of the attendees will be married."

"Well, that little detail never stopped me before," Lydia purred. They both burst into laughter as Jean grabbed the nearest parking place a few houses down from Barbara's.

They got out of the car and walked up the sidewalk arm in arm, swapping silly speculations about the party, laughing like school girls. Jean flinched and stopped mid-laugh, suddenly fearful of the discovery of Lydia's stash as a Posse car cruised by.

Lydia either didn't notice or didn't care, as she continued laughing and tugged Jean to keep up. They strolled up the walk to Barbara's door.

Jean reached up to ring the doorbell but hesitated. The front door was open, in spite of the air-conditioning being on, and a dull roar poured out into the quiet desert evening. Entering would be like diving into cold water.

"No need to ring the bell. Let's go in." Lydia swung the heavy screen door open and waved Jean in.

* * *

Helen, 5:15pm

TWISTING LEFT AND THEN RIGHT, Helen nodded in approval at the reflection of her party outfit in the full-length mirror on the back of the bedroom door. The turquoise silk blouse with boat neck and long sleeves was feminine, and the color complemented her hair. It would be cool, plus it covered her upper arms, which had begun to sag a bit in recent years. The lightweight charcoal-colored linen slacks with narrow leather belt accentuated her flat stomach. Dressy half boots finished the ensemble and gave her just a bit of extra height.

She was so glad she'd splurged with some of Lou's mad money and bought herself and Sally new duds for the party. Thank heaven the atmosphere had turned festive after Sally's disclosure. It gave Helen hope that things would work out.

Sally popped her head around the partially closed door. "Wow, Mom, you look really nice! A bit conservative, but classy."

Helen smiled. "I'm not young like you, missy. And I never was one to go strutting about in flashy clothes. I'm much more comfortable in something elegant but understated. You, on the other hand, are going to be the belle of the ball!"

Sally came in and walked up and down the length of the bedroom, pretending she was on a runway and striking poses. Helen couldn't contain her laughter. She eyed Sally's little black dress. The spaghetti straps showed off her tanned shoulders, and the simple style suited her. The cut of the dress accentuated her narrow waist and long legs. It was shorter than Helen would have liked, but she had to admit, Sally looked great. Her sparkly dress sandals added a touch of color. "I love how you've braided your hair up, Sally. It looks so formal. How are you able to do that yourself?"

Sally smiled smugly. "It isn't that hard once you learn. I got a book on braiding at the bookstore—in the children's section, would you believe?— and it had a bunch of wonderful styles in it. I've really enjoyed trying them out."

"You're going to be the youngest person there. I hope you won't be bored. We don't have to stay for long. You give me a sign if you want to come home."

"Really, Mom, relax. It's about time you got out and mingled. We'll have fun. What's not to like about free food and booze? I know, I'm not drinking any alcohol tonight. I've turned over a new leaf since I got pregnant."

Helen smiled in relief that they weren't going to have to argue about that. Giving a final appraisal to Sally's outfit, she made a decision. "Sally, let's get you some jewelry to wear with that pretty dress. Maddie gave me something that might be perfect."

"Oh, goody, jewelry!" Arm in arm, they giggled their way into the walk-in closet and stopped at the shelf with Helen's two jewelry boxes. Helen searched through the drawers as Sally watched in rapt attention. "What is it, Mom?"

"Maddie gave me a necklace and earrings that are gorgeous, but they aren't in a color I'm likely to wear. Let me find them and show you." She continued to rummage around and then murmured with success. "Here they are."

She pulled out a medium length necklace of graded black onyx beads that had red Swarovski crystals and gold beads for accent. Sally gushed with excitement. "Oh my God, it's beautiful! I love it." She reached for the necklace and put it on. It was just the right length for the neckline of her dress.

Helen held out her hand. "Here are the earrings." A single large onyx dangled from the french earwires with a small red crystal above it, separated by a gold bead. "Now that looks really fancy. They even match your shoes." The dressy sandals had fake crystals, and some were indeed red.

Sally hugged her impulsively. "Thanks, Mom. These are super. Will your friend Maddie be at the party?"

"No, she and Stanley don't go out much."

"I was just hoping I could show her."

"She loves giving away her creations, as she calls them. I have more than I'll ever be able to wear. These lizard earrings are among my favorites. They go with anything." She pushed her hair back from her ears to show Sally.

"Yes, I really like those as well."

"Well, these, I'm keeping. But you can have that set if you like. I never wear black near my face if I can avoid it. It makes me look pasty. Yet it suits you tremendously. I'll tell Maddie I gave them to you. She'll be pleased."

"Oh, thanks so much, Mom. I love them!" Sally bounced up and down like a little girl.

"Well, now that we have our finery on, let's walk to Barbara's and see what's happening at the party."

Helen put her arm around Sally's shoulders and they walked out to the living room companionably. Sheba was curled up on the sofa, and Helen went over to her. "Sheebs, we're going to go next door for a little while. You just relax."

Exiting through the sliding glass doors in back, they crunched across the gravel to Barbara's yard. It was still smolderingly hot, even though the sun was getting lower, its rays painting long shadows in front of them as they approached Barbara's patio.

"She has a really lovely yard, doesn't she?"

"Yes, Barbara has such a good eye for decorating." They stopped on Barbara's patio, surveying the back yard. The bougainvillea bushes were a riot of fuchsia. A spreading desert tree took up a large part of the yard. An empty fire pit was centered in the large, flagstone-paved patio that extended well beyond the patio cover. Lawn furniture was set up in several conversation areas, but they were all currently empty. Turning towards the house, they could see a mass of people through the windows and glass doors.

They entered through the sliding glass door and plunged into the crowd as the sounds of smooth jazz and the buzz of many conversations washed over them. Barbara spotted them from across the room and rushed over to greet them.

"Helen, Sally, so glad you could make it. Isn't it marvelous? I believe

139

almost everyone we invited is going to come. Even Owen, if you can believe that." Barbara gave Helen and Sally each a hug and grabbed Helen's arm to tug her in the direction of the bar. "Ben is on drink duty, so give him your orders and then get some snacks. Oh, but silly me, I want to introduce you to Alexander before we do that. He's our resident travel/food writer—and most eligible bachelor—and even though he's already a world-class chef, he takes the gourmet cooking classes in Palm Lakes just for fun. You mentioned you had enrolled in the next class, and I thought you'd like an introduction to someone who will be in it, so you don't have to feel like a complete stranger going in."

Helen's heart filled with gratitude at the thoughtfulness. "That's so kind of you! Yes, I'd love to meet him."

Barbara guided her and Sally away from the sea of people to the small parlor at the front of the house which was quieter and less crowded than the great room, having only half a dozen people. Barbara steered them towards a couple who were engaged in what appeared to be a lively discussion. As they drew closer, the woman and man stopped talking and looked their way.

Helen's first reaction surprised her. She wasn't one to ogle men. But this man, who must be Alexander, was stare-worthy. At least 6 ft tall, with broad shoulders, wavy silver hair swept back from his high forehead and piercing green eyes, he was so handsome she couldn't take her eyes off him. His clothes looked expensive, even though they were casual. The black and white Hawaiian print shirt seemed to be made of silk, and his black trousers had a sharp pleat. He wore no jewelry except for a thin gold watch on his tanned wrist.

Barbara parked them in front of Alexander and his companion. "Ladies, I'd like you to meet Alexander Stirling and Sophie Forrest. Sophie, Alexander, I'd like you to meet Helen Mueller and her daughter Sally, who's here for a visit. Alexander, Helen is the one I spoke to you about. She's taking the cooking class, and she doesn't know anyone in it. You're such an old hand, I thought maybe you could shepherd her through it."

Helen took his outstretched hand and shook it, still a bit awed. "I really appreciate both of you doing this. I haven't participated in any classes before, and I'm a bit shy about being in a new group of people."

He held her hand just long enough to make her feel he was truly pleased to meet her. "I know how it feels, Helen. You can partner up with me if you like. They always split the class into couples working together. It keeps the cost down for materials. I think you'll enjoy it. I always do." Alexander smiled, showing beautiful white teeth and charming laugh lines around his glittering green eyes.

It was overwhelming to have any man act nice to her, much less one who looked like him, but she managed to respond. "That's very generous of you, Alexander. I accept. I think I'm getting the best of the deal, though. Your reputation precedes you."

He brushed off her self-deprecating remark with a wave of his hand."They're a very welcoming group, and it doesn't matter what experience you have."

Barbara took Helen by the arm again. "Well, I waylaid these ladies on their way to the food and drink, so I'm going to take them back now; just wanted to make sure you two got to meet."

Helen smiled one last time at Alexander. "See you in class, Alexander."

"Looking forward to it, Helen." His smile made her weak in the knees.

They wound their way back to the great room and the bar, where Barbara handed them over to Ben. "I have to run and greet someone else, but I'll be back. Oh, and watch out for Bernie. He's had a few already. Ben, I think it's time you cut him off."

Ben saw Helen's worried look."Don't worry, Helen, you can't miss Bernie. He and I play golf together. He's a bear of a guy, balding, overweight and socially inept, especially after he's had a few. He's annoying but harmless. So, ladies, what can I get you to drink? We have just about anything heart could desire."

Sally spoke while Helen was processing the information about Bernie. "I'll take a Diet Coke, thanks."

Ben reached for a large glass, putting ice cubes into it, then poured the soda. "This is a vintage Diet Coke, Miss Sally. I believe you'll love it. It's bold, but not pretentious." He gave it to her, then turned to Helen. "And what can I get for you, lovely lady?" Helen laughed at his blatant flirting because she knew it meant nothing. "A red wine for me, Ben, any kind is fine. By the way, where's Jack?" She glanced around, looking for a furry whirling dervish.

He grabbed a wine glass and filled it. "This is a delightful merlot that I just know you'll like. Jack's at the sitter's house. Barbara felt it would be better all around if he wasn't under foot."

Helen accepted the glass and nodded her thanks, and she and Sally moved in the direction of the other end of the great room, where a sofa sat invitingly empty. Helen sat down and patted the cushion next to her. "Have a seat. Give yourself time to get the lay of the land."

Sally joined her and sat with perfectly crossed legs, sipping her soda. They hadn't been there a minute when a bearlike creature emerged from the crowd in front of them. *Bernie. It has to be. The receding hairline and combover; the bulging middle hanging over his belt; the clothes slightly disheveled and wrinkled, almost as if he slept in them; the somewhat unfocused eyes. It will cinch it if he does anything obnoxious.*

He looked at Sally and Helen and immediately put his hands out in front of him, though one held a glass with what looked like whiskey in it. The empty hand was making a squeezing motion. Considering he was implying doing it with both hands, his intent was pretty obvious. *Yes, Bernie for sure.*

Before either woman could say anything, he sat down close to Sally. Sally didn't budge, not that there was room to. Helen was annoyed, but wasn't used to remonstrating with a man about his behavior, so she held her tongue.

"I'm Bernie Rivers. R-I-V-3-E-R-S, but the 3 is silent." He laughed at his joke. Obviously, it was one he used a lot and of which he was quite proud. Neither woman laughed, but he did not appear chastised in the least. "I golf with Ben and live a couple streets that way." He exaggeratedly pointed to his left. "What are your names, lovely ladies, and how do you know Ben and Barbara?"

"I'm Helen, and I live on this street, and Barbara and Ben are good friends. This is my daughter, Sally, who is here for a visit."

Bernie ogled Sally, who seemed undisturbed by his attentions. "I can't believe I never met you before, Helen. And how fortunate that Sally was visiting today. Can I get either of you beautiful women a refill?"

Helen sighed to herself. It was obvious neither of them was ready for another drink, though enough time with Bernie might speed that timeline up. "No, thanks, Bernie."

Sally stood up, and Bernie almost fell over onto the vacated spot on the sofa. He must have been leaning on her. "Me, neither, Bernie. Nice meeting you. But I think we're going to have to go now. Mom promised to introduce me to everyone, and we only just got here."

Bernie's face fell. Helen found herself feeling almost sorry for him, but not sorry enough to stay. "Nice meeting you, Bernie," she said, and she and Sally headed for the snacks across the room.

Helen whispered as they plowed through the crowd. "Thanks for saving us, Sally."

"No problem, Mom. He wasn't much of a challenge. You did pretty good yourself, not telling him your last name."

They reached the granite counter that was filled with platters of delicious-looking finger foods, and she and Sally filled their plates with nibbles, commenting on the excellent variety and presentation. Pointing to the small crock pot, Helen told Sally, "I do love hot crab dip, and Barbara makes the best. You'll have to try some." Sally put some on her plate, and they took their refreshments to an area far from Bernie where two chairs were empty. "This should keep Bernie at arm's length," said Helen, laughing. They sat down, putting their glasses on the table between the chairs.

"This dip *is* great, Mom! Do you have the recipe? Where did she get crabmeat here in the desert?"

"Yes, I do, and a specialty grocery store downtown has just about anything you could want for putting on a great party. I'm sure Barbara got it there."

Helen glanced around the room. Tanya and her hubby were standing at one edge of the crowd, Tanya peering predator-like at the other guests. Helen assumed she was scoping the crowd for someone particular. She wondered if it could be Owen. Just as that thought occurred to her, she spotted Owen by following Tanya's now-frozen gaze. He was standing alone in a corner across the room, nursing a drink and looking very out of place. *Hmmm.*

Tanya turned to her husband, said something, then tottered across the room towards Helen. She was wearing 4-inch stiletto heels (did she ever wear anything else?) with black leggings and a very revealing blood-red blouse with lots of ruffles. She'd clearly had work done and liked to flaunt it. Her knuckle-buster rings were garish, and her makeup was applied way too thickly for Helen's taste.

A fake smile plastered to her face, Tanya asked in a singsong voice, "Helen, is this your daughter? What a pretty girl she is! She'll be the hit of the party for sure in that tiny black dress. All the old farts will love it, but watch out for Bernie! What's your name, honey?"

Sally appeared shocked but recovered quickly. "I'm Sally."

"Well, honey, watch out for Bernie is all I can say. In fact, watch out for all of them—or rather, most of them. There's still some life in some of them." She looked pointedly back at her husband with disdain, then turned back with the fake smile. "They rarely see a sweet young thing like you in Palm Lakes. That's one reason the wives like living here. Me included." She didn't wait for a response but lurched away in a direction that Helen couldn't help but see would eventually lead to Owen.

"She's terrible, Mom."

"She lives down the street. I think she drinks, and that doesn't help. I don't think she's a happy person." She kept to herself that she suspected Tanya had Owen in her sights for an affair. It wasn't fair to talk about things she didn't know. Maybe she'd read too much into what she'd seen. But as she chastised herself for making unpleasant assumptions, she saw Tanya weave over to Owen, touch his arm and stand close to him. Her body language said she was coming on to him. His body language was conflicted. He seemed both attracted and repelled. He stayed in place, allowing the contact, but seemed even more tense than usual, if that was possible. Wonder what that meant? And why was he here? Trust Barbara to be so forgiving and include him in the party, but why would he accept the invitation? He didn't seem the party type, but then, neither was she, and she was here.

Helen cast a glance towards Tanya's husband, who could easily see what was going on but showed no signs of concern. There was something nondescript about him that reminded Helen of something she'd read in a spy novel about a good spy not standing out in any way. Tanya's husband could be a great spy, because he seemed to blend into a crowd as if he were a ghost. Poor man.

The tête à tête between Owen and Tanya ended with no obvious outcome, and Tanya moved on to speak briefly to another couple. Shortly after that, Helen saw Owen leave in a rush. Tanya continued to mingle. Maybe Helen was imagining things because she didn't get out enough and watched too much TV. It was silly to imagine illicit romances going on in Palm Lakes. It was a retirement community, after all, not some soap opera.

Just then, Barbara came up to them with two ladies in tow. "Helen, Sally, I'd like you to meet my special friends Lydia and Jean. We're in yoga class together, and we have so much fun. I thought you might like to join us in the next class, Helen."

Helen was touched at being included. "I would love to do that, Barbara."

Barbara smiled encouragingly. "The people are so easy to be around; the teacher is gentle and kind. And yoga just makes you feel terrific." Barbara patted Helen on the shoulder and went back to mingle with the other guests.

The next couple hours were filled with laughter, entertaining stories and a growing sense of closeness to Jean and Lydia. Suddenly for the first time in her life, Helen had friends. She was being included in a group. It had all happened so fast her head was spinning.

After saying goodbye to Barbara and Ben, inviting them to dinner soon (*why did it never occur to me to do that before?*), Helen and Sally walked the short distance across the moonlit yard to the back door of Helen's house and let themselves in.

"That was really fun, Mom. Thanks for inviting me."

"Barbara's the one to thank. You could call her tomorrow if you like. I'm glad you were here. I doubt I could have brought myself to go alone. I did enjoy meeting Lydia and Jean and Alexander. I hope we weren't too boring for you."

"Ah, Mom, free food and drink in a lovely setting with nice people? What's not to like? And Jean and Lydia were fun. Alexander? He's hot for an old guy! Maybe you and he can go out on a date sometime. He's like movie-star handsome, and he seemed real nice."

"Heavens, Sally, your Dad hasn't been gone that long."

"Yeah, Mom, I know, but you and Dad had nothing, at least as far as I could see. Why not get out and live a little?"

Helen was shocked by Sally's directness, but she couldn't argue. "Maybe someday, but Alexander is way out of my league. He's being nice, but that doesn't mean anything. The women must be beating a path to his door, and I'm no great catch."

"Look in the mirror sometime, Mom. I don't know how you manage to convince yourself you're no catch. You look great for your age. You're a nice person. You put up with Dad for years. You're smart and kind. You're a catch."

"Thanks for the pep talk, Sally. I appreciate the vote of confidence. I agree he is handsome. It will take me time to be willing to go beyond noticing that."

Sally shrugged. "I'm going to hit the sack now. I get tired easier these days." She gave Helen a brief hug and went back to the guest room.

Helen reached down to pet Sheba, who was meowing incessantly. The meows stopped, but Helen knew what Sheba wanted, so she picked her up and snuggled her. "Who's my Precious? Didn't we come back like I promised?" The purring response was loud and strong, but Sheba felt even lighter than usual, her bones sticking out as if she were a rescue cat. "When did you get so skinny, Precious?" Worry stabbed Helen again. She couldn't imagine life without Sheba. Things were still so unsettled, and Sheba was her one true friend. "I'm going to get an appointment with the vet to check you out; Sally's visit distracted me." Then she walked back to the master suite, hugging Sheba and whispering reassurances to her.

Once in the bedroom, she gently deposited Sheba on the bed and changed into her nightgown, an old cotton one with flowers and a scooped neck. They'd never had money for nice clothes, so she didn't have much of a wardrobe, but she didn't really mind. Shopping wasn't her thing, and she rarely went out. It had been fun shopping with Sally today, but she couldn't see herself getting addicted to it.

She went to the walk-in closet and opened a built-in drawer and shoved aside the clothing, exposing her journals. Thank heaven she'd thought to remove them from the office when Sally called unexpectedly. She loved seeing Sally, but she had no intention of sharing her journals with anyone.

Grabbing her pen and the latest journal, she went back to the bed and crawled onto the covers, propping the pillow behind her back to cushion it from the headboard. It wasn't a comfortable position, but she really wanted to write tonight.

Saturday, August 26, 1995

Tonight was the first night in ages that I went to a social function. Lou never liked them, and I have to admit I'm very reserved in groups, so I didn't really mind avoiding them. But today was part of the program to discover the new me. I thought the party would entertain Sally, and I wanted to try to mingle more. I've never been good at mixing with people, especially strangers. And until you mingle, everyone's a stranger.

The night went far better than I could have predicted. I didn't find myself tempted to drink more than a couple glasses of wine. It was fun putting on brand new clothes and going to a real party. Sally looked so pretty. Jean and Lydia were delightful company. I can't wait for that yoga class. And Barbara was so kind to introduce me to Alexander, who offered to partner with me in the cooking class, though I can't imagine why he'd want to be saddled with me. Life is suddenly looking very attractive for the first time in decades.

It's not without its challenges, though. As soon as I began to work out some of my problems, Sally shows up. Her life is in a bigger shambles than mine. I'm still very conflicted about what to do. I find it hard to say 'no' to her. She was always my favorite, but it's more than that. She has no husband, no job, no place to live. She's a grown woman with a good education, and I'm sure she can survive, but somehow I feel it's my job to help her, to say 'yes' to her. I just know that I don't want to leave Palm Lakes and be her child's nanny. How much is a mother obliged to do?

She paused briefly as a scene from the past came back to her in a rush. It had happened years ago. She was sitting in the doctor's examining room, shivering in the chill in a silly paper gown, hoping that Lou would stay in the waiting room. He'd yelled at her so much that day, and she was terrified. She never handled his rage well. He wouldn't do anything in public; when they got home was another matter. But she wasn't going to give in.

She began to write again.

Sally being pregnant has brought the memories back. It's hard to believe it was nearly 31 years ago this happened...

It was still as fresh as wet paint to her, and she didn't really like to touch it, because of the way it made her feel. She forced herself to continue writing.

It seemed like I waited hours that day in the doctor's office, but finally, he came back. "Congratulations, you're pregnant!"

The doctor had no idea that Lou was going to be angry about the news. Lou had told me he was going to make sure I got an abortion if I was pregnant, that we couldn't afford another mouth to feed. I'd hidden the pregnancy as long as possible; I wore my loosest clothing to cover the bulge.

I smiled faintly at the doc. He probably wrote my bland reaction off to morning sickness. "Shall we bring Lou in and tell him the good news?" I nodded, knowing Lou would be unlikely to overreact in front of the doctor. Anyway, I hoped he wouldn't. He was always so afraid of what people would think.

The doctor brought Lou back and broke the news. Lou's mouth was a savage slit and his eyes glittered with rage. "Can we get an abortion?"

The doctor had looked surprised at the coldness of Lou's question, then after searching both our faces, he must have realized what was what. "No, it's too late for that."

Lou's dark expression darkened further. "Fine." Turning abruptly, he left the room, and it fell to me to smooth things over with the doctor, in spite of my heart being in my throat. I was so relieved I had held out long enough to keep my baby.

I never told Sally how her father had tried to have her aborted. From the moment I conceived, she was my special little miracle, and I wouldn't let anything happen to her. He threw a fit when we got home, saying two kids was enough, but with time, he accepted it. He actually treated her special after she was born, which was a blessing. She was always able to wrap us both around her little finger and often did.

Now that she's in a family way, I find myself asking if an abortion is the best course of action for her. I never liked the idea, and I wouldn't encourage her to, but would I discourage her from it? Fortunately, she never expressed it as an option. It would certainly take me off the hook. The only thing that is making it so hard for me to say 'no' to her is the baby. I want my grandchild to have a good life. But does it have to mean giving up mine?

I wish it were easier to know what to do. I feel selfish, wanting to do what I want. I feel angry that I never really have had a chance to do that. Lou did what he damn well pleased his whole life. I've watched my kids make their own decisions and create their own lives. Sally has lived a carefree, full life until now. I never got that. Of course, it's my own fault for marrying so young, but when will it be my turn?

I want to find a way for both of us to have what we want. I want to help Sally, but I want to stay in Palm Lakes and explore this new life I've been given. I'll go apartment hunting with her if she likes and maybe give her some of the extra furniture when I move. She loves some of these pieces. It will annoy Lena no end, but too bad. I can give them to Sally to help her get a good start here and feel supported. That should soften the blow, and if I can get a decent job and downsize enough, maybe I can continue to give her a bit of money to help out, along with some babysitting. It all comes down to her finding a decent job, which I believe she can.

Helen put the pen down and closed the book. She knew what she wanted to do, but she wasn't sure she'd be able to stick to her guns if Sally couldn't find a good job and place to live. Life had sure gotten challenging the past several months. She got up and put the journal back in its hiding place and bedded down next to Sheba.

* * *

Jean, 12:20am

JEAN AND LYDIA were driving along the moonlit streets, enjoying the quiet, a welcome change after hours of music, talk and laughter.

Finally, Lydia broke the silence. "Want to come in and share a joint with me?"

"No, thanks, Lydia. I really don't smoke. Richard probably wonders what happened to me. It's past midnight, and I never stay out late. Not that I think he'll be jealous."

"Too bad. Maybe we should arrange to make him jealous. We could have gotten you a date with Bernie, I'm certain."

They both tittered. "Yeah, Bernie would be a real catch. Poor guy. Makes me feel lucky to have Richard in a way."

"Sometimes being alone is better than being with someone you're incompatible with," Lydia said with conviction.

"Speaking from experience?"

"Tons of it. I seem to be incompatible with long-term relationships. I've tried often enough. None ever took. But I'm happy on my own, really. I have no one to answer to, no need to compromise and no one to fight with. Life is good."

She didn't sound too convinced, but Jean didn't want to invade her privacy, so she let it slide. "I don't know where my marriage is heading. I'd like to save it, but I'm wondering if there's anything left to save."

"You'll figure it out. Just be true to your heart and be kind to yourself. Whatever you do, I'm here for you."

"Oh, Lyd, I have no idea how I could deal with this otherwise." She pulled up in front of Lydia's condo and parked the car. "Thanks for going with me this evening. I would never have gone on my own."

"It was a blast, wasn't it? There weren't many eligible bachelors, but the food and drink were super, just like the company. I think Helen will be a great addition to our little group. I really like her."

Jean smiled. "I do, too. She seems so sweet, though a little scared in crowds like me."

Lydia patted her on the arm. "It's OK to be shy with strangers. How would it look if everyone wore lampshades at parties? Leave that to us extroverts." They both dissolved into laughter.

Lydia opened the car door and got out, reaching back for her humungous purse. "See you soon! Call me if you need anything." She slammed the door and walked up the sidewalk, digging through her purse for her house key.

Jean sat waiting for her to get in, then put the car into gear and pulled away from the curb.

Moonlight was spilling across the landscape, black shadows contrasting with pools of otherworldly light. It gave the trees and cacti an alien look, monochromatic and forbidding. No one was out at this time, even on a Saturday. No cars and no people. Typical retirement community. It was as if she were the only person on a movie set.

She enjoyed the quiet and solitude of the short drive home, the car windows rolled down and a warm breeze blowing through them. The garage door went up, splitting the silence eerily as she turned into the driveway. She noticed that Richard had left the light on for her, or maybe he was still up.

The garage door came down noisily behind her and clunked shut. She got out of the car and grabbed her purse from the back seat. The car door sounded louder than usual as it slammed shut in the stillness of the empty garage. *Why do things sound different at night?* Dismissing the odd thought, she went through the office and saw the living room light on through the doorway. Her attention was grabbed by the computer display. It had gone dark like it did when it went to sleep, but there was a small image on the center of the screen, and it caused her eyes to bug out.

It was a picture of a naked woman and man, his genitalia displayed as the main attraction. She couldn't bear to look at it; she barely registered it as her heart pounded in her ears.

Richard's voice snapped her out of shock. "So you're home! How was the party?"

She stepped through the doorway into the hall and stared blankly at Richard, who sat in an armchair in front of the TV in the great room, a book in his hand as if he'd been reading. But clearly, he hadn't. He had just left the office, shutting down a porn site. He wasn't that computer literate, which had led to her discovery of his addiction in the first place. He didn't realize a popup had appeared after he shut the site down. He was in too much of a hurry to get into the living room and look relaxed when he heard the garage door go up.

Her heart pounded in her throat. She had imagined any number of scenarios, but it really hadn't occurred to her that he would lie to her. It felt very much as if a line had been crossed. And it was up to her whether to confront him or let it slide.

"What's the matter, Jean? You look like you saw a ghost. Was the party that bad?" Richard oozed charm, and she marveled at how she would have been taken in if only that popup hadn't appeared and given him away. She couldn't let it pass. This was intolerable.

"I guess I did see a ghost of sorts. The ghost of our marriage. You've been on the computer watching porn again. No, don't deny it. Just go look at the computer. How could you lie to me? I trusted you to keep your promise!" She was annoyed that her voice sounded whiny. Why should she plead, when he was the wrongdoer?

Richard seemed unnaturally calm. "What do you want me to say?"

"You don't know?" She let out a huge sigh of exasperation. It hit her suddenly: he wasn't even going to try. "I'm going to move into the guest bedroom. I need some space and time to sort out this mess in my head. It's late. I've had a few drinks, so it isn't the right time to talk about this." Not that it would ever be.

She stalked back to the master bedroom and grabbed her nightgown and toothbrush and went to the smaller guest room with its adjoining bath. Tears streamed down her face as she realized there probably wasn't any way to save her marriage.

She heard him in the master suite getting ready for bed. She wondered what was going through his mind. Why didn't he come try to talk with her? Didn't he care? She began to cry again.

She could have fought another woman, but this porn thing was impossible. She was actually wondering what she had done to drive him to this. What an idiot she was! She lay down and closed her eyes, and after a while slipped into a troubled sleep.

RENAISSANCE: CHAPTER 5

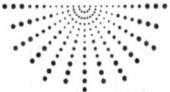

THURSDAY, SEPTEMBER 7, 1995

Helen, 9:54am

*H*elen sat in her car at the Recreation Center, giving herself a pep talk while letting the cool air blast her face. The first session of the International Gourmet Cooking Club was starting in several minutes. Thank heaven Barbara had arranged for her to meet Alexander at the party, and God bless him for offering to partner with her. That really did take a lot of the panic out of the experience, but it was surprising how the prospect of walking into that room full of strangers still terrified her.

She had always known she was shy, terribly shy, but she'd told herself it was Lou who had kept her home. Now she realized he had merely been a convenient excuse.

Afraid of being late (that would only make things worse), she turned the car off and went into the building looking for Room 107. When she found it, she paused in the doorway, taking in the scene.

In the open part of the room were several islands which each had a sink and countertop. Along one wall was a restaurant-sized stovetop, a couple of wall ovens, a microwave, a large refrigerator, automatic dishwasher, double stainless steel sink and rows of floor-to-ceiling cabinets and shelves, plus plenty of counter space. Everything was spotless and new-looking.

There were locks on most of the cabinets, but one set was open, and she could see pots, pans and cooking implements.

The room opened up beyond the cooking area into a dining room with round tables that would seat at least 8 people, each surrounded by comfortable-looking chairs. The far side of the room was a bank of floor-to-ceiling windows that gave a spectacular view of the golf course. Over a dozen people were scattered around the room, talking in small groups.

She spotted Alexander in the center of the largest bunch. She recalled that Barbara had told her he was a writer for a food and travel magazine. It suddenly hit her that her partner was probably the most popular person in the club. The women surrounding him radiated interest, and why not? Alexander was a bachelor. In Palm Lakes, if you were a single man, you had to beat them off with a stick. Unless you were someone like Bernie, she amended. She saw two other men in the room, but most of the students were women.

She propelled herself through the doorway and headed over to Alexander, noting once again how attractive he was. He could make the most casual outfit look like something from a fashion magazine, and he didn't even seem aware of it. His maroon polo shirt, black pants and black leather shoes were a counterpoint to his longish silver hair and emerald eyes. There wasn't an ounce of fat on his frame. She wondered how he managed to stay in shape when so many men his age carried extra weight around their middle. There was no doubt about it; he was gorgeous, and his apparent lack of vanity made him even more appealing.

Finally, his eyes met hers, and he smiled warmly and waved her into the group, introducing her to all the ladies like she was his oldest friend. She shook hands with each of them, swiftly forgetting their names in the tension of the moment.

She got her panic under control as the students began to quiet down and the teacher called the class to attention. "OK, everyone gather 'round me. Let's get started." A few minutes passed as the people stopped their conversations and moved in the direction of the teacher, a grandmotherly woman with gray hair who looked like someone who not only enjoyed cooking, but eating what she cooked, as well.

"I'm Alice, and I'm your teacher. I see the usual suspects are here. Alexander. Nora. Ray. Alan. Welcome back. I hate to make it seem like you're back in school, but I have to take roll call, so we might as well use that as a chance to get to know each other. Let's stick with first names and just briefly say what you hope to get out of this class. That will help me do a better job."

Helen was relieved at the chance to learn names again, and this time, she focused on remembering them. It still went by in a blur, and she was nervous about having to speak, but as she listened to the other students, she relaxed and got into the swing of it. Before she knew it, she was standing with Alexander at one of the islands with several pots and other necessities for their project.

Alexander smiled, the laugh lines around his eyes crinkling his tanned skin. "I saw you taking in the place when you arrived. It's impressive, isn't it?"

"I didn't expect something this grand. What's the dining area for?"

"All the clubs are entitled to have celebrations here, so you'll find that many of them vie for the space around New Year's Eve and other holidays. We have a dinner here annually. You'll have to plan on attending. Assuming you enjoy the club, that is."

"You're so gracious, taking me on not knowing what you're getting into. I'm sure I'll love it. I love cooking, and I really want to expand my culinary horizons."

"Well, this is the place!" Alexander started organizing the implements and looking over the written instructions for today's lesson, but she was too distracted to concentrate.

The room buzzed with conversations, and Alice was teaming unpaired students based on interest and experience, so Helen and the old hands were in a holding pattern.

Ray and Alan were at the island adjacent to theirs, and it was obvious they were going to be the class entertainment. She watched in rapt attention as they did impressions for the people at the next island over, Nora and another woman whose name she had already forgotten.

"Oh, Alan, you know your mother can't compare to mine. *Mine* takes the prize." He was camping it up in a voice that sounded gay, and it occurred to her that maybe Ray and Alan *were* gay.

"I beg to differ, Ray, my mother was the *height* of hypocrisy. He posed as if answering a phone... 'Oh Nora, so nice you called. Of course, dear, anything you like will be fine with me...Sure, tomorrow's fine...'" He mimed hanging up the phone and rolled his eyes disdainfully. "Bitch."

It came out such a contrast to the hypocritical niceness that Helen sputtered with laughter. Class was going to be highly entertaining if this was a sample. She looked at Alexander, whose eyes flashed with amusement. "You're in for it, Helen. This is just the beginning."

To her surprise and pleasure, the class passed swiftly. Working with Alexander was how she imagined dancing would be, never having done much dancing. They had a rapport that was...graceful. Though she hardly knew him, it was as if they anticipated each other's thoughts and intentions, and as they worked, the smooth efficiency acted like a balm to Helen's nerves. She'd never imagined working with another person could be so pleasant and rewarding.

They'd created some lovely paté and were busy cleaning up by the time she came back to reality. She hadn't thought to bring something to put food in for later. *Was that in the paper I got about the class? What's the matter with my memory these days?*

Alexander saw her looking around and divined her issue. "It's so easy to forget everything you're supposed to bring the first day of class. Kind of like being a kid again, isn't it? I tell you what. I'm going to make a special dinner tonight because I got some salmon at the store...just couldn't resist, since you don't often see good fresh fish on offer here. Do you like salmon? I can take the paté home with me. You can have dinner at my house and bring a container to take your share of the paté home, or whatever is left after we eat. How's that sound?"

His invitation sounded so normal, so casual, but...why he was asking her to dine with him? She hoped he wasn't asking because he wanted a date. Part of her was intrigued; the other part was petrified. She had no idea how to respond.

He watched her patiently, and she got the distinct impression that he knew she was scared. He'd been so nice, it wasn't fair to act ungrateful.

"That's thoughtful of you, Alexander. I have no plans for this evening, and I would really like that." She hoped she hadn't sounded too wooden, but her vocal cords were partially paralyzed by shock.

"Wonderful. I'll pick you up at 5:30, if that's all right? I want to drive so I can make sure you get home safely, because I have a couple of lovely wines for you to sample." He rummaged through the drawer of the island and found a blank piece of paper. "Why don't you write down your phone number and address for me. If I get lost, I'll call you."

She nodded and numbly began to write on the paper. She knew he was OK because Barbara had introduced them. And he hadn't been at all tactile or forward during the class. He probably was just being friendly, and she could use a friend. She handed him the paper. "It isn't that far from here, and I don't think you'll have a problem finding it. Can I bring anything?"

"No, thanks, I have it covered. But you can help me cook. It will be good practice for class." He chuckled as he said it, and she felt the tension drain from her body. So it wasn't a date. "I hope you don't mind eating later in the evening. I know most people eat early around here, but when you're cooking a nice meal, it takes time. Is a late night all right?"

She wasn't used to being consulted about her preferences and struggled to answer. "I don't keep a regular schedule. It's always a pleasure to have a real meal and someone to share it with."

They walked out to the parking lot, and he pointed at a silver Mercedes a few rows over. "That's my car. I'll swing by and pick you up at 5:30."

"OK. Thanks." She watched as he strode across the tarmac towards his car, then reached into her purse for her keys and walked to her station wagon. It wasn't until she got in the car that she remembered Sally was at home, and she'd have to explain to her why she was going out tonight.

* * *

Samantha, 10:00am

SWITCHING her clipboard to her right hand, Samantha pressed Barbara's doorbell once. Instantly a small dog started yapping. The door swung open, and Barbara smiled in welcome. "Samantha, how nice of you to help me out like this."

"It's my pleasure." Samantha followed Barbara into the large, elegantly decorated great room.

The Jack Russell terrier was hopping up and down around Samantha, so she finally gave him her full attention. "What a cute guy you are. What's your name?"

"He's Jack. Imaginative, right? We can sit down for a minute and talk about my vision for the yard. I'm eager to hear what you suggest. I'm not that knowledgeable about desert landscaping. Oh, and how about I get you a drink? A soda? Lemonade? Iced tea?"

"That's kind of you, but I have water in the car." She wondered if Barbara always put people at ease like this, or if it were just because Samantha was Maddie's girl.

As if reading her mind, Barbara asked, "How are Maddie and Stanley doing? I only see them rarely. They didn't come to my party, but your Mom said they don't socialize."

"That's right. They pretty much stay at home. They don't even go out to eat, which is unusual in this town."

"I'm sure they're happy to have you living here."

"Yes, they were surprised and pleased when my husband said he wanted to retire here. We did enjoy our visits here a lot, and of course, how could anyone complain about the winters? We were pretty tired of snow."

"Ben and I were blessed that way. Winters are mild in Southern California. But Ben wanted to live in a golfing community, and he fell in love with the desert. It's very different from our old home, but I'm getting used to it."

"It certainly does take time to adjust, especially to the summers."

"That's why I called you. I know we've only been here going on five years, but now that I've lived here a while, I'm ready to make some improvements to our landscaping. I really love the hummingbirds. We have a feeder out, but I'd like to put in some plants that would attract them. We spend a lot of time outdoors, and we love watching them. Plus there are a couple bushes I just don't like and want to replace."

"I'll need to look at the various locations before I suggest anything in particular, but there are a number of nice flowering bushes I can recommend."

"Great. Why don't we go out back? That's the main area I'm interested in updating at the moment."

They rose and exited through the sliding glass doors, Jack close behind them, onto a spacious patio with a slatted patio cover. Samantha's eye was caught by the lovely Texas ebony tree which dominated the back yard, its spreading canopy nearly as impressive as a palo verde or mesquite. They walked around the yard as Samantha questioned Barbara about her likes and dislikes.

When they returned to the patio, Samantha eyed the yard for a few minutes as she came up with a new design. "I'm not sure how radical a change you want." She verbally sketched which plantings she'd remove and what she'd replace them with, explaining the pros and cons as she went along.

Barbara nodded, taking everything in. "That sounds exactly like what I wanted, especially those dwarf bottlebrush. We had the full-size version back home, and those sound cute. They'll be perfect around the patio extension."

Samantha looked around as if searching for something. "Where's Jack?"

"Oh, he probably wandered off. He does that sometimes."

"Shall we go find him? People around here get touchy about neighbors' pets in their yards."

"Don't I know it! He'll be back soon. He never goes far. So what do you think about the job? Any further suggestions?"

"I would suggest we do just that much and then go from there. You might not want to do anymore. Or you might. But it's hard to picture huge changes, so why not do it a little bit at a time?"

"I like how you think, Samantha. What will it cost me and what are the details?"

"Give me a minute to work up an estimate."

Barbara turned to go inside. "Let's get out of this hot sun so you can do your math."

Samantha followed her back into the house, smiling that it hadn't occurred to her that it was all that hot. She was still concerned that Jack had run off, but Barbara didn't seem worried.

Ten minutes later, she bid Barbara goodbye and drove the short distance to park in front of Mom's house. Samantha enjoyed doing appointments in her parents' neighborhood because it made visiting much more convenient than finding time outside of working hours. She'd be able to get a couple visits in while doing Barbara's redo, as Julio was very family-oriented and encouraged her to see her folks when she could.

She pressed the doorbell. Right on cue, Beau's deep bark began. It wouldn't stop until he saw her. The door finally opened (Mom was getting slow with her arthritis), and Beau greeted her effusively as she came into the house. A hug for Mom, a pat for Beau. "Where's Dad?"

"In his office, reading."

"I was at Barbara's giving an estimate on some work and figured you'd both be up by now. She's hired me. I'll be able to come by while I'm supervising that job."

"That will be nice."

Mom had obviously been making jewelry, as the light on the dining room table was lit, and bits and pieces of jewelry were lying out on white cloths. "Making a new design?"

"Yes, I got a shipment of some nice tourmaline, and I'm trying to decide what to do with it."

They wandered back to the table together. Samantha really admired her Mom's beautiful and original designs. For this project, she had some lovely gold findings she was mixing with the purple, green and goldish tourmaline chips. "That's going to be really lovely, Mom."

Mom smiled and sat down. "Can you stay a bit?"

"No, I'm still on the clock, and I shouldn't stay longer than to say a quick hi to you both."

"Go see your Dad, then. But come back and say bye before you leave."

"OK."

Samantha straightened her shoulders and walked back to her Dad's small office. As she rounded the corner, she could see him sitting at his desk reading a book. He looked up and waved her in.

"Close the door. I have something I need to talk to you about."

She resisted being drawn in. "Dad, I can't stay. I'm just stopping to say hi."

It was obvious resistance was futile. "This won't take long. You need to see this."

She sighed, then hoped his failing hearing hadn't caught her. It was as if he didn't remember that every time she came, he gave her the same unpleasant lecture.

Stanley pulled out a tablet and began to write numbers which he'd obviously committed to memory. "You need to understand the facts because it's likely that I'll be the first to go, since your mother is much younger than me. You need to know what the financial situation is, because she has no interest in it, and someone has to take responsibility. Otherwise, she'll end up in big trouble. She doesn't know the first thing about paying bills or saving. And there's no way she'll ever be able to live on a budget. After I'm gone, the survivor's portion of my pension will be a fraction of what we now get. The house is paid for, and this is how much money will be coming in each month." He pointed to a number on his pad. "This is approximately what the bills cost each month." He pointed to another number. "As you can see, there won't be a lot left. She'll need to use that for food and incidentals."

Samantha stared at the numbers yet again, wondering how her money-obsessive, control freak father had ever gotten into such bad financial condition. He claimed to have very little savings, and he had no life insurance, no catastrophic or long-term care insurance, nothing as a safety net. It was as if he planned to drop dead one day instead of needing special care. If anyone could plan that, he could. But what she didn't understand was why he couldn't have planned better for Mom.

Displaying more confidence than she felt, she offered, "I think she'll do OK, Dad, but of course, I'm here to help."

"She's going to need it. Mark my words." It sounded almost as if he wanted Mom to fall on her face.

"I need to get back to work, Dad. I'm only supposed to take quick breaks to visit you. Arthur and I will come by Sunday. I'll be back a few times over the course of Barbara's redo."

"OK, see you then." Stanley's white head was already bent over his book as he waved a hand at her in dismissal.

Out in the dining room, Mom labored over her project, her jeweler's magnifying glasses like a miner's helmet. Her failing eyes only slowed her down a little; the doctor had said it was macular degeneration, but maybe he was wrong. She was still doing quite well with her jewelry. Samantha hoped it never got too bad. Making jewelry was what kept Mom sane.

"I'm leaving, Mom. I'll come back when I can. Arthur and I will stop by on Sunday. Do you have anything you want me to pick up at Price Club or anywhere?"

"I can't think of anything this time."

"I'll fertilize your citrus trees Sunday. I'll pick up the fertilizer and you can reimburse me."

"OK," Mom said distractedly.

"I have to do mine anyway, and that way you don't have to lug heavy things around and crawl around under your trees."

"I could do it, but if you insist..." Mom's resentment was palpable. Samantha knew that Mom wasn't happy about accepting help with the yard, but she also knew she was getting too infirm to do many of the things she used to do. It made for a mutually unhappy situation.

Samantha patted Beau and left to finish the rest of her workday.

When she got home, Arthur was sitting in a wing chair in the great room, reading the paper. He looked up briefly to acknowledge her return, but said nothing and went back to reading. She registered an inexplicable annoyance towards him.

Her mind went back to her Dad's spiel, and she got the connection. Arthur hadn't mentioned anything about providing for her, yet he was nearly 20 years older than she.

Why hadn't Arthur prepared for the future? Here she was working full time while he played tennis most days, and he had never taken out life insurance or talked about anything that would protect her ability to stay in their home if he died. When he died.

She swallowed her concerns and went back to the bedroom to take a shower.

* * *

Sally, 11:10am

SALLY PUT the phone down and did a little victory dance around her Mom's living room. The job offer was everything she could have asked for and more. She could hardly believe she'd gotten such a wonderful job so fast!

Too bad Mom wasn't home to celebrate, but she had her cooking class and then was taking Sheba to the vet. Now would be a good time to rent that apartment they'd looked at yesterday, the one she liked so much. Worried that someone else might get it if she delayed, she decided to go without Mom. It would be easier that way, anyhow.

She got her purse, checking that she had the cash Mom had given her, and headed out to get her new place. The apartment complex was a trying

20-minute drive west on a heavily traveled four-lane highway that was always choked with traffic, or at least had been every time Sally drove down it. Today was no exception.

She arrived at the Desert Palms apartment complex, filled out paperwork and placed a deposit, then let herself into her new home and walked around the apartment, savoring the sense of freedom and the adventure of starting a new life. Her unit on the second floor had two bedrooms and a nice view of the pool and inner courtyard. It even had a stacked washer and drier. Standing in the empty space, she could feel herself expanding and relaxing.

Mom meant well, but 13 days of living with her had shown Sally how ill-suited they were for living together. Once she got into her apartment, she could do what she liked; no prohibitions against alcohol, no worries about bringing a man home with her. She'd forgotten how restrictive living with parents was.

She shuddered to think what living with Mom full time would have been like. Desperation had nearly driven her to do something colossally stupid. Pretense was natural to her (isn't that how everyone manages to live with family?), but keeping it up 24/7 took a toll. After nearly two weeks with Mom, it was clear living with her would mean full-time acting, and she wasn't up for that. Now she wouldn't have to.

She locked up and headed back, stopping for a bite to eat on the way, since she'd missed lunch.

A couple hours later, Mom walked through the door carrying Sheba's travel crate, a sad look on her face.

"What's wrong, Mom?"

"The vet says she has a mass, and it's probably cancer, but they're doing some tests to make sure. At her age, there isn't much we can do about it. Just keep her comfortable for as long as possible." She put the crate down, opened the door and coaxed Sheba out. Sheba walked arthritically towards the master bedroom.

"I'm so sorry, Mom. I know how much Sheba means to you." This was going to take the fun out of her announcement.

"I'm having a hard time accepting it. I know she's old, but I don't know what I'll do without her." Helen picked up the crate and carried it to the garage to put it in a cupboard.

When she came back in, Sally went over and hugged her. "That's terrible news, but I have some good news. Do you want to hear it?"

Mom smiled weakly. "I could use some good news."

"I got a job offer, a really good one. They were impressed with my experience, and they'll give me maternity leave, and they have an on-site day care center. My boss is really cool! It couldn't be better!"

"That's terrific news! Congratulations. Now you can choose your apartment." Mom was making an effort, but her voice was flat.

"Already did that. As soon as I heard, I went and rented that one I liked so much. I didn't want to lose it. I can move in this weekend."

Mom looked stunned. "Wow, it all happened so fast!"

"I can hardly believe it myself." Sally wanted to jump up and down, but tamped down her excitement, since Mom was still reeling from all the news, good and bad.

Mom sat down and sighed. "What are you going to do about your belongings back home?"

"I put them in storage before I left. I was thinking maybe I can coax Warren into loading up a U-Haul and bringing it down sometime. Do you think he'll come for Thanksgiving?" Sally sat down on the sofa and patted Mom's arm encouragingly.

"Maybe. I've suggested they come down, but they haven't committed yet." Mom was looking a bit lost at the pace of change.

"I can make do with minimal stuff for a while."

Mom's blue-green eyes finally sparked with interest. "You need furniture. I'll take you to some estate sales. You can pick up good stuff that way."

It thrilled Sally that Mom was getting with the program. "That's a great idea! We might even be able to do that this weekend since I don't have a lot of stuff to move. I'll get an airbed or futon and maybe a small dining set, some dishes and things like that. But I don't need a lot."

"When I move, you can have furniture I won't need." Sally clapped her hands together in excitement, and Mom smiled. "I have an appointment with a realtor next week, and I'm hoping to find a smaller place here in Palm Lakes."

They walked out to the kitchen, and Mom made iced tea for them to take out to the patio. It was still pretty hot, but Sally liked watching the hummingbirds come to the feeder.

"So how was your cooking class with Mr. Movie Star?"

"Oh, really, Sally, don't dramatize it. We're just partners in the class, which was really fun. We made paté."

"So do I get to try some?"

A look crossed her mother's face. It almost looked like guilt. "Well, I forgot to bring a container with me, so Alexander took it all home...We're having dinner at his place tonight."

"Wow, that was quick! You already have a date with him?" Sally raised an eyebrow appraisingly. "I underestimated you."

"It's not a date, Sally."

"Sure sounds like it to me." Sally started giggling, and Mom smiled.

"Neither of us is interested in dating. He's just a friend." Mom paused, seeming to contemplate something. "It was really strange. I expected to feel awkward, and I did at first, but after a while, it was like we'd known each other forever. We didn't need to talk a lot; we worked together surprisingly well. I felt funny when he asked me to dinner, but he managed to put me at ease about it. Now that I'm talking with you, I'm nervous again."

Sally patted her hand encouragingly. "So what are you having for dinner?"

"He hasn't given me details, but it's salmon, and I have to help cook."

"Is he coming to pick you up?"

"Yes, you'll have to say hi."

"Hell no, Mom. That would spoil the whole thing. He'd feel he had to invite me as well. I'm going to stay out of sight. I'll keep Sheba company. When you get home, if I'm still up, you can tell me all about it."

"There won't be a lot to tell, but I'll be happy to share."

"So what are you wearing?"

Mom looked at her with confusion. "I guess I'll wear what I wore to the party. I don't have anything else."

"That's just wrong! You need something different. You can't let him see you in the same outfit twice in a row!"

"He's coming to pick me up at 5:30. I don't have time to shop, and since it isn't a date, I don't have to worry about rules like that. I'm going to wear what I wore to the party."

They sat in silence for a few minutes, then Mom spoke up. "What do you say we shop the estate sales this weekend and go out for a meal Sunday to celebrate your good fortune?"

"I'd love that!"

"Then it's a deal." She watched as Mom got up and took the glasses back into the house. Alexander would be here in less than two hours. She needed to give Mom a pep talk. She was too timid; no wonder, given what Dad was like.

Eligible men seemed scarce here, and if Alexander was interested, Mom should go for it. Maybe she should give her a safe sex talk...Nah, Mom was too old-fashioned to fall into bed with him on a first date. But it would be nice if it worked out for her, not only because she deserved some happiness. Having a boyfriend would also keep Mom from focusing too much on Sally's life.

Now if only she could find a hunky guy for herself.

* * *

Alexander, 5:29pm

WHEN ALEXANDER PULLED into Helen's driveway, the sun was getting low, but the air was still oppressively hot. She opened the door dressed in the same outfit she'd worn to Barbara's party.

She was a beautiful woman, and there was something about her that hinted at hidden depths and mysteries, which intrigued him. Even more attractive was her total lack of interest in dating him. Her fear of him, or rather, men in general, put him strangely at ease, something he hadn't felt with a woman in a very long time.

"Alexander," she said nervously. "Would you like to come in?"

"Not necessary, Helen. I'm ready to put you to work in my kitchen if you're ready to go. Do you have a container for paté?"

She laughed at his joke while stepping back to get her purse and a small plastic container off a nearby chair. At the car, he held the door open for her. She paused as if she wasn't used to such chivalrous treatment. He almost cracked wise but decided it might unnerve her if she realized he could read her so easily.

She sank into the rich leather seat and reached to touch the dashboard, which had real wood trim. She brushed her fingers over his car phone. It was charming to see her sense of awe at the little luxuries. She broke the silence about halfway to his house. "So, you're going to have to tell me soon what we're eating." It was rewarding to see she was anticipating the evening with interest.

"We're having a coconut seafood curry on jasmine rice accompanied by a very nice bottle of Riesling."

"I thought you said we were having salmon?"

"It's a salmon curry. You said today that you like ethnic dishes with exotic flavors. I took you at your word. Is curry OK?"

"As long as it isn't too hot, I would like it very much."

They chatted about the weather and cooking class and soon arrived at his house. As he pulled into the driveway, he surreptitiously watched her reaction.

Her jaw partially dropped as she took in the grand front entry and the casita nestled next to the house. He drove into the two-car garage that had extra space for his golf cart. The floor-to-ceiling cabinets kept the garage spotless, and the pink epoxy-painted cement made it feel like an extension of the indoors instead of a garage.

"Oh my God! This is beautiful!"

Her admiration tickled him. "Thank you. I'm glad you like it. I'll give you the nickel tour when we go inside."

He got out and rushed around to open her door. She beat him to it, but he offered his hand to help her get out of the seat. She hesitated before accepting. Her hand was cold and dry, and she took it back from him as soon as possible, but instead of offending him, her behavior made him feel more protective towards her. Everything about her said she was frightened of men.

It was a perfect time of day to show her the house. The late afternoon sunlight poured in through the bank of picture windows in the great room. She oohed and ahhed as he led her to the kitchen and showed her the walk-in pantry, wine cooler and 6-burner range plus 2 wall ovens. She ran her hand along the dark granite counter top and touched the oak cabinets briefly.

She opened the refrigerator door and suddenly closed it as if she'd been caught snooping. "I'm sorry. I didn't mean to be nosy. I just got carried away."

"Help yourself, Helen. The kitchen is my favorite room."

She continued to look admiringly at everything. When he felt she'd had her fill, he said, "Let me show you the rest of the place before we cook." He pointed for her to go through the doorway at the other end of the kitchen, and they stepped into the large living room that looked out on the golf course. "I have such a nice view, and that's important to me. I know they say you can't eat scenery, but somehow it feeds my soul."

She sighed in pleasure. "I know exactly what you mean. I've always wanted to live somewhere with a view. This is spectacular." As he guided her across the room, they passed a chair where a large Siamese cat lay sleeping.

"Oh, I love cats. I have one myself. I should have made you come in and meet my Sheba. Who is this?

"That's Fido."

"Not really? That's a dog's name." She looked at him skeptically.

Alexander chuckled. "He's as faithful as any dog ever was. I've had him for seven years. He was a feisty young thing when I moved to Palm Lakes. I was kind of ignorant. I let him run loose. I almost lost him to a coyote through my own stupidity. I'll tell you the story one day. He stays in the house now. He's my best buddy."

"I know just how you feel. My Sheba is much older than Fido. She's my best friend in the whole world," she said with a catch in her voice.

He showed her the rest of the house, and she became more relaxed, asking him questions about his mementos from his travels. When they got into his office, she asked to see his books. He pulled out copies, and she admired them, so he told her he'd give her a signed copy of any one she wanted.

The expansive glow was replaced by embarrassment. "I didn't mean to be hinting for that."

"I know you weren't. I'd be pleased to give you a copy of any of them you want."

"You can't be doing that for everyone."

"I don't." He paused and looked into her eyes. "You're the first person I've had visit."

Her eyes widened in surprise. "You're kidding me!"

"Why would I kid about that? I socialize a lot, but I'm a very private person, and I don't share my home with people. Maybe I'm an urban hermit."

"Then why me?" Curiosity put two small wrinkles between her eyebrows.

"I honestly don't know. It just seemed natural." He nodded to the book she held. "You can let me know anytime, and I'll get you an autographed copy. Let's get to work now."

Back in the kitchen, he pulled all the ingredients and necessary tools out of cabinets, refrigerator and pantry and placed them on the counter and island in a fashion that would divide the labor between them. She watched intently, commenting on the fancy stainless steel pots and pans.

"Would you be willing to do the chopping of veggies while I prepare the fish and measure the spices and other ingredients?"

"Sure, I can do that. Just tell me how much and how you want them chopped."

"I've placed the right number of garlic cloves, onions and serrano chilis there, along with a chunk of fresh ginger. Mince the garlic; chop the onions small; peel and grate the ginger; strip the seeds out of the chilis and then chop them small. A copy of the recipe is on the counter so you don't have to remember. Be careful of the chilis. Wash your hands and use the silver bar by the main sink to remove the juice, or you'll get a nasty surprise later when you touch your eyes or nose."

She seemed a bit overwhelmed, but all she said was, "What silver bar?"

He took her gently by the shoulder and walked her to the main sink, reaching past her to pick up a silver soap-bar-shaped object that lay in a shiny metal container that also held a sponge and vegetable brush. "After you use the soap to wash, pretend the metal bar is soap and wash your hands in water with it, rubbing any surface that touched the peppers. It absorbs smells from fish or garlic and even neutralizes hot pepper juice."

Even though he only had a partial view, he could see her face transform as if he'd given her a magic wand. "I've never heard of such a thing. I can't wait to try it." Her wonder was so joyful, he impulsively patted her shoulder. Instantly, her body tensed up, so he removed his hand, making a mental note to give her more space at the same time as feeling challenged to do whatever it would take to win her trust.

He reached for an open wine bottle that sat way back on the counter by the sink and filled two glasses with red wine. Handing her one, he smiled and said, "Here's to a lovely meal and a great evening."

They clinked glasses. He watched her sip the wine, waiting for her reaction. She didn't disappoint him. "Oh my heaven, this is good! What is it? I don't think I've ever tasted wine this good before."

"This is a good Beaujolais. It will go nicely with some of this fine paté we made." He pointed to a platter of paté and crackers on the counter, and they each sampled some.

"I can't get over how good it is. Did it cost a lot?"

"Yes. But remember, this is what I do, so it's tax deductible." He smiled teasingly at her, but she didn't seem to realize he was pulling her leg.

"Well, I never would have guessed. I confess I thought it was a lot of pretense about expensive wine. Maybe I was being snobbish because I couldn't afford the good stuff. Thank you so much for sharing this with me."

They fell into an easy rhythm as they prepared the meal, and a short while later, he plated the food on elegant china. "Do you mind taking these to the dining room while I open the Riesling?"

"Glad to do that. The sooner I can taste this, the better." She grabbed them and headed for the dining room.

Her enthusiasm was contagious. "I'm really looking forward to it, too. I never tried this recipe, and I'm hungry."

She stopped in the doorway and turned to him, her mouth open in surprise. "You're kidding! Not about being hungry...about never making this recipe before."

"No, I'm quite serious. You're a guinea pig tonight." He turned to the counter to open the wine.

The evening sped by. Dinner was excellent, but then he knew it would be. Helen was rapturous about the whole experience. Obviously, she didn't dine often like this. She was alternately shy and expressive, but both suited her.

She didn't want to leave the cleanup to him, so he had to promise that next time, she could help do dishes instead of being treated like a guest.

She seemed surprised at his assumption of a future invitation, which further convinced him she had no designs on him, as if he needed proof. She was the most genuine person he'd met in a long time.

They repaired to the living room to sit in comfortable chairs and chat for a while. He went over to the bar. "What can I get you to finish the evening off? I have a nice sherry if you like that."

"I'm not sure I should drink anything else. I fear I may have overdone it tonight."

"I'll be driving you home, so do whatever feels best to you. I'm going to have a small sherry."

"I'll have one, too, then. But you are leading me into temptation."

He laughed as he carried the two glasses over and set hers by her hand. Almost as if on cue, Fido got up and came to sit in his lap.

Helen's eyes brightened. "He seems devoted to you."

"Yes, he is very affectionate. He sleeps with me and is usually much more talkative. I think he's being reticent because he isn't used to having company."

"That reminds me of Barbara introducing us. It seems like a long time ago we were at her party. I've only just met you, but I feel we've known each other forever...I'm blathering on because I drank so much. Sorry. It's just that I really appreciate your taking me under your wing in the class, and this invitation was so kind and unexpected. I don't get out much at all, and this has been so wonderful." She paused and looked downward.

He pretended he didn't notice the tears welling in her eyes. "I have a bit of a confession to make. I don't mean to brag, but with the ratio of bachelors to single women in Palm Lakes, I'm under siege much of the time, and I've had to develop strategies to avoid getting flooded with casseroles, dinner invitations and even offers of sexual comfort. Barbara's suggestion was a godsend. She told me you're recently widowed, and she sang your praises, and I felt that I would benefit as much as you by the partnership. I assumed you wouldn't be looking for a relationship, and it was an unexpected bonus that we hit it off so well. It's nice to have a friend. It's been a long time for me."

She stayed quiet for a minute, then looked up at him, her damp eyes glistening in the half-light. "I'm glad you feel you're getting something out of it. You're right. I'm not looking for another husband. I doubt I'll ever marry again. It was an unpleasant experience. My husband was abusive. I've never told anyone else, but I want to be honest with you." She began to twist her pants leg. "I'm not looking for sympathy. It was my choice to stay with him. But I never had friends, so this means a lot to me." She paused as if wondering what else to say.

That explained a lot. "Anything you say to me stays with me, Helen. And I appreciate your trusting me enough to share that." He was certain something else was bothering her but didn't want to press.

"I'm sorry. I had too much wine tonight. I'm becoming maudlin. I don't want to be bad company."

"You're not bad company. You've been through a lot lately. I'm happy to listen if you feel like talking. I promise to keep whatever you say between us."

She suddenly burst into tears, gulping air like she was drowning. Even though he'd anticipated it, it shook him up to see her so upset. He went to the bar, grabbed the box of tissues and offered them to her. She took them and pulled a couple out, struggling to get control. He wondered if he should put his arm around her, or if her natural shyness would make that a bad move. So he just stood there quietly waiting for a couple of minutes.

"Gosh, I am *so* sorry. I'm not used to being treated kindly." She wiped her eyes delicately and blew her nose. "I'm not usually such a high maintenance person. I guess things have been piling up on me lately, and today the vet told me that Sheba has cancer and there isn't much she can do to help. She wants me to consider euthanizing her, and Sheba is all I have at the moment."

She scrunched up the kleenex in her hand and pulled a new one from the box. "Plus I'm going to have to sell my house. I don't have the money to maintain it. Then my daughter showed up out of the blue; that's a whole 'nother story. There's just been so much change, and most of it very trying. Lou used to say I couldn't handle the real world. Maybe he was right."

She paused as if overcome with emotion, and began to cry again, this time less violently. "Please forgive me for dumping all this on you."

"I'm so sorry to hear about Sheba. I would feel terrible if something happened to Fido. Please let me know if I can help. I can drive you to the vet, so that whatever you do there, you can focus on Sheba and not worry about driving. Would you let me do that?"

"I don't want to impose on you, Alexander."

"It would be my pleasure to help. We're friends, right? Friends help each other through times like this."

"OK. I'll let you know." She seemed embarrassed at her outburst.

He contemplated sharing about himself, but it just seemed too early and too risky. If they remained friends, he'd have to, but maybe he could put it off for a while. Instead, he decided to offer sympathy.

"Years ago, I lost someone who meant the world to me, and ever since, I've wondered if I will ever find love again; in fact, I promised myself I never would, because it hurt too much. The years have dulled the pain, but it's still there. Now and then I still have a good cry about it. Yet I wouldn't give up one moment with my lover. They were the best times of my life. I know it sounds like a platitude, but everything changes, so it won't always be like this for you. I hope you'll let me be part of your support network."

He sat down and reached for his glass and held it up, indicating he wanted to make a toast. She smiled weakly and lifted her glass.

"Here's to good friends."

"Yes," she seconded quietly. They sipped their wine in a companionable silence. The storm seemed to have passed and left in its wake a deeper sense of intimacy between them. She sighed as if a weight had been removed from her.

He could tell she was wrung out. "Are you feeling tired? It's been a long evening. I'm not trying to get rid of you, but you look exhausted. I can take you home."

She looked at him with gratitude. Nodding in assent, she put her glass down.

"You promise I can help clean the kitchen next time?"

He smiled that she referred to a next time. "Of course! You're family now, and you can't get away with leaving the dirty dishes all to me, woman."

Her laugh was genuine and uninhibited. "I'll be a good helper."

"Let's get you home." He stood up and went to where she had laid her purse and handed it to her. Then he got her container with her share of the paté.

They didn't speak on the short drive, but it felt comfortable. He pulled into her driveway and quickly went around to open the door. This time, he beat her to it. He handed her out and then walked up the sidewalk with her. After a minute fumbling for her house key, she got the door open and turned to him. "Thank you for the best evening I've had in years."

He was flattered and at the same time sad that she felt that way. She was hesitating as if wondering what to do next, so he put his arms around her and gave her a brotherly hug. At first, she flinched; then she leaned into him.

"You get a good night's sleep and pet Sheba for me. Call me anytime, and promise you'll let me drive you to the vet."

"I will." She went into the house, and he waited to hear the deadbolt close.

He walked back to the car and drove home. It was pretty obvious he'd have to tell her soon. First, he'd have to figure out for himself exactly what was going on. She'd dropped into his life as if fitting into a spot made just for her. What exactly *was* the spot? And what would she say if she knew everything about him?

FIND OUT WHAT HAPPENS NEXT

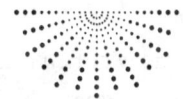

G et a copy of Renaissance by Maggie McPhee and find out what happens to Helen, Alexander and the other residents of Palm Lakes retirement community. Just click the cover image or the link above, which will take you to the store where you downloaded *Death in Autumn*. The whole series is also available in paperback.

ABOUT THE AUTHOR

Maggie McPhee is a writer of contemporary 'boomer' women's fiction. She also writes nonfiction using her real name, Maggie Percy.

www.ingramcontent.com/pod-product-compliance
Lightning Source LLC
Chambersburg PA
CBHW071236130626
46556CB00003B/1041